The Woman Who Walked in Sunshine

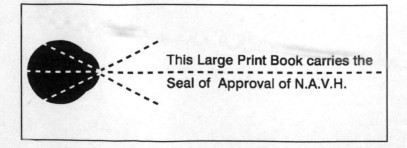

This Large Print Book carries the
Seal of Approval of N.A.V.H.

THE WOMAN WHO WALKED IN SUNSHINE

ALEXANDER MCCALL SMITH

WHEELER PUBLISHING
A part of Gale, Cengage Learning

GALE
CENGAGE Learning·

Farmington Hills, Mich • San Francisco • New York • Waterville, Maine
Meriden, Conn • Mason, Ohio • Chicago

GALE
CENGAGE Learning®

LIBRARY OF CONGRESS CATALOGING-IN-PUBLICATION DATA

McCall Smith, Alexander, 1948-
   The woman who walked in sunshine / Alexander McCall Smith. — Large print edition.
      pages cm. — (Wheeler publishing large print hardcover) (The No. 1 Ladies' Detective Agency)
     ISBN 978-1-4104-8305-8 (hardback) — ISBN 1-4104-8305-3 (hardcover)
    1. No. 1 Ladies' Detective Agency (Imaginary organization)—Fiction. 2. Ramotswe, Precious (Fictitious character)—Fiction. 3. Women private investigators—Botswana—Fiction. 4. Botswana—Fiction. 5. Large type books. I. Title.
   PR6063.C326W66 2015b
   823'.914—dc23
                                                 2015035701

Published in 2015 by arrangement with Pantheon Books, a division of Penguin Random House LLC

Printed in the United States of America
1 2 3 4 5 6 7 19 18 17 16 15

This book is for Alistair Moffat.

CHAPTER ONE:
IT IS IMPORTANT FOR
CHILDREN TO LEARN
ABOUT ELECTRICITY

Mma Ramotswe remembered exactly how it was that the subject of taking a holiday arose. It was Mma Makutsi who started the discussion, with one of her inconsequential observations — those remarks she made à propos of nothing — remarks that had little to do with what had gone before. She often said such things, quite suddenly making a pronouncement that seemed to come from nowhere, her words dropping into the stillness of the afternoon air like stones tossed into a pool.

It was mid-afternoon in the offices of the No. 1 Ladies' Detective Agency in Gaborone, in late October, one of the hottest months in what was proving to be one of the warmest years in living memory.

"It is very hot, Mma Ramotswe," observed Mma Makutsi, as she leaned back in her chair, fanning herself with a wilting copy of the *Botswana Daily News.* "When it is this hot, it is very difficult to work."

From her side of the room, where, if anything, it was slightly hotter because of the pool of sunlight that penetrated the window and fell directly across her desk, the begetter and owner of Botswana's only detective agency cast a glance in the direction of her erstwhile secretary, later assistant, and now, by dint of the latter's sheer tenacity and perseverance, her colleague. In normal circumstances, if a member of staff said that it was too hot to work, an employer would interpret this as a strong hint that it was time to close the office and go home. When it came to Mma Makutsi's utterances, though, one could quite easily be wrong, and so Mma Ramotswe merely said, "Yes, it is very hot, Mma — very hot indeed."

She knew that there was no reason for Mma Makutsi to stay at work if she felt inclined to go home. Following her marriage to Mr. Phuti Radiphuti, proprietor of the Double Comfort Furniture Store and owner of a substantial herd of cattle, Mma Makutsi had no need of the modest salary Mma Ramotswe paid her; indeed, had that salary stopped for whatever reason, she probably would not even have noticed it. Nor was she technically obliged to keep certain hours: her contract of employment with the agency was a very informal one — so informal, in fact, that there was even some doubt as to whether it existed at all.

"People who trust one another do not need to put things in writing," Mma Ramotswe had once said. "It is enough that they should have given their word."

Mma Makutsi had been quick to agree. "That is very true, Mma," she said. But then, as she began to think about the proposition, she started to discern the problems that might come from a failure to reduce understandings to writing, no matter how well understood they might have been. "Except sometimes," she added cautiously. "You can rely on somebody's word in many cases, but not in all. That is why it is safer to have everything in writing."

"I'm not so sure . . . ," began Mma Ramotswe.

But Mma Makutsi was just getting into her stride. "No, you must almost always put things in writing. This is because people forget what they said and then they start to rewrite history and end up blaming *you* for not doing something they think you said you'd do, but haven't done. They never accept that they may be remembering things incorrectly." She looked at Mma Ramotswe reproachfully, as if the other woman were widely known to be one of the very worst offenders in this respect. "That is why you should have everything in writing — preferably in duplicate, in case you lose the original." She paused, still looking at Mma Ramotswe, as if now challenging her to disagree. "They always taught us at the Botswana Secretarial College to put everything in writing. That is what they said, Mma. They said: 'What's written down on paper is written down in stone.' "

Mma Ramotswe frowned. "Stone and paper are very different, Mma. I'm not sure —"

Mma Makutsi cut her off. "You see, Mma, when something is written in stone, it means that it cannot be changed. They do not mean to say that you have to copy everything down from paper and then carve it in stone. That would take a very long time."

"Very long," muttered Mma Ramotswe. "And every business would have to have a secretary *and* a stonemason. That would not be practical."

The joke passed unnoticed, and now, on that hot October afternoon, the conversation suddenly took an unexpected slant.

"I met Mr. Polopetsi the other day," Mma

Makutsi remarked. "He was walking along when I saw him. You remember how he used to walk? Those small steps of his — like an anteater. You remember how he walked, Mma?"

Mma Ramotswe looked up with interest. She had never thought of Mr. Polopetsi as resembling an anteater, but now that Mma Makutsi had mentioned it . . . "Mr. Polopetsi? Now, there's a good man, Mma."

Mma Makutsi agreed. Mr. Polopetsi had worked in the agency a few years ago and had been as popular with clients as he had been with those with whom he worked. He had been recruited by chance after Mma Ramotswe had knocked him off his bicycle while driving her white van. When she heard the story he had to tell, she had been moved to offer him a temporary job to make up for what she saw as the shocking injustice of his undeserved conviction for an offence of negligence. Mr. Polopetsi had been a hospital pharmacist who had been sentenced to a term of imprisonment for a dispensing mistake made by somebody else — a grossly disproportionate punishment, thought Mma Ramotswe, even if he were to have been negligent.

He had survived the unwarranted sojourn in prison, and although his dispensing

11

licence had been taken from him, after he left the agency he had been able to find work in a chemist's shop. That job had not lasted long, as the business had run into financial difficulties. Fortunately, his wife had recently been promoted in her civil service post, and her increased salary meant that the family was comfortably enough off. Mr. Polopetsi, Mma Makutsi revealed, had found a part-time position that suited him very well — teaching chemistry in a high school. The regular chemistry teacher there, a man of great indolence, was only too pleased to have an energetic and popular assistant to take over on those afternoons when he wanted to watch football matches on television. The full-time teacher never bothered to enquire as to the reasons for Mr. Polopetsi's popularity with his pupils; had he done so, he would have discovered that there was nothing Mr. Polopetsi liked more than to end a chemistry lesson with as loud and as spectacular an explosion as he could get away with, given the resources — and fragility — of the school laboratory. The inner pyromaniac that lurks in most boys was present in him as much as it was in the male pupils, just as it was, perhaps to a slightly lesser degree, in the girls, who enjoyed any experiment that generated col-

12

oured smoke in any quantity.

"He was very happy," said Mma Makutsi. "You remember how he liked to smile? Just like a nervous rabbit? Well, he was smiling like that when I saw him the other day. He was walking along with that strange walk of his, smiling just like a rabbit."

"I'm glad that he's happy," said Mma Ramotswe. "He deserves to be happy after what happened to him, poor man."

Mma Makutsi looked thoughtful. "I'm not sure if we get the happiness we actually deserve," she said. "There are some people who look very happy but certainly do not deserve it. Look at that woman . . ."

Mma Ramotswe knew exactly whom Mma Makutsi meant. "Violet Sephotho?"

Mma Makutsi nodded. As she did so, a small ray of sunshine caught the lens of her large round glasses, sending a flash of dancing light across the ceiling. "Yes, that is the lady I was thinking of," she said. "If you look at her, she seems to be very happy. She is always smiling and . . ."

". . . and looking at men," supplied Mma Ramotswe. "You know that look that some ladies give men. You know that look, Mma?"

Mma Makutsi did. "It is a very encouraging look," she said. "It is a look that says, *If you are thinking of doing anything, then do*

13

not hesitate to do it. It is that sort of look."
She paused. "And yet she's happy. All that
smiling and laughing looks very happy, I
would have thought."

They both fell into silence as they contemplated the sheer injustice of Violet
Sephotho's apparent happiness. Mma Makutsi opened her mouth to speak, but
thought better of it and closed it again. She
had been about to say, "But God will surely
punish her, Mma," then had decided that
this was not the sort of thing that people
said any more, even if it was what they were
thinking. The trouble was, she thought, that
God had so many people to punish these
days that he might just not find the time to
get round to dealing with Violet Sephotho.
It was a disappointing thought — a lost opportunity, in a sense: she would very will-
ingly have volunteered her services to assist
in divine punishment, perhaps through
something she would call *Mma Makutsi's
League of Justice* that would, strictly but
fairly, punish people like Violet.

Mma Ramotswe's own thoughts were far
from retribution, divine or otherwise. She
returned to the subject of Mr. Polopetsi.

"So what did our friend have to say for
himself?"

Mma Makutsi shrugged. "He said that he

14

likes being a part-time teacher. He works three afternoons a week, at the most. He said that he was teaching the children how to make a battery and they were enjoying it."

"That is a very useful skill," said Mma Ramotswe. "It is important for children to learn about electricity."

"Yes, Mma, it is. But then he said that he had just been on a week's holiday. He said that he was still feeling the benefit of that."

Mma Ramotswe was interested to hear this. But even as she pictured Mr. Polopetsi on holiday — she had no idea what he would do — she began to ask herself whether she knew anybody else who had been on a holiday. Had anybody she knew been away, or even stopped working and stayed at home? Mr. J.L.B. Matekoni had certainly never had a holiday, at least not as long as she had known him. She was certain, too, that Mma Potokwane, the indefatigable matron of the Orphan Farm, had never taken a break from her post, with the exception of the few days when she had gone away following a dispute with the Orphan Farm's management board. That had not been a holiday, of course — it was more of a retirement, even if a very short-lived one.

"What did Mr. Polopetsi do on this holiday of his?" she asked.

"He said that he did nothing," answered Mma Makutsi. "He said that he just stayed at home and lay down on his bed for much of the day. He said that it slowed his heart down and that was a good thing because it had been beating too fast for many years. He said that you cannot make a truck go at sixty miles an hour for too long. Eventually, he said, it gets tired and stops."

That was very true, observed Mma Ramotswe. "But was that all he did? Stay at home and lie down on his bed?"

Mma Makutsi did not answer the question. "He also said to me that people who take holidays live much longer than people who do not."

"Well, that sounds very interesting," said Mma Ramotswe. "But what about people who are running their own businesses? What do they do about holidays?"

There was a brief silence as Mma Makutsi considered the question. Then, rather tentatively, she gave her reply. "Somebody else in the office takes over," she said. "Most businesses have more than one person working in them, you know, and so when the owner goes off on holiday, one of the others takes over."

"I see," said Mma Ramotswe.

"So," Mma Makutsi continued, "if there is, say, a manager at the top and he — or she, of course — needs to go off on holiday, then it will be the deputy manager who takes over. It is usually a very smooth process — no bumps or hiccups — and the customers never know that it is the deputy manager in charge."

Mma Ramotswe looked up at the ceiling, her occasional resort when Mma Makutsi was in full flow. "I am sure they don't," she muttered.

Mma Makutsi's spectacles flashed again — a shard of steely light. "And I believe that this is sometimes how deputy managers become managers." There was a long, meaning-laden pause at this point, and then she continued, "It is because they do the job so well when they are given the chance. Then somebody says, 'Oh, that person — that deputy manager — could just as well be a full manager.' That sometimes happens, I believe."

"Really?" said Mma Ramotswe.

Mr. J.L.B. Matekoni was late home that evening, having had to attend a meeting of the Motor Trades Benevolent Association, on the committee of which he served as treasurer. Mma Ramotswe had fed Puso and Motholeli early, and had then run them both to their cub scout and guide meetings in the hall of the Anglican Cathedral; they would not be ready to be collected until nine, by which time she would have served dinner for her husband and herself, washed the dishes, ironed Puso's shirt for the following day, and performed a number of the other chores that went with running a household and that never seemed to be finished no matter how methodical and hard-working one was. She did not resent these tasks, of course — to iron the shirt of a little boy like Puso, or to make a packed lunch for one's good husband whom one loved so much, was no great hardship; she merely wished that there would be some break between them, some brief moment when one might recover one's breath and one's energy before embarking on the next round of domestic duties.

Mr. J.L.B. Matekoni's meeting had not been an easy one. "The members of the Benevolent Association are always complaining," he said as he sat down at the kitchen table. "They expect the committee to deal with all their problems — not just one or two problems, but all of them."

"Some people can be like that," said Mma Ramotswe, as she mashed the potatoes for their shepherd's pie. "Perhaps it is because we have become spoiled. We have so much these days that we think it is our due."

"And I am just the treasurer," said Mr. J.L.B. Matekoni. "I have about twenty-seven thousand pula in the common good fund at the moment, and so I can't do everything. But they are always asking me to pay for their grandfather's funeral, or to cover the school fees of the children of a late mechanic, or even to fund people's weddings. They expect all that, Mma! That is what they ask for."

"You cannot do it, Rra," said Mma Ramotswe. "There is not enough money in Botswana to pay for half the things people want paid for. It just isn't possible."

Mr. J.L.B. Matekoni sighed. "Sometimes I feel like throwing everything in, you know. I feel like getting all the papers together — all the accounts and receipts and so on — and passing it over to the members and saying: 'Here you are. You do it now.'"

Mma Ramotswe laughed. "Maybe you should do just that, Rra. That would show them." She paused. "Maybe . . . maybe you could take a break."

"From being treasurer?"

"From everything," she said. "You could take a break from being treasurer and . . ."

She turned round from the stove to look directly at her husband. "And you could take a break from the garage too. A holiday, in fact."

He stared at her, puzzled. "Me?" he said. "Me?"

"Yes, why not? Everybody needs a holiday at some time. We're not meant to go on working until . . . until we drop."

She uttered the words "until we drop" with her heart in her mouth. Men did drop — they dropped rather often and with very little notice — and no woman with a husband should tempt Providence by talking lightly about such things. She knew many men who had dropped, often without the chance to say goodbye to their wives; they just dropped, more or less where they stood.

"But some of us have to go on working," said Mr. J.L.B. Matekoni. "Some of us have to carry on, because if we did not, then everything would come to a stop. What would happen at Tlokweng Road Speedy Motors if I said that I had had enough and was going to stop working? It would come to a grinding halt, Mma, and that would be that. It would be Tlokweng Road Speedy Motors (Now Late), Mma, that is what it would be."

She took a moment to think about this.

What Mr. J.L.B. Matekoni said was probably true. There was Fanwell, of course, who was now a qualified mechanic even if she — and others — still called him an apprentice. And there was Charlie, who had recently been seconded to the No. 1 Ladies' Detective Agency because there was not enough work for him in the garage. But could either of these — or indeed both together — manage the business in the absence of Mr. J.L.B. Matekoni? She thought not. Charlie had always needed close supervision or he would lose his temper with an engine and start hitting it with a hammer; he would be no use. Fanwell was a much better, much more patient mechanic, but he was reticent in his manner, and it was difficult to see him coping with some of the more assertive customers, particularly those who objected to the size of the bills that had to be issued for servicing or repairing a car. Cars were expensive things, and anything to do with their maintenance was correspondingly costly, even if a garage was modest in its charges. Fanwell was too gentle, she thought, to fight that particular corner.

Mma Ramotswe returned to her task, but she had planted a seed in Mr. J.L.B. Matekoni's mind. He sat in his chair, looking up at the ceiling, drumming his fingers

21

lightly on the table. Then he stood up, crossed to the window, and looked out into the yard. It was dark outside, and the light in the kitchen prevented his seeing the stars that hung, in great draperies of silver, above the land.

Turning away from the window, he addressed Mma Ramotswe. "Of course, you could, you know. There's no reason why you shouldn't."

She stirred the pot with the wooden spoon she had owned since the age of eight — an artefact of her childhood that still reminded her of the aunt who had given it to her. It was another world, the world of childhood and of Mochudi — a world of openness and innocence, a world in which the old Botswana ways were not just the customs that people remembered with fondness but the precepts and habits by which people led their day-to-day lives. *We have lost so much,* she thought. *Our dear country has lost so much.* But everybody had lost something — it was not just Botswana, which had perhaps lost less than others. So many people had lost that sense of identification with the land that gave meaning to life; that fixed one firmly to a place one loved. At least we still have that, she thought: at least we still have land that we can call *our place;* acacia trees

22

that are *our* acacia trees; a sky that is *our* sky because it watched over our mothers and fathers and took them up into it, embraced them, when they became late. We still have that, no matter how big and frightening the world becomes.

The thoughts inspired by the simple wooden spoon gave way to his question. What had he suggested she do? Or not do, perhaps?

"Me? Do what, Rra?"

"Take a holiday, Mma. You work so hard —"

She cut him short. "A holiday? No, I was not talking about myself, Mr. J.L.B. Matekoni. I was talking about other people taking a holiday — maybe even you."

He shook his head. "And I told you I cannot, Mma, but then I thought: *Why doesn't Mma Ramotswe take a holiday herself?* That's what I thought, Mma."

Mma Ramotswe laughed. "But I can't possibly take a holiday, Rra. Who would look after the agency?"

Mr. J.L.B. Matekoni did not hesitate. "Mma Makutsi."

Mma Ramotswe laid down the wooden spoon. Mma Makutsi had many virtues — she was the first to admit that — but the thought of leaving her in sole charge of the

23

No. 1 Ladies' Detective Agency was absurd. Judgement was needed to run something like a detective agency, and she was not at all sure that Mma Makutsi had that. Yes, she was keen and hard-working, and yes, her filing was probably second to none in all Botswana, but the agency dealt with some very delicate matters and Mma Makutsi had never been renowned for her tact. If she were left in charge, there was bound to be a point at which she would say something ill-considered or even downright confrontational. Look at how she always succeeded in riling Charlie when anybody with any *real* sense would know that a young man like that has to be handled with circumspection. If you criticised somebody like Charlie or, worse still, shouted at him, you would be guaranteed to get nowhere; in fact, you could more or less be assured of going backwards. No, she could not countenance leaving Mma Makutsi in charge of the agency, and she explained to Mr. J.L.B. Matekoni why this should be so.

He listened courteously, as he always did when she — or anybody else, for that matter — addressed him. Once she had finished, he smiled. "Everything you say may be true, Mma," he conceded. "It is true that Mma Makutsi can be a little bit difficult from time

24

to time, but in spite of that she is still very good at her job. And remember that she got ninety-seven per cent in the —"

"Oh, I know all about that," said Mma Ramotswe. "We have all heard about that ninety-seven per cent. But that was for things like filing and shorthand. I'm talking about ordinary human skills now."

"Well, I think she has those too," said Mr. J.L.B. Matekoni. "And even if she doesn't have them at the moment, how is she going to develop them if you never give her a chance? How does somebody who is down at the bottom" — and here he gestured with one hand to demonstrate the lowest rung on the ladder — "how can somebody who is down there get up here?" His hand was raised to above his head — a social and professional elevation separated from the starting point by an ascent beyond scaling.

He waited for her to respond, but she did not. She realised that he was right: people had to be given their chance.

"Well, Mma?" pressed Mr. J.L.B. Matekoni.

"I still don't think I need a holiday," she said. "Everything is going very well at the moment, and I don't want to put a spanner in the works."

Mr. J.L.B. Matekoni's eyes lit up at the use of the mechanical metaphor. "Talking of putting spanners in the works," he said, smiling in pleasure at the recollection, "one of our clients brought his car in today. We had serviced it only six months ago and so I wasn't expecting it."

"And?"

"He said that the engine was making a strange noise."

"Ah."

Mr. J.L.B. Matekoni's tone changed. He was now the concerned doctor, conveying to the family of a patient some item of bad news. "So I drove it round the block and listened. And yes, the engine was making a very discouraging noise — a sort of clanking sound that meant that all was very definitely not going well. So I took the vehicle back to the garage and opened up the engine compartment. And you know what I found?"

Mma Ramotswe could not resist answering. "A spanner? There was a spanner in the works?"

He looked crestfallen. "Well, yes, that's exactly what I found. It had been left there by Charlie when he serviced the car some months earlier, and it had become entangled with all sorts of bits and pieces."

Mma Ramotswe rolled her eyes heavenwards. "Charlie is very slow to learn, isn't he?"

"He is, I'm afraid," said Mr. J.L.B. Matekoni. "But remember that he is still very young and things could get better."

"Do you think they will?" asked Mma Ramotswe.

Mr. J.L.B. Matekoni thought for a moment. "I don't think so," he said at last.

It was not the answer that Mma Ramotswe would have given. She was of the view that things were getting better, even if there were temporary setbacks and even if there was very little light at the end of the tunnel. But in her opinion, the last thing one should do was to bemoan the fact that things were changing. She would not slip into a position that failed to see any progress in human affairs. There was a great deal of progress being made, right under their noses, particularly in Africa, and this progress was good. Life was much harder for tyrants than it had been before. There were more civil liberties, more literacy, more children surviving that first critical year of infancy; there was a lot of which one could be proud. And Charlie would be a better young man eventually — all he needed was time, which was what we all required.

Mr. J.L.B. Matekoni tried another tack. "But you deserve it, Mma. We all agree about that. We all think you deserve a holiday."

She smiled at the kindness, but then, as she turned back towards the pot on the stove, the implications of what he had just said sunk in. *We all think you deserve a holiday . . .* This meant that they had been discussing it among themselves. Why had they done this? Was it a . . . she hardly dared say the word to herself, but now she forced herself to face it. Was it a *plot*?

She closed her eyes and for a moment saw Mma Makutsi lurking in the shadows somewhere with some faceless ally, her presence only betrayed by a glint of light catching the glass of her spectacles. And she heard her saying, "Well, that's got rid of her for the time being. She'll be off for . . ." And the other conspirator would say, "She'll be off forever, not that she'll suspect it."

The resentment welled up within her, but subsided very quickly when she reminded herself that she was putting these words into Mma Makutsi's mouth and there was no evidence, not one scrap, that suggested that her colleague — or anybody else — wanted her out of the way. Even so, she saw no reason at all to take a holiday — none whatsoever. And Mma Makutsi would never betray her; she just would not. There were some people about whom one could say that sort of thing — and Mma Makutsi was one such person — but generally one had to be careful about trusting the rest of humanity; sometimes the people who were closest to you were also those who were furthest away. One should remember that, she told herself: there were no plots being hatched against her — there just were not. *But how do you know that?* asked a tiny voice, from somewhere down below. *How can you be so sure?*

She looked down at her shoes. Had they spoken? If there were any speaking shoes, then they belonged to Mma Makutsi, not to her; unless, of course, the condition, whatever it was, were an infectious one, and she had now caught it. No, that was ridiculous — patently so. She knew that any utterances that came from down below were almost certainly no more than tricks played by the mind, even if the questions they asked, or the observations they made, seemed penetrating and acute. One might hear anything, if one allowed one's mind to wander; people said, for instance, that if you stood out under the stars above the Kalahari, under those great silver-white fields of distant light, you could hear a *tsk-tsk* sound that was the stars calling to their hunting dogs. But in reality there was no sound — or if there was, it came from somewhere closer at hand, from scurrying insects, timid creatures whose job it was to whistle and whisper in the darkness.

"I just know," she muttered.

"More fool you," said the shoes.

CHAPTER TWO:
THE BIRDS HAVE
THEIR WORK TO DO

The events that preceded Mma Ramotswe's holiday happened in such rapid succession that later it was difficult for her to identify the point at which she had reached the decision to take the holiday. In fact, when she came to think about it, she even wondered whether she had actually made such a decision, or whether it had somehow been made for her.

The day after her discussion in the kitchen with Mr. J.L.B. Matekoni, she had gone into work early, expecting to be the first to arrive in the office. But she was not — not only was Mma Makutsi already there, seated at her desk, but Charlie was there too, leaning nonchalantly against one of the two filing cabinets, a mug of steaming tea in one hand and a half-eaten sandwich in the other.

"So!" exclaimed Mma Ramotswe as she entered the office. "So, here we all are already — and I thought I would be the first one in." She glanced at her watch. "It's only seven-fifteen, I see."

"It is always good to start early," said Mma Makutsi brightly. "If there are many things to do, then it is best to start them early in the morning — chop, chop — and get them finished. That is the way to do things."

Charlie nodded his agreement. "Chop, chop," he said.

Mma Ramotswe smiled. "That is a very good way of approaching things. Yes, I agree." She paused. "But are we particularly busy at the moment? I thought things were a bit quiet. Have other things come in?"

Charlie glanced at Mma Makutsi. She was unfazed by this, and shook her head as if to say that one could never be too careful. "You never know," she said. "We are often quiet, and then the next moment we are very busy. You can never tell."

"True," said Mma Ramotswe. "What goes up can also come down."

"Or what is down can always go up," added Charlie.

"Yes," said Mma Ramotswe, crossing to her desk. "That is also true."

She sat down at her desk while Mma Makutsi switched on the kettle to make her

32

a cup of red bush tea.

"Somebody is coming in at eight," she said.

Mma Ramotswe turned a page of her desktop diary — a gift from the Botswana Stationery Company. "I don't see anything in the diary."

"No, it is not there yet," said Mma Makutsi. "I have not had time to put it in. But I shall do that now."

She crossed the room to Mma Ramotswe's desk, took the diary from her, and made an entry. Then she handed it back and Mma Ramotswe read: *8 a.m. — Mr. Polopetsi.* She looked up enquiringly at Mma Makutsi. "A social call, Mma?"

Mma Makutsi busied herself with the teapot. "Not exactly."

"So did he just ask for an appointment about something?"

Mma Makutsi affected a casual shrug of the shoulders. "Actually, I suggested that he come in. I asked him, Mma."

Mma Ramotswe frowned. "You didn't hold out the prospect of a job, did you?" She glanced at Charlie. "You know that we can't really take anybody else on. You know that, don't you?" Charlie was expensive enough, and his wages were paid as an act of charity more than anything else. He was useful enough — in his way — but a small business such as the No. 1 Ladies' Detective Agency had very little spare cash to spend on salaries.

Mma Makutsi was quick to reassure her. "Mr. Polopetsi is all right, Mma. He does not need to earn more money because his wife has got that very good job now and she is well paid. He also gets something for his afternoons teaching chemistry. No, he is not looking for a full-time job."

"Nor a part-time one," muttered Mma Ramotswe. "At least I hope he isn't."

"No, he is not looking for anything involving money. I can assure you of that, Mma. This is not about money."

"Then what is it about, Mma?"

The kettle had now boiled, and Mma Makutsi was filling the teapot set aside for red bush tea. "It's to do with that holiday you were talking about, Mma."

Mma Ramotswe drew in her breath. The breezy effrontery of Mma Makutsi was quite extraordinary; it deserved a response, but what could one say to somebody who took such liberties with historical truth? "That I was . . ." She trailed off.

"Yes," said Mma Makutsi with all the casual confidence of one who was simply recalling what had happened rather than spinning a web of half-truths and distortions. "Yesterday. Remember? You said you were thinking of taking a holiday."

Mma Ramotswe was genuinely perplexed. She could not recall her exact words when the subject had been raised; it was always possible that she had been misinterpreted, or that she had said something she had not intended to say. "Did I say that?" she asked.

Mma Makutsi nodded. "I agreed with you, Mma. Remember? I said that when the person in charge of a business needs to take a holiday there is always somebody else in the office who can take over."

Mma Ramotswe remembered that part of the conversation, but even if the discussion had been along those lines, that was still a far cry from her actually saying that she intended to take a holiday. "I don't think I went so far as to say that I —"

Mma Makutsi did not allow her to finish. Appearing to ignore the beginning of Mma Ramotswe's protest, she launched into a further encomium of those who took holidays. "People who take holidays often do so not just for themselves, Mma. Oh no, they are not selfish people, these holiday people; they are often thinking of the good of the company, you know. They realise that if they take a holiday they will be better at their job when they come back — they will avoid getting stale." She paused, looking intently at Mma Ramotswe before continuing, "It is not a good thing to get stale, Mma. It is not a good thing at all."

Mma Ramotswe looked down at her hands, folded passively on her lap. Was she getting stale? She looked at her shoes, at her faithful brown shoes with their broad soles and their flat heels. Were these the shoes of a stale person? She did not feel in the slightest bit stale, but then did stale people ever recognise their own staleness? That was the problem with human failings — they were often more visible to others than to those whom they afflicted.

Her gaze shifted to Mma Makutsi's shoes. Mma Makutsi had always been fond of bright shoes — of shoes that some might even go so far as to describe as extravagant shoes. When she first came to the agency, in the days when she was simply the agency's secretary, her taste for glamorous shoes had been constrained by poverty. But then had come the gradual improvement of her financial situation, initially through her setting up of the Kalahari Typing School for Men. That venture had not lasted all that long, but it had been profitable while it lasted, and it had enabled her to treat herself to a few luxuries, including more fashionable shoes. After her marriage to Phuti Radiphuti, of course, any need for parsimony had disappeared, and she had acquired a whole rack of glamorous shoes, in a wide range of styles. That morning Mma Ramotswe noticed that Mma Makutsi was wearing a pair of bottle-green patent sandals with wedge heels. The crisscross straps of the sandals were numerous, but thin — impossibly so, thought Mma Ramotswe — and could not be much stronger, she felt, than the gossamer of a spider's web. If one had to run in such shoes, surely the straps would sunder, toppling the wearer where she stood. And yet no matter how impractical such sandals might be, they were clearly not the sandals of a stale person. No, a stale person was far more likely to wear broad brown shoes with low heels, or no heels at all.

Suddenly she felt weary. Ever since leaving school at the age of sixteen, Mma Ramotswe had worked. She had kept house for her father, the late Obed Ramotswe; she had worked in a small local store, selling matches and soap and paraffin for stoves. She had tried her best to make a home for her first husband, Note Mokoti, and had continued with that until violence and the fear it bred had forced her out. Through all that she had never stopped working and had continued to do so even after her father's death, and the small inheritance she received from him had enabled her to start her own business, the No. 1 Ladies' Detective Agency. And then there had been Mr. J.L.B. Matekoni and the foster children to look after and all the burdens of making a success of a small business. All of that had taken its toll, but she had never once thought of that, never entertained any idea of taking a break of more than a couple of days. Well, perhaps now it was catching up with her and she was becoming stale, just as Mma Makutsi was effectively suggesting.

She sighed. "Maybe we should talk about it later, Mma Makutsi," she said. "I have to drink my tea, and sometimes it is difficult to drink tea and talk at the same time."

Charlie laughed. "If you do that, the tea can go up your nose," he said.

Mma Makutsi looked at him scornfully. "There is no need to bring noses into this, Charlie," she said. "There are letters for you to take to the post."

Charlie put down his mug. "Where will you go on your holiday, Mma Ramotswe?" he asked. "There are plenty of places, you know. You won't want to go somewhere too

38

exciting, of course, but there are some good places for . . ."

He did not finish, inhibited by Mma Makutsi's disapproving stare. Mma Ramotswe said nothing, but thought: *Plenty of places for stale people. Yes, there probably are — quiet places where the stale people sit in their chairs, warmed by the afternoon sun, undisturbed by any loud noises or activity. There would be plenty of places like that.*

Mr. Polopetsi arrived exactly at eight, entering the office after calling out, in the traditional way, *"Ko! Ko!"*

"I am here," he said. "It is only me, but I am here."

Mma Ramotswe rose to her feet and greeted him warmly. "*Dumela,* Rra! It is very good to see you again."

Enquiries were made as to the health of various members of everybody's family — again as required by custom — and then he sat down opposite Mma Ramotswe while Mma Makutsi prepared the tea.

"You will be surprised to see me," said Mr. Polopetsi. "But it seems as if it's only yesterday that I was here, helping you ladies with your work. Remember those days, Mma Ramotswe? You answered the phone and wrote the letters while Mma Makutsi did the secretarial work . . ."

He was interrupted by a cough from Mma Makutsi. "I am no longer a secretary, Rra. That was a long time ago."

Mr. Polopetsi turned round to face her. "Oh, really? So you are an assistant now?"

Mma Makutsi shook her head. "Co-director," she said.

"Well, well," mused Mr. Polopetsi. "That is very good news. I have always thought that you would be a very important detective one of these days. I have always thought that, Mma."

Mma Makutsi beamed with pleasure. "And now you have been proved right, Rra."

Mma Ramotswe helped the conversation on. "Well, it is certainly very good to see you again, Rra. And I hear that you are teaching chemistry at Gaborone Secondary School. That must be very interesting work."

"It is very enjoyable, Mma," said Mr. Polopetsi. "The children are very keen to learn about chemicals. Maybe we shall have many chemists in Botswana in future years. You never know, do you?"

"That would be very good," said Mma Ramotswe. "And then there is your wife — I have heard that she is very senior now in the government offices."

"She has two secretaries," said Mr. Polopetsi, again turning to impart this information to Mma Makutsi, and then repeating it. "Two secretaries, Mma."

In Mma Ramotswe's mind there formed the sudden mental image of two Mma Makutsis — each with an identical hairstyle and big round glasses — sitting at a desk, pencils poised above their notebooks. How would she cope if Mma Makutsi were *doubled*? It would be very difficult, she thought; perhaps even impossible.

"I am glad to hear that," said Mma Makutsi. "It is good that there are many jobs for secretaries these days. In my day it was more difficult. You could graduate from the Botswana Secretarial College with a really good result . . ."

Mr. Polopetsi remembered, and grinned at the memory. "Yes, of course: with ninety-seven per cent . . ."

"Exactly," continued Mma Makutsi, acknowledging the implicit compliment with a nod of her head. "And yet even with that result you might find it hard to get a job. Even with that sort of result."

"They were difficult times," said Mma Ramotswe. "Things are easier now."

There was silence as Mma Makutsi decanted the freshly boiled water into the two teapots, stirred each briskly, and then

41

poured the brew into mugs.

Mr. Polopetsi sipped appreciatively at his tea. From the other side of the desk, Mma Ramotswe eyed him fondly. She had always liked Mr. Polopetsi — they all liked him — and had her business been more profitable she would have employed him without hesitation. But it was barely profitable — indeed, at the end of some months it did not even break even, and employing him would have sent the accounts deeply into the red.

She waited for him to speak, but he did not; instead he took another sip of his tea, exhaled a slight sigh of satisfaction, and continued to look at her with a sort of benign politeness — as if to imply that being in her company was all that he wanted.

Eventually she broke the silence. "So, Rra," she began, "have you come to ask me anything in particular?"

He seemed surprised by the question. "Why, no, Mma. I have no questions to ask."

She nodded. "I see."

"Yes," he said. "There is nothing that I want to ask of you."

Her relief was evident. "I am glad to hear that, Rra. Many people only go to see other people when they want to ask for some favour."

"Except for one thing," Mr. Polopetsi continued quickly.

"Oh."

"And it is not a favour. Well, it is not the sort of favour that people usually ask other people for. I think that you might call it an offer."

She raised an eyebrow. "An offer?"

"An offer of help." He paused before continuing, and threw a glance over his shoulder at Mma Makutsi, who nodded encouragingly. "You see, Mma Makutsi told me about this holiday you're taking . . ."

Mma Ramotswe threw a glance in the direction of Mma Makutsi, who smiled innocently.

Mr. Polopetsi noticed the glance, but continued nonetheless. "She explained that you would be taking this holiday, and I thought that I might come and work here while you are away and the agency is short-handed."

Mma Ramotswe held up a hand. "No, hold on, Rra. There is no money for a new post — even a temporary one. If there were such money, Rra, you would certainly be the first person I would turn to, but there just isn't. It is a simple fact of business life."

She put her mug firmly down on the table after she had finished this statement — a decisive gesture intended to make it clear there could be no further discussion of a possibility precluded by economic reality. Yet Mr. Polopetsi was not dismayed. "But, Mma," he protested, "this is not about money. I do not want to be paid. I just want to help . . . and to have something interesting to do. I am feeling bored at home, Mma. That is the problem for me. I am like a woman who has a rich husband and just sits about at home all day. I am like such a person, Mma."

After he had finished, for a few moments Mma Makutsi looked at him admiringly before she turned to Mma Ramotswe. "You see, Mma," she said, "it is all pointing one way. You must take a holiday. You can be sure that I shall run things here. I shall have Mr. Polopetsi to help me. I shall have Charlie as well. It will be a first-class team."

Mma Ramotswe stared through the window at the acacia tree that grew behind the building. It was home, on and off, to a pair of Cape doves, gentle, cooing creatures that led their innocent uxorious existence in its branches. But they were not there then, their place having been taken, briefly, by a small, unidentifiable bird that perched hesitantly on a swaying twig before launching itself into the air again. *They have their work to do,* she thought. *The birds have their work to do.*

Behind and above the branches of the tree was the sky, the great, empty sky of Botswana, indifferent, as the sky always was, to the things that went on beneath it: to the sudden animal dramas of life and death that took place on the plains of the Kalahari, to the grubby conflicts of the human world, the cruelties, the plotting . . .

Plotting. She looked at Mma Makutsi. She had done everything she could for her, right from that fateful day when she had appeared and more or less barged her way into the job of secretary to the fledgling No. 1 Ladies' Detective Agency. She had advised her, supported her, paid her when there was very little in the coffers and it had meant the curtailing of her own drawings; she had done all that, and now here she was plotting with Mr. Polopetsi of all people — although Mma Ramotswe accepted that he might be an innocent pawn — to dispatch her on some open-ended and possibly even permanent holiday; and all of this so that she, Mma Makutsi, could run the business as managing director.

Mma Ramotswe was not a vindictive woman — anything but — yet now she felt that something had to be said, even if her words might be little more than a mild reproach. Mma Makutsi could not be allowed to get away with this; could not be permitted to imagine that her machinations had not been seen for what they so clearly were.

"You know, Mma Makutsi," Mma Ramotswe began. "You know, anybody who listened to all this could well say: 'Why do they want to get her out of there?' Such a person might listen to all this and ask herself: 'Why are they so keen to send her off on a holiday that she does not want to take?' And then, if such a person got round to answering that question, the reply might be: 'Because a certain person wants to run the place and there is another lady in the way.' But if you get that lady out of the office, then everything will be in place to go ahead with the plan to do whatever it is that you want to do. Perhaps to change everything. Perhaps to do things that the other lady would not permit. Things like that." She paused briefly to take a breath. "What does the hyena do when the lion is away? He does all the things that hyenas would like to do but that lions will never allow. That is what he does. We all know that, Mma — we all know that."

She finished. She had held Mma Makutsi's gaze throughout the speech, but now she lowered her eyes and looked instead at the floor. She still felt the other woman's eyes upon her, though, and saw, at the edge of her field of vision, the flash of light from the large round lenses.

Mr. Polopetsi shifted awkwardly in his chair. "Oh, I don't know, Mma. I don't know —"

He was cut short by Mma Makutsi. "Mma Ramotswe," she blurted out. "I am very, very sad that you think that. I would never, never do anything like that, Mma. I would never do that. You, who have been my mother — yes, my mother, Mma — who took me on when I was just a nothing and gave me my chance. How could I forget that, Mma? How could I ever forget that?"

Mma Ramotswe swallowed. She looked up and saw that Mma Makutsi had removed her spectacles and was dabbing at her cheek with a handkerchief. It was not an empty gesture; it was not an affectation. Mma Makutsi was in tears. And she knew immediately, and with utter clarity, that she had been wrong.

"I was only thinking of you, Mma," Mma Makutsi continued, the words coming out between the sobs that now began to erupt. "I have been worried, you see, that you work all the time and never have a rest. You are always thinking of other people, Mma, and you never think of yourself. Well, you have to do that, Mma. You have to have some time to rest. You have to, Mma, or one day you will die, Mma. You will fall over like a cow and die, Mma."

She paused, which was the opportunity for Mr. Polopetsi to voice his view. "She is quite right, Mma Ramotswe. She did speak to me about it — yes, she did, but all she said was, 'I am very worried about Mma Ramotswe. She is working too hard.' That is what she said, Mma. That was all there was to it. And she is right when she said you could fall over like a cow. You could, you know, Mma. Just like a cow."

Mma Ramotswe rose to her feet and, brushing past Mr. Polopetsi, she crossed the floor to where Mma Makutsi was seated, head lowered in private anguish, wiping her glasses furiously to demist them. She bent down and put her arm about her friend.

"Oh, Mma Makutsi, I am so sorry," she said. "I should never have thought all that . . . all that nonsense. You are right, Mma — I need a holiday and you have been the one to tell me that. I can see that now. I am so sorry, Mma."

Mma Makutsi sniffed. She reached up and

48

put a hand on Mma Ramotswe's arm. "I am the one who should say sorry, Mma. I am the one who sometimes is not as tactful as I should be. They have always said that, you know. They said it up in Bobonong — they said you must not speak so directly. You must be more careful. And I think I know everything when I actually do not, Mma. I do not know everything."

"You know a very great deal," whispered Mma Ramotswe. "You got ninety-seven per cent, remember? You cannot get that mark if you do not know a lot."

Mr. Polopetsi voiced his agreement. "That is true. That is absolutely true."

"So," said Mma Ramotswe. "I shall start my holiday soon. I shall hand everything over to you and Mr. Polopetsi and I shall go and sit under a tree."

Mr. Polopetsi clapped his hands. "That is just the thing to do, Mma." He paused, and then added, "Which tree, Mma?"

Mma Ramotswe, surprised by the question, waved a hand airily. "Oh, there are many trees in this life," she said. "It does not matter too much which tree you choose, as long as you choose the right one."

Mma Makutsi and Mr. Polopetsi both nodded. They thought the answer very wise, although, on contemplating it a little later,

Mr. Polopetsi felt that it required a bit of further consideration: *if it did not matter which tree you chose, then . . .* But that was not the time for such reflection; not then.

Chapter Three:
The Great Man-Eater
of the Kalahari

"So, Mma," announced Mr. J.L.B. Matekoni over the breakfast table. "So, there we are."

Mma Ramotswe nodded. She was not sure exactly what he meant, but she saw nothing to disagree with in what he had said. "Yes," she replied, shelving the freshly washed cooking pot in which she had prepared his sorghum porridge. "Here we are."

"The first day of your holiday," he went on, licking a small amount of butter off a finger. "That is always a good feeling, isn't it? It's like a Saturday with a whole lot of other Saturdays stretching out beyond it. Just like that, don't you think, Mma?"

She was not quite sure she agreed. It was actually a Wednesday, as she had finally left the office late on a Tuesday afternoon, and as far as she could make out the day had nothing about it that distinguished it from any other Wednesday.

51

"One thing I do know, Rra," she said. "I feel that I should be going off to work, although I realise that I don't have to."

He chuckled. "A lady of leisure — that's what they call ladies who have nothing to do, isn't it? A lady of leisure." He paused, looked at his watch, and then rose to his feet. "There are many ladies like that in Gaborone, I think. You see them in their cars, driving around, but I'm not sure that they have anywhere to drive to. Some of them, I think, just drive round the block several times and then go home. That makes them feel they've been out."

There was a lot she could say about that observation. She might start by pointing out that the women in question had, in fact, plenty to do; that they were driving purposefully to do something useful at the other end of their journey; or that they were actually driving to their work as doctors or accountants or even the pilots of Air Botswana planes; or that they were in the middle of ferrying children about; or that they were going to shops to buy the supplies that they would subsequently cook for their men who *never* bothered to help in the kitchen. She could point all that out and then remind Mr. J.L.B. Matekoni that it might only be men who formed the view that these people were driving around aimlessly because they — the men in question — had no idea what women really did, but she said none of that because she knew that Mr. J.L.B. Matekoni was not one of those men who belittled women and that his remark had not been intended unkindly, and that, when all was said and done, it was probably just a little bit true: there were at least *some* women in Gaborone who had nothing to do but to drive around in that way. So she left all of this unsaid and went on, instead, to say, "I will not drive around like that, Rra — you know that, surely."

He was quick to agree. "Of course not, Mma. You will have many things to do, I think. You'll . . ."

The unfinished sentence hung heavily in the air, and Mma Ramotswe thought: *I cannot let it be like that.* She would never be one of those ladies of leisure with their driving round aimlessly until it was time for lunch with other ladies of leisure. No, she would do something with this holiday; she would . . . She faltered. It was difficult to think what she could possibly do. It was too hot to do any work in the garden, other than in the first half hour or so of light before the sun floated up above the line of acacia trees that made the horizon. Once that happened it would be too late; the very earth that one worked would become too hot to touch, and the only place to be, if one were outside, would be in the pool of shade cast by a tree.

Of course she could always go for morning tea at the President Hotel. She could sit out on the verandah, which was blissfully shaded, and watch people in the square down below, but there was a limit to how much time you could sit there, eking the last drop out of the teapot, before the waiters began to fuss about you and encourage you to give up your table to somebody else.

Apart from that, what was there to do? Her friends would all be busy, as they had things to do during the day — jobs to go to or children to look after — and of course none of them would be on holiday. But an idea came to her nonetheless, and now it struck her as being exactly the sort of thing one should do if one found oneself on holiday.

"I shall go to see Mma Potokwane," said Mma Ramotswe. "I have not been out to see her for some time, and I think I should."

A slightly doubtful expression crossed Mr. J.L.B. Matekoni's face. "A visit to Mma Potokwane? Well, perhaps . . . but don't you think that might not be the most restful thing to do, Mma? Whenever I go out there I am given something to do — fix the pump, please; make the windscreen wipers on the minibus work again, if you don't mind; could you look at a light switch in one of the houses, now that you're here, as it's sending out sparks when you turn it on, and I am worried about sparks when there are children about, Rra, as I'm sure you'll understand . . . That sort of thing, Mma."

Mma Ramotswe smiled. "That is because she knows you can do all those things, Rra. It is different when I go out there. Then she likes to eat fruit cake and talk. That is a good way of passing the time if you're on holiday — eating fruit cake and talking."

"That is all right, then," he conceded. "But remember, Mma, holidays are for doing even less than that. They are also a good time not to eat fruit cake and not to talk."

"I shall try to remember that," said Mma Ramotswe. And then a thought occurred to her. "Of course, they are also a good time not to have to do work in the kitchen."

He began to show his agreement, but faltered. "Within reason, Mma," he said. "But you are right about that. Women have so much work to do in a house and they deserve a holiday from that; of course they do. But . . ."

She waited. "But what, Mr. J.L.B. Matekoni?"

"But they cannot stop altogether, because if they did, then what would happen to the men, Mma? What would they do?"

"That is what women sometimes wonder, Rra," she said.

He cleared his throat. "They would never . . . they would never leave us altogether, would they, Mma? These ladies who call themselves feminists, are they saying that all women should get up and walk away? Is that what they want, do you think?"

Mma Ramotswe tried not to laugh at his sudden anxiety. She understood why some women should want to walk away — she herself had walked away from the dreadful Note Mokoti — and there were many of her sisters who would do well to walk away from their drunken and abusive husbands. But there were also many men — and Mr. J.L.B. Matekoni was one of them — who had done nothing to deserve such a response. "Of course not, Rra. There may be some ladies who say that all women should walk away from men altogether, but they are very few in number, I think."

He still looked worried. "Are there any such ladies in Botswana, Mma?"

She nodded. "Yes, there are, Rra. There

are ladies like that."

He shook his head in dismay. "Are they happy, do you think, Mma?"

"They say they are."

"But do you think they really are? Happy inside?"

She hesitated. "I think some of them are, Rra. And some of them, anyway — not all of them, but some of them — may not like men very much, Rra. They may prefer to be with other women, you see."

He stared at her. "Somebody told me that one day. I have heard such a thing."

She shrugged. "Different people like different things, Rra."

He lowered his voice, although there was nobody else present. "Do *you* know any ladies like that, Mma?"

She nodded. "Yes, I do, Rra. They are just like anybody else, you see — they are ordinary people."

He looked at her doubtfully. "Except for . . . well, they are unlike other ladies who are fond of the company of men."

"You could say that. But these days, Rra, things like that are not very important. There are parts of Africa, I'm afraid, that are being a bit unkind about these things and do not want people to be happy . . . in the way they want to be happy."

57

"That is very unkind."

They had negotiated the trickiest part of the conversation and come out on the other side more easily than she had imagined. She loved her husband, not least for his kindness, which had been evident in what he had just said. Unfortunately, there were many men who were not so kind, and they were often the ones who were in a position to make others unhappy; and would continue to do so, she imagined, until women asserted themselves more and then gently, very gently, took the reins of government into their own hands, or at least took their fair share of power — which was exactly half. Would that ever happen, she wondered? She thought it might be beginning — there were places where it was and they were working well. As long as the right sort of women became involved, of course, and not people like . . . She shuddered. She did not like to think of Violet Sephotho, but every so often she did.

"Violet Sephotho," she muttered.

Mr. J.L.B. Matekoni looked up sharply. "Is she one of those ladies, Mma?"

Mma Ramotswe smiled. "I do not think so, Rra. She is one who is always chasing men."

"I hope that the men she chases are fast

runners," said Mr. J.L.B. Matekoni.

"Some of them cannot run fast enough, Rra. Then they are caught. It is the same way in which a lioness catches one of those tiny antelopes they like to eat . . ."

"Duiker," said Mr. J.L.B. Matekoni. "Their meat is very sweet."

Mma Ramotswe remembered something. "I have heard certain ladies being referred to as man-eaters, Rra. Have you heard that expression?"

Mr. J.L.B. Matekoni nodded. "I have heard it."

"I think that people might call her that," she said. "They might call her 'The Great Man-Eater of the Kalahari.' "

He glanced at his wife. She was a kind woman — none kinder in Botswana — and it was unusual for her to make an uncharitable remark. And even as he thought this, Mma Ramotswe felt a sudden pang of guilt. Nicknames were popular, but they were often cruel. Did Violet Sephotho deserve such a cutting nickname? The answer, she realised, was probably *yes*. But no, that was no excuse. "Perhaps we should not call her that," she said, sounding a bit disappointed.

"Perhaps not," said Mr. J.L.B. Matekoni, adding, "Even if it does suit her rather well, Mma."

He looked at his watch. "It is time for me to go to work," he said. "I am not on holiday."

"I will make you some lunch," offered Mma Ramotswe. "That will give me something to do."

"I shall be back at lunch time, then." He paused. "Don't look for things to do, Mma Ramotswe. Remember that this is a holiday and you must not look for things to do on a holiday."

She promised him she would not. "I am already beginning to unwind," she said. "I am like a big spring that is unwinding slowly."

"That is good," he said. "That is exactly how it should be."

But that was not how it was — at least not on that first day of the holiday, and indeed not on the second or third day either. Shortly after Mr. J.L.B. Matekoni had driven off to work in his battered green truck, Mma Ramotswe found her way into the kitchen. She looked about her, at the cutting boards and the cupboards, at the stove with the discoloured heating plates, at the stacks of crockery on the shelves. Kitchens were quick to look shabby, and although Mr. J.L.B. Matekoni had painted theirs barely eighteen months ago, it was already looking slightly down at heel. Part of the problem, of course, was the absence of proper ventilation. Modern kitchens — and hers could not really be described as such — had extractor fans that took all the smoke and smells out. Mma Makutsi's kitchen in her new house was like that: she had two large metal hoods coming down from the ceiling in just the right place to catch the steam laden with fats that would otherwise be deposited on the walls and ceiling, the fingerprint of countless meals. That steam was ushered out of Mma Makutsi's kitchen, but in Mma Ramotswe's it swirled about until it settled in a thin layer over everything. If you fried a lot of foods — as Mma Ramotswe had to admit to doing — then you soon noticed the effect.

"Open a window," suggested Mr. J.L.B. Matekoni. "That's what I do in the garage when I run an engine. I open a window to let out all the carbon monoxide."

She admitted that this would help, but it was not a complete solution. The trouble with opening a window in Botswana was that even if you let certain things out, you also let other things in — and sometimes those things you let in were things it would be decidedly better to keep out. There were mosquitoes, for example, that loved open windows, even if the window was fitted with a metal mesh screen precisely to keep them out. Such screens were an inconvenience to mosquitoes, but nothing more than that; inevitably there were holes at the corners or there were places where the tiny wires that made up the screen had buckled or moved, creating a good place for mosquitoes to fly through.

Then there were those large black insects with wings. You never learned what these insects were; they made a lot of noise with the beating of their wings, and they had sharp points protruding from their heads, but they did not appear to belong to any known category of insect. Some people said that they were harmless and that it was bad luck to step on them and crush them; others said that if you let them crawl around your house they would just find a place to set up their own homes and breed their own families. "People have been pushed out by those insects," somebody once told Mma Ramotswe. "I know a woman who let one or two of them come into the house and then did not deal with them. Then two days later there were five hundred, and a few days after that all her walls were covered with them and she had to move out."

Mma Ramotswe did not believe that story; people exaggerated for effect, especially when it came to the creatures they encountered. If people said that they almost stepped on a snake in the bush, then that snake would always be a black mamba — it would never be one of those more numerous, but less dramatic, grass snakes. Those ordinary snakes were scared of people and would do anything to avoid an encounter, but they, for dramatic reasons, seemed never to feature in people's stories.

Mind you, that was no reason to be complacent about black mambas. Most people had seen one at one time or another, as black mambas were to be found now and then, along with cobras, puff adders, and other potentially lethal snakes.

As she looked around at her kitchen that morning, Mma Ramotswe wondered whether there were any places where a black mamba might lurk if it were to decide to come into the house. It was not at all fanciful to entertain such a possibility: snakes did come into houses, especially during the hot weather when even a cold-blooded creature like a snake might find the blast of the midday sun too hot to bear. She remembered a snake coming into the house in Mochudi when she was a girl and Obed Ramotswe spotting it. He had whispered to her to stand quite still while he reached for his *sjambok,* that hide whip used to drive mules and oxen. The snake, though, had seen his movement and had raised its head, ready to strike. Fortunately, it had thought better of it, and had turned tail and shot out of the house. She had not seen a snake in the house since then, but it was bound to happen sooner or later.

She noticed that there was a small hole between the floor and the base of one of the cupboards. She had not seen it before, and it occurred to her that the bottom of a cupboard, the dark place below, would be an ideal place for a snake to hide. Coiled up in such a refuge, cool and concealed, a snake would be well placed to take advantage of any scraps of food that might fall off the well-stocked shelves above . . . if snakes liked such things. Presumably they did. And of course there was nothing a snake liked more than a hen's egg, and there were always plenty of eggs in that particular cupboard. It would be simplicity itself for a reasonably lengthy snake — and black mambas were often as long as a person is tall — to slide the upper part of its body up to the bowl of eggs, open wide its hinged jaws, and swallow one. A black mamba might find such living quarters highly congenial and might live there for months, for years indeed, before the unfortunate householder detected his presence. And that would be the point at which the uninvited guest said to his unwilling host: "I'm sorry, but now it's time for you to go," and those wicked little fangs would be exposed and . . . She shuddered.

She crossed the kitchen to stand immediately in front of the cupboard. Very gently, she eased open the cupboard door and gazed at the shelves on which the various foodstuffs were stacked. Right at the top were the sweet things — the jars of produce she bought from the sale of work out at Kgali Junction: melon jam, cumquat spread, marmalade made out of bitter oranges from the Cape. There was the tin of Lyle's Golden Syrup, with its picture of a contented lion on the label; there was the box of sugar lumps; there was the sticky cordial that she had made for the children.

On the shelf below, she kept tinned foods: sardines from the fisheries of Namibia, bully beef from the factory down at Lobatse, tins of baked beans in tomato sauce. And then, on the shelf below, were the perishables — the packets of flour, the container into which she decanted the maize meal, and the bowl of eggs. She bought these eggs from a man who called round on his bicycle every week, a man who wore a crumpled hat not unlike the hat that her late father had worn; she could never turn down a man in a hat like that. He told her that they came from his hens at Mochudi, and she had bought them on the grounds that Mochudi eggs would have been the eggs she ate as a child, but then one day she discovered a supermarket stamp on one of them and her faith in the egg-man had been dented. His prices were still competitive, though, and she liked him in spite of his unreliability on that point.

She looked at the eggs. Suddenly she noticed that one of them had two small holes — two puncture holes — on its top. It was, she thought, exactly the sort of mark a snake would make if it had tried, and failed, to swallow an egg. She looked more closely, nestling the egg in the palm of her hand while she peered at the tiny punctures. The shell was slightly speckled at that point, with fragments of white mixed with the brown, and she decided, with a surge of relief, that these were not holes at all but imperfections in the surface: the egg itself was quite intact.

She replaced the egg and gazed at the food cupboard, trying to remember when it was that she had last tidied it. Never, she thought; I have never tidied the food cupboard. The thought made her smile. How many women were there in Botswana walking about with the guilty knowledge that they *had never tidied the food cupboard*? Everybody had some secret or other — something they had never confessed to another, even to those who were closest to them. In her work, Mma Ramotswe had learned this and had discovered, too, that even the most inconsequential of secrets could weigh heavily on a person's soul. An act of selfishness, some small unkindness, could seem every bit as grave as a dreadful crime; an entirely human failing, a weakness in the face of temptation, could be as burdensome as a major character flaw: the size of the secret said nothing about its weight on the soul.

She tried to think of any other secrets she might have, but she could think of nothing. She had a weakness for fat cakes, but then that was hardly a secret to anybody who knew her, and indeed half the population of Botswana — no, more than that — almost the entire population had that weakness. Perhaps further secrets would surface. And as for her friends, what about them? What secrets did Mma Makutsi have? The answer

67

to that came to her quickly: Mma Makutsi had more shoes than she would own up to having. She had claimed the other day she possessed only six pairs, but Mma Ramotswe was sure that this was not true. And Mr. J.L.B. Matekoni: What were his secrets? None, she thought — apart, perhaps, from the subject of at least some of his dreams. He was quite happy to tell her when he had had a dream about gearboxes and engines — which was almost every night, as far as she could work out — but there were some mornings when he said he did not remember what he had been dreaming. She was not convinced, but never pressed him on the matter.

And then there was Puso. He was such an odd little boy, with such an active imagination; one might suppose that his was a life filled with secrets, but she knew that this was far from true. Puso still had the honesty of childhood and tended to reveal without hesitation what was in his mind. But there was a secret — and now she remembered it. *Puso drank the bathwater when he was still in it.* She had seen him doing it, and had been about to admonish him when she stopped herself. Children needed at least some corners in their lives where there was no adult footfall. That might be one.

She reached out to the top shelf of the cupboard for a packet of spices. The date by which the contents were to be consumed was printed on the packaging. It was more or less exactly three years earlier. She picked up a jar of apricot jam. The children did not like apricots, and she and Mr. J.L.B. Matekoni were not great jam-eaters. She opened the jar: a crust of mould, cream and beige in colour, covered the jam, which could not even be seen beneath it. She shuddered: mould looked the way it did for a reason — it was a warning. She put the jar down on the floor, the beginning of what was to be a large stack of out-of-date or inedible foods.

The task of tidying the food cupboard took close to two hours, at the end of which the shelves were transformed, the foodstuffs arrayed in neat rows. It was just the sort of cupboard that a house-proud woman would keep — akin, she thought, to the well-ordered files in which Mma Makutsi took such pride.

It was half past ten on the first morning of her holiday. She had tidied the food cupboard, drunk two cups of red bush tea, and given her teeth a slightly longer-than-usual brushing. Now what? She walked into the living room and gazed out of the window, through the verandah, to the garden beyond. The day was well under way, the sun high in the sky, and there was not very much she could do in the garden in that heat. Even the verandah might be a bit uncomfortable, she felt, in spite of the shade it provided.

She sat down in one of the living-room chairs and looked about her. The room was tidy and the floor, made of squares of smooth cement, had been polished only a couple of days ago by Rose, her part-time cleaner. She had applied red polish until the floor was like a smooth red mirror, as slippery and almost as reflective. She looked up at the ceiling for cobwebs or for fly-spots: the white ceiling-boards, although buckled here and there, were pristine. The maid had cleaned even there.

Mma Ramotswe sighed. There was nothing to do in the house and nothing to do in the garden. She could read something, of course, but the magazines in her living room were well thumbed and familiar. There were several old copies of *Reader's Digest* and a *Drum* magazine from over the border, but even had she been in the mood to read she would have found nothing new there. She had read the *Reader's Digest*s from cover to cover, and *Drum* was more for the eyes than

70

for the mind, in spite of the irresistible headline displayed so prominently on its cover: "Man Mysteriously Loses Nose." Even yesterday's *Botswana Daily News,* brought home in the evening by Mr. J.L.B. Matekoni, had been thoroughly perused. And there was never anything really surprising in the newspaper because people were always doing the same things. People show no inclination to change, thought Mma Ramotswe; they do the things they've always done time and time again. It would be more newsworthy if people did not do the things one expected of them. That would be news indeed: "Finance Minister Makes No New Promises," or "No Sign of an Increase in Crime This Year," or "Minister of Water Affairs Says Nothing About Possible New Pipeline." People would be most interested to read *real* news like that.

She glanced at her watch. The last ten minutes had been very slow, and now it was only twenty to eleven. At this rate a day would seem like a week; a week would seem an eternity. No, she would not spend any more time sitting about the house, even if she was on holiday. She would go to the President Hotel and have mid-morning tea, with perhaps one or two of their fish-paste sandwiches to keep hunger at bay before

71

she returned to cook Mr. J.L.B. Matekoni's lunch. There was always a group of ladies having tea at the President Hotel — she had seen them there — and she knew one or two of them slightly. She could join them and enjoy a bit of stimulating conversation. Time always passed much faster when there was talk to be listened to.

CHAPTER FOUR:
YOU MUST NOT
SPANK ME, MMA

She parked under a convenient tree near
the President Hotel. As she locked the van
behind her, a young boy appeared out of
nowhere and stood in an attitude of expectation. "Two pula, Mma," he said.

"Two pula for what?" she asked. "Why are
you offering me two pula?"

The boy grinned, showing a set of brilliant white teeth. "I am not giving you two
pula, Mma — you are giving two pula to
me!"

"Oh, really?" said Mma Ramotswe. "And
why am I giving you two pula?"

"For deposit. Two pula now, and then two
pula when you leave. To look after your van."

Mma Ramotswe arched an eyebrow. "But
my van is all right. My van does not need
any looking after. It is not going to run
away."

The boy laughed. "Vans do not run away,
Mma! No, vans get damaged. That is the

problem for vans — they get damaged."

"And who damages them?" asked Mma Ramotswe, pulling herself up to her full height.

The boy moved back slightly. His cocky air was now somewhat dented. "Bad people," he said. "There are bad people who damage vans."

"Oh, I see," said Mma Ramotswe, advancing even further. "Then we shall have to get the police onto these bad people, I would say. Or maybe you can tell me who they are, since you seem to know so much about this."

"You'll be sorry," said the boy, his voice lowered. "If you do not give me four pula, then you will find that some bad person will have damaged it. Scratched it. Maybe put a nail in the tyres. There are many nails about here, Mma — many nails."

Mma Ramotswe's eyes narrowed. "If this van is damaged, young man, there will be a lot of trouble for you. I will give you a big spanking. I am very good at spanking people like you and you will be very, very sorry."

The boy took a step back.

"So now," she continued, "you just give me two pula right now — come on, hand over two pula. And if the van is not damaged when I come back, you can have your two pula back. If not, then you will get a very big spanking. I will find you. I am a detective, you see, and a detective can find a boy like you and give him a big spanking. Understand?"

The cowering boy reached into his pocket and extracted a couple of coins.

"Thank you," said Mma Ramotswe. "You will get this back later. It is a deposit for good behaviour. Understand?"

The boy nodded, and Mma Ramotswe, struggling to conceal a smile, began to make her way into the President Hotel. The trouble with the world today, she thought, was that people were not prepared to stand up to bad behaviour. They looked away, they pretended they had not seen anything, and hardly anybody bothered to deal with badly behaved children, with the result that they could run wild, could go on the rampage unchecked. It was not necessary to spank children — she did not approve of that and would never do that herself — but it was sometimes necessary to *threaten* to spank them. That, after all, was how young male lions were kept in order by the senior lions — and it worked. There were things, then, that lions knew, but that we did not; or that we did once know, but had now forgotten; not, she thought, that we should try to learn too many lessons from lions.

On the well-shaded upper verandah of the President Hotel, looking out over the traders in the square below, Mma Ramotswe negotiated her way between tables. The hotel was busy, and would become even busier at lunch time, when a buffet would be laid out. The customers for that were yet to arrive, the tables currently being occupied mostly by women meeting their friends before returning to their houses for lunch.

Mma Ramotswe looked about her. Gaborone had grown in recent years, but it was still in some senses a village, as many cities are, with a great deal of village intimacy surviving. It was rare for somebody like Mma Ramotswe to go about the town without spotting familiar faces, and here in the President Hotel there were plenty of these. There, for instance, was Mma Phumele, wife of Mr. Spots Phumele, owner of Deep Clean Cleaners ("We Do the Dirty on Dirt"). Seated next to her, expostulating on some topic of the day to an attentive audience, was Mma Gabane Gabane, mother of a senior government minister and rumoured, probably correctly, to be the formulator of virtually every policy of her

76

son's ministry. Then there was a lady un-known to Mma Ramotswe, but on the right of that lady was an old friend of Mma Poto-kwane's — a woman from Molepolole who had for many years been a matron at the Princess Marina Hospital and who was always selling raffle tickets for the nurses' benevolent fund.

Mma Phumele caught Mma Ramotswe's eye. "Come over here, Mma," she called. "There is a seat here for you."

The other women looked up. "It's Mma Ramotswe," said Mma Gabane Gabane. "Are you here on detective business, Mma? Are you going to investigate us?"

This was greeted with good-natured laughter.

"I am on holiday," said Mma Ramotswe. "I am not working at the moment."

"Then we shall be able to speak freely," said Mma Gabane Gabane.

Mma Ramotswe sat down and gave her order to the waitress who had been hover-ing round the circle.

"Mma Gabane was just telling us about a very silly woman," said Mma Phumele. "Tell Mma Ramotswe what you told us, Mma."

Mma Gabane Gabane seemed to be very pleased to be invited to repeat her story. "Well, Mma," she began, "this woman comes from up north, from Francistown. She came down here to work with the diamond people, and she met this very nice man who works as an accountant there. He has a very good job and is very solid. He is like a big tree, Mma."

"As solid as a big tree," said one of the other women. "You know the sort of man."

"And then," continued Mma Gabane Gabane, "they buy a really comfortable house out towards the airport — you know those new houses out there. It was very convenient for their work — both are in the Debswana building, you know. There is no problem parking there. So they get in the car in the morning and drive round to the diamond building and park very easily. Then they are inside, working away all day, until five o'clock, when they come out and drive their car back to the house just down the road. That is their life."

"And a very good one too," said Mma Phumele.

Mma Ramotswe nodded. She saw nothing wrong in such a life, but she had a feeling that something was shortly to go wrong. People who live near their work and have easy parking arrangements . . . well, even if they have husbands who are as solid as a tree, things can go badly wrong. Sex, she thought. That is what is going to go wrong here.

And she was right. "This woman," Mma Gabane Gabane went on, "this foolish, foolish woman met a young man who worked in the same office. He wasn't an accountant — nothing like that — he was a trainee, Mma Ramotswe, just a trainee. He was eighteen."

There was a sharp intake of breath from Mma Phumele, who looked at Mma Ramotswe to gauge her reaction. She would be every bit as shocked as the rest of them, she imagined. And Mma Ramotswe was shocked. "He was eighteen, Mma? Just eighteen?" she said.

"Eighteen," said Mma Gabane Gabane. "Eighteen years old, Mma. Can you believe it?"

"I can," said Mma Ramotswe, with a sigh. "I have seen things like that in the course of my work."

All eyes turned to her. "You have seen many such things?" asked Mma Potokwane's friend. "Eighteen-year-old boys with . . . with ladies over thirty?"

Mma Ramotswe lowered her eyes. She was not enjoying this conversation, but she had to say something. "There are many shocking things that happen," she said. "I see them in my work."

One of the ladies exhaled loudly. "You must tell us about these things some time, Mma," she said. "You must tell us about some of these shocking things."

"Yes," said another. "We are very keen to disapprove."

Mma Gabane Gabane asserted her control once more. "They were carrying on, Mma Ramotswe, in one of the cupboards." She paused, letting the full effect of this detail sink in.

"The stationery cupboard," said Mma Phumele.

Mma Ramotswe imagined what Mma Makutsi's reaction to that would be. *Stationery, Mma? They were carrying on in the stationery cupboard?* There was no doubt that Mma Makutsi's secretarial soul would be deeply offended by the very idea of conducting an affair in a stationery cupboard.

"But what if somebody came to get some paper?" asked one of the women. "Or a pencil? What then?"

"I think they probably locked it from inside," said Mma Gabane Gabane. "These people are very cunning once they start to get up to their tricks. They think of all the angles. I have seen it so many times before."

80

Now all eyes shifted to her; eyes widened at the thought of the subterfuges of those engaged in illicit affairs. What exactly had Mma Gabane Gabane seen? And would she share it with them?

But the conversation had to move on.

"What happened then?" asked a woman who up to that point had said nothing. "Were they found out?"

Mma Gabane Gabane drew in her breath in preparation for the denouement. "I will tell you what happened," she said. "The husband had no idea that his wife was having an affair with this . . . this boy. He had no idea at all. But — and here she's going to learn her lesson, ladies — but what she didn't know, that shameless woman, was that because of all the security they have to have in the diamond building, there were closed-circuit television cameras all over the place, including in the stationery cupboard. They have them there in case anybody might be tempted to take some diamonds in there to conceal them about their person."

"Ah!" exclaimed Mma Phumele. "They take that very seriously at the diamond place. If you go out to the mines, you know, you have to be X-rayed in case you swallow any of the diamonds."

81

"It is very important," said Mma Ramotswe. "We do not want people to steal our diamonds. We do not want any of this smuggling that goes on elsewhere."

"You are right, Mma Ramotswe," said Mma Gabane Gabane. "My son is always telling me about that. He says that we must keep our diamonds clean. He says that our Botswana diamonds are the cleanest in the world." She paused. "So there was a camera in there, and it was recording all the goings-on between this woman and this boy. And the man in the security department who looks at all these recordings is the cousin of that good man who is like a strong tree. He went to him and said, 'Your wife, Rra, is becoming a film star.' That is what he said, Bomma. Those were his actual words."

"Ow!" said Mma Phumele. "Was that the end for that woman?"

Mma Gabane Gabane nodded. "It is a big offence to carry on in a stationery cupboard. Not a criminal offence, of course, but an offence in terms of company regulations. That woman was fired from her job and her husband sent her home to Francistown. He was very, very sad. What is the use of having a good job and a nice house and then finding that your wife is meeting a young lover

82

in a stationery cupboard?"

"That man must have been very let down," said Mma Potokwane's friend. "I feel very sorry for him."

"You are right," said Mma Gabane Gabane. "He was very sad and he lost a lot of weight. I saw him a few days ago. He is thin, thin now. He is a very unhappy man."

"Well," said Mma Phumele. "People who do that sort of thing may reap what they sow, but they also destroy the harvest of those who are around them."

"That is very true," said Mma Gabane Gabane. "But I need more tea now, I think. Who is ready for more tea? Once we have more tea we can come back to this lady in the stationery cupboard."

Tea was poured, and the conversation drifted along. Then Mma Gabane Gabane said to Mma Phumele, "I see there is a new place."

Mma Phumele asked her what the new place was. "Everything is new these days," she said. "You close your eyes and there is some new place. What new place are you talking about?"

"It's a school of something or other," said Mma Gabane Gabane.

"I've heard there's going to be a school of fashion," said Mma Potokwane's friend.

"That will be very popular, I think. Why study mathematics or engineering or whatever when you can go and study what people are wearing?"

Mma Gabane Gabane found this amusing. "You could sit here in the President Hotel and write down notes on the clothes you see. That would be your homework."

"I think it would be more difficult than that," said Mma Phumele. "Fashion is a very complicated subject. You have to know about design and materials and all that sort of thing."

Mma Gabane Gabane nodded. "This new college is nothing to do with fashion. It's business, I think. Business or accountancy. They say that there will be many students coming to it."

She did not stay long. Making an excuse that was at least partly true — "I have to go home now to make my husband's lunch," the *now* being the untrue part — she walked back down the outside staircase that led onto the square below. She had not enjoyed her time with these ladies, whose conversation had been limited to the scandals of the day. It was not edifying to dwell on the failings of others; they might be lightly touched upon but should not be recited with such delight as these ladies had shown. At the end of the debate on the woman from Francistown and her trysts in the stationery cupboard, Mma Ramotswe felt sorry for her rather than disapproving or censorious; we might all have our heads turned by a young man, we might all yield to the temptations that the stationery cupboard offered; none of us was *above* all that. If this was what the world of idle women had to offer, then Mma Ramotswe was glad that she was fully employed, even if on holiday.

She walked round the side of the hotel to the place where she had left the van. It was still there, partly shaded by the tree under which she had parked it. That was good, as a vehicle left fully exposed to the sun in this hot weather would be a furnace inside once one opened the door. Sometimes it was impossible to get in until the interior had cooled down; sometimes it was necessary to spread a cloth or blanket over the seat or one might scald oneself on sitting down at the wheel. Sometimes the wheel itself was like a hoop of foundry-heated iron, far too hot for the human hand to touch.

Standing beside the van, feeling for the key in her bag, her eye was drawn to the side of the driver's door. It was unmistakable: a scratch, deep enough to be a gouge, had been made in the paintwork. On the ground below, a small line of white flecks marked where the fragments of paint had fallen.

She caught her breath. Then, dropping her bag, she emitted an involuntary wail as she bent down to examine the damage. Then she saw the nail, the instrument with which this assault on her tiny white van had been perpetrated. This had been tossed casually aside, as the knife of a careless murderer might be left at the scene of the crime — a further insult to the feelings of those who came upon the victim.

"My van," she muttered. "My van."

She stood up and looked around her. There was no doubt about the identity of the culprit; the boy had warned her of this, and now he had done exactly what he had threatened to do. The car park was largely deserted, although there was a man approaching from the square. He was heading towards a large Mercedes-Benz at the other end of the car park, and it occurred to Mma Ramotswe that the boy might be watching, hoping to collect his tip for looking after that car. She took a step away from the van to take advantage of the cover provided by the tree. She was not fully concealed — she was appreciably wider in girth than the tree

— but she was certainly less obvious.

The man approached his car, and as he did so the lights flashed in obedience to his remote unlocking fob. And that, it seemed, was the signal for the boy to appear, as he did seemingly from nowhere, but probably from behind a parked truck on the other side of the road. Running towards the man, he held out his hand and was rewarded with a couple of coins. He inclined his head gratefully, and then skipped back to his station on the other side of the road, unaware that Mma Ramotswe had returned and was watching him from behind her tree.

Mma Ramotswe lost no time. Striding out from behind her tree, she quickly crossed the road and intercepted the boy just as he was looking in the other direction and was therefore unaware of her approach.

"Now, young man," she said, reaching out and grabbing him by the scruff of the neck. "You are going to come with me. I want to show you something."

The boy struggled, but, had this been the boxing ring, he was a bantamweight in the grip of a champion heavyweight. He tried to kick himself free but was simply lifted up off the ground and held there while his scrawny legs kicked uselessly at the air. Then he was slowly lowered and the grip around his collar was reinforced by Mma Ramotswe's other hand grabbing the seat of his trousers. Carried bodily through the air, he was taken back to the van and lowered beside his handiwork.

"Why did you do this to my van?" she asked. "Why did you do it?"

The boy opened his mouth to speak, but managed no more than a half-strangled groan.

"Why?" repeated Mma Ramotswe. "Why have you done such a wicked thing to my van?"

The boy now began to whimper, and then, with a sudden shudder, started to cry. Between his sobs words could be made out — the truncated, isolated words of one who weeps as he speaks. "You must not . . . spank me, Mma. I do . . . not want to be spanked. I am . . . a bad boy, but you must . . . not spank me, Mma."

Mma Ramotswe slackened her grip.

"Please, Mma," sobbed the boy. "Please."

"I am not going to spank you." She sighed. "You will not be spanked."

The boy continued to cry. "I am very sorry, Mma. I am a rubbish, no-good boy."

She abandoned her grip altogether. "You must stop crying," she said. "It is no good crying."

She wanted to put her arms around him. She wanted to pick up this ridiculous little boy and comfort him. You could not harden your heart to tears such as these, whatever the boy had done — even if he had taken a nail to an innocent van. You simply could not.

"Listen," she said. "You stop crying and then you can tell me some things. I will open the door, and once the van is cool, we can sit in there and you can tell me who you are and where you live."

"I live nowhere," he said between sobs. "I am just a rubbish boy."

She reached for the handkerchief she kept tucked into her bodice and wiped at his cheeks. "Hush," she said. "You stop crying and then we can talk."

He looked up at her. "You are not going to spank me, then, Mma?"

"I am not going to spank you. There is no need for spanking."

CHAPTER FIVE:
THIS IS NOT A RUBBISH BOY

The boy looked at Mma Ramotswe, shooting a glance at her and immediately dropping his gaze to his feet and the dusty rubber mat on the van's floor. Her eyes remained upon him, and in the brief moment that he had looked at her, he knew that he was looking into the heart of something that was much bigger than anything else, much kinder, something that had nothing to do with the things that made his life so difficult — the threats, the beatings, the shouted abuse, the constant and necessary furtiveness.

Mma Ramotswe reached out to touch him gently on the shoulder. He flinched, and she felt the instinctive, self-defensive contraction. A boy of this size, particularly one who lived like this, would be all sinew and muscle, a tight spring of humanity, ready to run. "Where is your mother?" she asked. "Is she near here or . . ." Her hand waved in

90

the direction of the hinterland, vaguely to the north and west, to some ill-defined land of absent mothers. It occurred to her that she might as well point skywards — there were so many children now whose mothers had fallen victim to that cruel disease.

She removed her hand. "Is your mother late?"

She realised that she did not even know what he was called, and this made her question seem cold. Before he could answer, she asked him his name.

"I am just called Samuel," the boy said. "There is a Setswana name that I do not use. It is one of those names that makes me look stupid. So I use my other name, which is Samuel."

Mma Ramotswe nodded. She knew about the habit of giving comic, sometimes absurd names to children. *The one who screams and screams.* Or, *The one who is always hungry.* People went through their lives with these names, and never got round to doing something about it.

She would not ask him his Setswana name. Instead she said, "Then you should forget about that name and just call yourself by your other name. Samuel is a very good name for a boy." She paused, and then added, "For a big man too. I know a Samuel who is very strong. When I hear the name now, I think of him — of this strong man who is called Samuel."

She saw that he was calming down. The readiness to flee, the tensing of the muscles, was draining out of him, and he now sat back a bit in the seat. She repeated her question about his mother, but now added his name. "Is your mother late, Samuel?"

The boy shook his head. "She is not late, Mma. She is living over that side, over there. Down near Lobatse."

He pointed south.

"That is not too far away," said Mma Ramotswe. "Just one hour maybe."

He nodded, but she could tell that it was not a journey that he made frequently — if at all.

"Tell me about her."

He looked up sharply. He opened his mouth to speak, but thought better of it, and looked down at the floor again, his brow furrowed.

"There is something wrong, isn't there?"

"There is nothing wrong, Mma. She is down there — that is all."

"All right, Samuel. Your mother is there. And your father? Where is your daddy?"

He simply shook his head, and again she

knew: he would have no idea who his father was.

"Is she working?" asked Mma Ramotswe.

The question seemed to encourage the boy. He looked up and announced proudly, "She is a prostitute, Mma. She has a very good job as a prostitute. An uncle told me that."

Mma Ramotswe caught her breath. *He does not understand. He does not know what he has said.*

She gazed out of the van window. The sun was now more or less overhead, foreshortening shadows, making the solid things of this world, the buildings, the cars, the fences and signs, sharp and distinctive against the washed-out background that heat can create. It was like looking at things against the light; you saw the thing, starkly outlined, but you did not see what lay behind it — just the glare.

Did the sun make a sound? She had heard some people say that you could hear the sun when it was high in the sky like this, that it made a faint sound — not too loud, but audible nonetheless; a sound that could reverberate in your head if you stood out there long enough; a sound like the beating of wings somewhere high in the sky. She did not think this could be so; the sun would make the noise of a great furnace, but it was so far away and you would never get near enough to hear what it really sounded like.

She turned to him. "You do not see her, do you, Samuel?"

He bit his lip.

"She is very busy."

Mma Ramotswe sighed. "Of course she is." She fiddled with her key ring; a loop of twisted wire to which a tiny lump of fur had been bound.

"That fur," she said. "You see it? It's from a dassie."

The dassie was a rock rabbit, a small, rather surprised-looking creature that lived in the crevasses at the foot of rocky hills; against all likelihood, the dassie was related to the elephant.

"It's the cousin of the elephant," Mma Ramotswe said, smiling. "That is very strange, isn't it? One is so small and the other is so big."

Samuel looked doubtful. "It cannot be true, Mma. The people who say that are not telling the truth. A very small creature cannot be the cousin of a very big animal. That cannot be true."

She shrugged. "Why are you not at school?"

He shook his head. "I do not go to school. They do not want me in that place."

"They do, you know."

"No, Mma, they do not."

She switched tack. "How old are you, Samuel?"

He hesitated, and she realised that he did not know.

"I think you are ten. That is how old you are, I think."

He appeared to accept this.

"And where do you live? Where do you sleep at night?"

His voice was flat as he gave his answer. "I sleep at a house over there." He pointed to behind the old police station. "There is a woman who lets me sleep in her yard if I keep watch. I wake up if there is anybody who comes to steal and I shout out."

"She gives you food?"

"She gives me food and she washes my clothes for me. She sometimes gives me money if I do things for her. I wash her car. She gives me money for that, but not very much, as she is always giving money to her three real children. I am not her real child."

Mma Ramotswe listened carefully. There were a thousand stories like this, just in this town. If you went out into the country, to the small, out-of-the-way places, you would find a thousand more, and a thousand after that.

"She is kind to you, Samuel? This lady with the house — she is kind to you?"

"Except when she beats me, Mma. She sometimes beats me — maybe each week. She has a stick."

"Beats you for what?"

"When I am a rubbish boy. When I break something in the yard, or when she has been drinking beer. When she is drinking too much beer, then she likes to beat me. It is a hobby for her."

Mma Ramotswe winced. She knew the world was far from perfect and there were things that occurred that could turn the stomach, and did. She knew too that these things had a way of happening under one's nose, even in Botswana, for all that it was a fine country that did its best by people. Seretse Khama, the first President of Botswana, who had led the country in the first days of independence, who had held its hand as it went through that doorway, had made it clear that people should treat one another with courtesy and decency, and this is what people, by and large, had done — except in a few dark corners, where that other side of human nature, the side that does not like the sun, had flourished.

She reached across again to lay a reassuring hand on him, and this time he did
not flinch. When, she wondered, had this
boy last had a human arm around his
shoulders; when had he last been able to lay
his head on a comforting breast; when had
he last felt that he was loved?

"And your money?" she said. "This money
that you get from people who park their cars
— what do you spend that on? Food? Fat
cakes? Coca-Cola?"

He did not answer immediately, and she
repeated her question. "What happens to it,
Samuel?"

She was not prepared for his answer. "She
takes it from me."

" 'She'? The lady with the yard?" *I might
have said,* she thought, *the lady with the stick.*

He nodded. "She says I am working for
her. She says if I try to run away she will
tell the police about me and they will come
and beat me. She says that if I am not careful she will make me go and live in the bush
and I will die . . . There are still lions in this
country, Mma. They will eat me, won't
they?"

It took Mma Ramotswe a moment to
compose herself. Then she said, "There are
still lions in Botswana, Samuel. Yes, there
are lions, but they are not close by. They are

not in the bush near here." And she thought: *Lions are harmless by comparison with the creatures that move among us.*

She made up her mind. There are some decisions that require a great deal of thought, and others that require little, or even none. Sometimes, in the case of this last group, you know in your heart, and straightaway, what you must do.

"Where is this place, Samuel? I want to see this lady."

He seemed unwilling. "She will be very cross with me, Mma, if I take you there."

I'm sure she will, thought Mma Ramotswe. She leaned forward so that she was looking directly into his face. He stared at her, eyes wide. "Listen to me, Samuel," she said. "I am going to take you away from that lady. She is very bad. I am going to take you to another lady who is kind-kind. She will not beat you. She will give you a place in a room that is very clean. There will be other children who will be your brothers and your sisters."

She paused. She was not sure that he was taking it in. And she wondered, too, whether she could commit Mma Potokwane in this way. It was all very well making such an offer, but did she know that there was a place in the children's home, or would there be a

98

waiting list? Everything, it seemed to Mma Ramotswe, had a waiting list — except the government taxman and the call, when it came, to leave this world. You could not argue with the agents of either of these: you paid, and you went. *But I am just on the waiting list . . .* No, there is no waiting list for these things . . .

Samuel was mute.

"I am telling you, Samuel," she continued. "There is a good place for you. I shall take you there, in this van, straightaway after we have seen this bad lady."

He gasped. "But you must not call her that, Mma. She is not a bad lady. She will beat you."

Mma Ramotswe tried not to laugh. "Will she?" she asked. "I do not think she should try, Samuel. It is I who will beat her if she tries anything. I am a traditionally built lady, you know, and if there are any bad people who try to push me around — or to beat me — then I can sit on them very quickly. And if I do that, then they cannot breathe — all the air goes out of their lungs and they cry out, 'I am not fighting any more, Mma.' "

He looked at her with astonishment, but she realised that she had won for him whatever battle he had been fighting within.

She decided to press home. "So, that is all fixed up, then. You tell me where this place is and we shall go and fetch your things. Then we shall go to this other place."

She looked at her watch. She should be back at home preparing Mr. J.L.B. Matekoni's lunch, but he would assume that she had been delayed and he would make himself a sandwich. He enjoyed any excuse to make himself a sandwich that would always have too much of everything in it — too much salad cream, too much cheese, too much ham (if there was any in the house), and too much butter. She called it his "Too-Much Sandwich," but he laughed at this and said that when you worked under cars all day a "Too-Much Sandwich" was justified, even if it was far from healthy.

"It is over that way," he said, pointing to a small road that ran off in the direction of Extension Two. "It is not far away."

The house had once been a good one — one of the larger bungalows built by the government in the late nineteen-sixties for an employee of one of its departments, and then sold on to its occupant. It would have been lived in by tenants, ending up by some circuitous route in the hands of the woman who now owned it. It had not been properly

100

maintained, and she saw at once that the yard was ill kempt, which spoke volumes, as it always did. If you did not keep your yard in reasonable order, then your whole life would be similarly untidy. A messy yard told Mma Ramotswe everything she needed to know about its owner.

She could tell that the boy was anxious, and she sought to reassure him. "You can stay in the van, if you like," she said. "You do not have to get out."

He looked grateful. "Can I hide, Mma? Can I hide down below the seat?"

"Of course you can. You do not need to see this lady. But what about your things? How will I know what is yours?"

"I do not have many things, Mma. You can leave them."

"If that is what you want."

He nodded. "I am frightened of that lady, Mma."

"Of course you are. But you need not be, now that I am with you. I am going to tell her that you are going. That is all. I am not going to talk to her about it — I am simply going to tell her."

She nosed the van into the short driveway of the house. There was a well-placed acacia tree that provided a wide circle of shade, and she parked under this. As she did so, the boy slipped off the seat beside her, to crouch in the footwell of the van. She patted him on the back and smiled. "You will be all right, Samuel. You will be safe there."

She got out of the van and walked up to the front door of the house. There was a gauze fly screen in its top panel, but this had been ripped and not repaired. She knocked and called out, *"Ko, ko!"*

Somewhere within the house there was stirring.

"Who is that?"

Mma Ramotswe cleared her throat. "I have come to see you, Mma. It is important. I have something for you."

In Mma Ramotswe's experience, that always worked. If you told people that you had something for them, then they always responded quickly. Now, from deep within the house, there came the sound of footsteps.

A woman of about Mma Ramotswe's age appeared. She was stocky, but much lighter than Mma Ramotswe, and she was wearing a faded pink dress and bright orange shoes. Mma Ramotswe's eyes ran down her to the shoes. She thought, *Even Mma Makutsi would think these shoes are too much . . .*

"Yes, Mma?" said the woman. "What is it you have for me?"

"I have something for you," said Mma Ramotswe. "But maybe it is best for you to invite me in."

Not to invite a visitor to enter was a grave discourtesy, but it did not surprise Mma Ramotswe at all.

"Of course," said the woman. "I am forgetting my manners, Mma. You must come in."

The other woman's tone had become unctuous. *She wants whatever it is I have,* thought Mma Ramotswe; *that is why.*

They entered the living room. It was untidy, and shabby too. Against one wall stood a stained and greasy sofa on which a number of magazines had been strewn. There was an empty beer bottle on the low table and an ashtray full of *stompies,* the stubbed-out ends of cigarettes. There was the stale smell of lingering tobacco smoke, mingled with cooking odours of an indeterminate nature.

Mma Ramotswe went right to the point. "There is a boy called Samuel. I have just met him."

The woman's reply was sneering. "Yes, there is that boy," she said. "So what? I am looking after him because his mother is late."

Mma Ramotswe frowned. "She is not late.

She is down in Lobatse."

The woman seemed genuinely surprised. "Oh no, Mma. That woman is late. She died last year."

Mma Ramotswe thought quickly. "But Samuel said to me that she is living down there. He said that . . . Well, I'm afraid that he said she was a prostitute. I don't think he understood."

The woman laughed. It was a crude, rather raucous laugh. "Yes, she was a prostitute. And that is why she died, you see. I have not told that boy that his mother is late. Why should he know? He will be unhappy if he learns that, don't you think?"

For a short while Mma Ramotswe was speechless. But then she recovered and said, "I am very sorry to hear that his mother is late."

"Well, many people die, Mma," said the woman. "He is lucky that I am here to look after him."

It was too much for Mma Ramotswe to bear. "You are not looking after him, Mma. You are using him as a thief — as *your* thief. That is what you are doing."

This elicited a sharp response. "How dare you say that, Mma! You come in here and you say things like that to me . . . in my own house. You watch your tongue, fat lady.

You just watch your tongue."

"But my tongue has some more things to say, Mma. I am taking that boy away from you. I am taking him to a safe place for children."

The woman let out a howl of rage. "You are not taking that boy! He is mine. You are not taking him, you big cow!"

As she hurled the insult, the woman advanced threateningly on Mma Ramotswe, and then, without any warning, launched herself upon her, intent on scratching her. Mma Ramotswe felt a nail scrape against her neck, and parried with her forearm. Then, exerting as much force as she could muster, she pushed her weight against the other woman.

It happened as if rehearsed one hundred times. As Mma Ramotswe's superior weight came to bear on her, the woman was momentarily unbalanced, and then, almost in slow motion, fell to the floor. Without waiting, Mma Ramotswe lowered herself to sit upon her opponent. It always worked; it always worked.

From beneath her there came muffled cries and a frantic thrashing movement. But there was no release.

"I am going to sit here for a few minutes," said Mma Ramotswe. "During that time, you can think about things. You can think about what you will say to the police if I go to tell them that you have been keeping that boy here and taking his money. You can think about what you will say when they ask you how he got that money."

There was silence.

"Have you started to think about that, Mma?" continued Mma Ramotswe. "Because once you have thought about all that, you can think about how it will be much easier for you if you let him go without any fuss. If that happens, then there will be no trouble for you."

She waited for a short time before she spoke again. "Have you thought about all that, Mma?"

The reply was terse — necessarily, as the woman was still winded. "I have thought about it. You can take him."

Mma Ramotswe rose to her feet, allowing the woman beneath her to gasp for air and reinflate. She did not enjoy sitting on people, but every so often it was necessary, and in this case it was entirely justified by self-defence. If people came at you and started to scratch you, then of course you had the right to sit on them. Even Nelson Mandela, she told herself, who was a good

and gentle man, would have agreed with
that.

CHAPTER SIX:
I THINK THIS IS A
COLLEGE FOR GHOSTS

Mma Ramotswe did not stay long at Mma Potokwane's — it was not necessary. Relieved at the ease with which her mission had been accomplished, she drove out of the Orphan Farm gate shortly after two o'clock, slightly light-headed at the significance of what she had achieved within the last couple of hours. A young life that had been bleak at eleven o'clock that same morning now had a very different feel to it. It was not a big change in the overall scale of things; it was not something that would be noted by more than a handful of people — at the most — but it was something to be pleased with, something even to sing about. And she did sing as she drove back along the Tlokweng Road, dredging up from memory a song she had last sung many years before, when she was still a young girl in Mochudi. A teacher had taught them the words of a traditional Setswana song about a boy who lets a trapped bird free and who is later saved by the very bird he liberated. The boy was lost in the bush, she recalled, and the bird remembered him and flew in front of him, leading him back to the path. We are all lost in the bush, she thought — every one of us, even if we do not know it. And somewhere there will be a bird that will lead us back to the place we need to be . . . Was that true? She smiled. Life was not that simple, even if there were songs that made us think it was. But we could still sing them; we could still open the window of our van and sing them out into the passing air, unconcerned as to whether people would be puzzled, or amused perhaps, at the sight of a traditionally built lady in a small white van singing out at the top of her voice for no discernible reason . . .

She felt vaguely guilty about not having been at home to make Mr. J.L.B. Matekoni's lunch, as she had promised she would. She knew that he would be content with the sandwich that he would have made, but it was not just the food, it was the breaking of a promise. Of course he would understand; in her work things were always cropping up and requiring a change of plans — except for one thing: she was now on holiday.

She considered dropping in on him to explain what had happened, but decided against it. It would not do, she felt, to turn up at the garage — which of course shared its premises with her own office — on the very first day of her holiday. It would imply that she did not trust Mma Makutsi to run things while she was away, and she did not want anybody to think that. No, she would telephone the garage when she got home and tell him then what had happened.

But before she returned to Zebra Drive there was shopping to be done. She did not have a long list, but there were things that needed to be bought for that evening's meal and to replace some of the ancient foods she had cleared off the pantry shelves. Desiccated coconut — something that Mr. J.L.B. Matekoni loved on the rare occasions when they had a curry — was no use if it had somehow absorbed moisture and turned hard and yellow. And brown sugar, normally so useful for making the banana loaf that Puso and Motholeli so hankered after, was similarly spoiled when ants had somehow worked their way into the package and established a thriving city, like a tiny termite mound, complete with tunnels and all the public buildings that ants create for themselves.

She parked in her usual place at River-walk, greeting Mma Motang, the elderly woman who was parking next to her and whom she recognised from church, the woman who always volunteered to help with tea after the service and who invariably succeeded in pouring almost more tea into the saucer than into the cup — which did not matter too much, as we all have our failings, and everyone simply poured the tea from the saucer back into the cup; and it cooled the tea too, and made it unnecessary to blow across the surface before taking a sip. That could have unfortunate consequences, as had happened when the chairman of the vestry, a solemn accountant, had inadvertently blown tea over the shirt of the Minister of Roads, who had been invited to the cathedral to give a talk entitled "Life's Journey: Taking the Right Turnings." The minister had made little of it, but his shirt was stained with small brown dots, and his wife, a rather sour-faced woman, had stared in a very hostile way at the chairman.

Her elderly neighbour's parking was not all that it might have been, and she bumped into Mma Ramotswe's van, braked sharply and reversed, scraping the paintwork as she did so. Mma Ramotswe turned off the van's engine and sighed. It was not the other woman's fault — well, it was, she supposed, but not her fault in any real sense. Things like this just happened, particularly if you were a bit shaky, as Mma Motang was. And did it matter all that much if the side of your van took the occasional blow? We all took blows in this life, and if you were a van, then this was just the sort of blow that came your way.

Mma Ramotswe got out of the van and walked round to Mma Motang. She saw that the other woman was sitting bolt upright, her hands covering her face in shame.

"Don't worry, Mma Motang," she said. "We all hit other cars. I do it all the time. Almost every day."

Mma Motang lowered her hands. "I am very stupid, Mma. I was paying attention, but I thought I had more room."

"That is not your fault," said Mma Ramotswe. "Cars are too big these days. That is why they are always bumping into things. If there is any fault, it is the fault of the people who are making all these big cars."

If there was comfort in this remark, it was not enough to console Mma Motang. "My husband will be very cross," she said, shaking her head. "He will tell me that I should not be driving. He says that women are

112

always bumping into other cars. He will say that this is just more proof."

Mma Ramotswe could not let that pass. "There are many men who say things like that. They are wrong. Women drive much more slowly than men. It is men who drive around at high speed and cause all those bad accidents. I have seen it many times, Mma. It is men themselves. We women just drive around and bump into things very slowly. We do not cause all that much damage."

"But he will not see it that way, Mma. He will not look at it like that."

Mma Ramotswe made a gesture that was unambiguously dismissive of those who thought as Rra Motang did. "There are some men who have not become as modern as they should."

"He is one of them," agreed Mma Motang. "That is definitely him."

"None of our husbands is completely modern," said Mma Ramotswe, with a smile. "They try — some of them — but they do not always succeed. The old Adam in them comes out, I'm afraid." She liked the expression "the old Adam," which she had heard somebody use on a Radio Botswana discussion programme. Others had heard it too, and it had been dropped, by

Mma Gabane Gabane, no less, into that conversation in the President Hotel, that conversation about that feckless woman from Francistown. "Let a man into a stationery cupboard and the old Adam comes out," she had said — or something like that.

Mma Motang was still considering the consequences of her accident. "He'll hear about it when the insurance claim comes in," she said. "He will be very upset by that."

"Insurance claim?" said Mma Ramotswe. "There will be no insurance claim, Mma."

"But I have scraped your paintwork, Mma."

Mma Ramotswe laughed. "That is always happening to me. It happened only this morning — a bad scrape — much worse than the one you made."

"But —"

"There are no buts, Mma. The insurance people are very busy with all sorts of serious claims. I do not want to make their life more difficult by going to them with a tiny scrape that will need a magnifying glass to see. I do not want to trouble those poor insurance people."

Mma Motang's relief showed immediately. "Then my husband need not hear about this?"

Mma Ramotswe had an idea. "No, he

need not, Mma. And if he asks you what happened today, you can simply reply: 'I bumped into Mma Ramotswe in the supermarket parking lot.' And he will think nothing of it, and you will have told him the whole truth."

It took Mma Motang a moment or two to appreciate the joke, but when she did her anxious expression became one of delighted amusement. "I bumped into Mma Ramotswe . . . Yes, I did, Mma, I did!"

They walked into the supermarket together. Mma Motang had a long shopping list, and bade farewell to Mma Ramotswe as they went their separate ways. "You are a very kind person, Mma Ramotswe," she said as they parted. "God bless and keep you, Mma."

Mma Ramotswe acknowledged the blessing with a smile, but said nothing. She had been reminded — there in the middle of the supermarket — of her last moments with her father, her dear daddy, the late Obed Ramotswe, who was now in that other Botswana, the one beyond this Botswana, where there were herds of slow-moving white cattle and where all the late people from Botswana were together once more; and she remembered how the minister had come to see him to say goodbye, and how he had used those precise words as he laid his hands upon her late father's brow: "God bless and keep you, Obed Ramotswe."

She stood quite still. Late people do not altogether leave us, she thought; they are still with us in memories such as that, wherever we are, no matter what time of day it was or how we were feeling, they were there, still shining the light of their love upon us.

She was not sure how long she stood like that, lost in thought and memory. Nobody paid her any attention, assuming that she was trying to remember whatever it was that she had come to buy and had forgotten. One woman almost asked her where the butter was, as she looked like one who would know about butter, but she saw how deep in thought she was and refrained from disturbing her.

It was the impact of a shopping cart that roused her from the reverie. A man had turned the corner too quickly, and the shopping cart he had been pushing, a cart piled high with the booty of half an hour's wandering the aisles, collided with Mma Ramotswe's still-empty trolley.

"Oh, I'm very sorry, Mma," said the man, and then, looking up, "Mma Ramotswe! It is you I have bumped into."

116

Mma Ramotswe was surprised to see Mr. Polopetsi. "Rra . . . I had not expected to see you." She had not expected to see anyone, but Mr. Polopetsi was even more unexpected than anybody else.

"I wasn't looking where I was going," he said. "I turned that corner and . . . well, it is very good to see you anyway."

"This is the second time I've been bumped into this morning," said Mma Ramotswe. "If things happen in threes, then I am going to drive home very carefully."

"It's always a good idea to drive very carefully," said Mr. Polopetsi. "Especially with all these lunatics they are putting on the roads these days." He shook his head in despair. Then he continued, "Sometimes, you know, I think that they have the driving licence office down at that place for lunatics near Lobatse. They give them all a licence when they let them out."

"It is not the lunatics who drive badly," said Mma Ramotswe. "It is young men." She thought of Charlie. "As for those poor people, many of them are very nice, Rra. I had a cousin who was a registered lunatic. He was very kind." She remembered him fondly — that quiet, rather withdrawn man, who told anybody who cared to listen that he was related to a family of zebras on his

117

mother's side.

Mr. Polopetsi looked abashed. "I am very sorry, Mma. I did not mean to be rude. And I know we shouldn't call them lunatics any more. I did not mean to be offensive."

She smiled at him to set him at his ease. "Of course not, Rra. How are . . ."

She started her question just as he began his. "How is your . . ."

She laughed. "You go first, Rra."

"I was going to ask how your holiday was going. Are you already feeling rested?"

"It is going very well, thank you. I am very rested already." But she thought: *My van has been damaged twice; I have been scratched by a violent woman and have had to sit on her; I have removed a little boy from near-slavery, and I have narrowly avoided being run over by a shopping cart . . .* She decided not to mention any of this, but instead asked him how things were going in the office.

"I was in this morning," he said. "I am not teaching chemistry this afternoon, and so I am doing the shopping for my wife. She gives me a big list, you see, and then I go round and buy the things on that list. That is what I have been doing."

Mma Ramotswe hesitated. She did not wish to seem too keen to find out what was

118

happening in the agency, but she could hardly miss this opportunity.

"Were things busy this morning?" she asked, trying to sound as casual as possible.

"They are always busy," said Mr. Polopetsi. "You know how it is."

It was not a very satisfactory answer. Mma Ramotswe wanted to know exactly what was going on, and this vague response told her nothing much.

"Anything in particular?" she asked.

"Oh, there is always something," replied Mr. Polopetsi. "One thing comes in and then another thing, and then you sort out one of them and you are still left with one thing. You know how it is."

She found herself becoming annoyed by the repeated refrain of "You know how it is." She tried to make light of her irritation. "I'm not sure that I know how it is," she said. "That is why I'm asking you."

Mr. Polopetsi frowned. "Asking me what, Mma?"

She decided to be frank. "I'm asking what is going on — that is what I'm asking." She paused. "You see, I'm still the owner of the agency. I have not sold it to Mma Makutsi. I am the owner."

"But you're on holiday. I don't want to burden you with petty details. I don't want to say to you, 'Oh, we had a telephone call from such-and-such a person and then I made tea and then Charlie fetched the mail.' You don't need to know that when you're on holiday, Mma Ramotswe."

There were very few people whom Mma Ramotswe wanted to shake; indeed, she could not remember when she last wanted to shake anybody, but now she felt the urge to shake Mr. Polopetsi. She would not shake him vigorously — she did not want to hurt him in any way — she just wanted to shake the desired answer out of him. But of course she would not, and so, after taking a deep breath, she simply said, "Let me put it this way, Rra: Was there any new business today? Any new clients?"

Mr. Polopetsi looked apologetic. "I can see that I should have told you in the first place, Mma. You have every right to know."

She relaxed. "Thank you."

"And the answer is no."

She felt a mixture of relief and disappointment. She was relieved that there had been no new clients because that saved her from feeling anxious as to whether Mma Makutsi would deal with them properly, but she was disappointed for the lack of news, for the lack of something to think about.

"Well, Rra," she said, "I hope everything

goes well. I know that you are a good pair of hands to leave things in."

He beamed at the compliment. "I do my best, Mma. I will always do my best for you — you know that."

And she did. Mr. Polopetsi, she felt, was one of those people who would never allow his own ego to get in the way of duty. He was a modest and unassuming man; he was the sort of man who would loyally serve an employer, who would never jockey for promotion or seek personal advantage. He was a good man.

She looked at her watch and explained that she would have to get on with her shopping. He said he must do the same, as he was cooking the evening meal for his wife.

"There are not many men in Botswana who can say that," said Mma Ramotswe.

Mr. Polopetsi acknowledged the compliment, but bowed his head as if to accept responsibility for the failures of all the other men. "I only have one recipe, Mma. Maybe I will get another one some day."

"That would be nice," said Mma Ramotswe.

She loaded her purchases into the back of the van, taking care to shelter the butter and milk from the direct rays of the sun. In this heat, exposure to even a few minutes of direct sunshine could turn milk sour and reduce butter to an oily puddle. There would have to be rain soon, she thought; the land was crying out for it. It would come, of course, as there had been rain further north and people were talking of a good season, but until that happened the heat would drain the life and energy from everything. What they would see first would be a darkening of the sky in the east — a change from empty blue to a grey-white that would gradually shade into a heavy, inky purple. And then there would be a wind — the wind that preceded a storm and carried the smell of rain on its breath. Leaves on the ground would be lifted, would dance briefly in tiny eddies of agitated air; trees would begin to sway as if bowing to the approaching shower. That would come suddenly, in a white sheet moving swiftly across the sky, accompanied by peals of thunder and brilliant flashes of silver lightning.

That would all happen, but its time was not yet. And so the van exhaled oven-hot air when she opened the door; and so the steering wheel was almost unbearably hot to the touch; and so the heat off the tarmac was a dancing shimmer. Her groceries stacked away, she drove out of the car park and began to make her way back to Zebra Drive.

Not far from the side gate to the university, a sign at the edge of the road caught her eye. She slowed down to read it. *Coming soon. The new headquarters of the No. 1 Ladies' College of . . .*

She did not have time to finish reading before driving past. And for a moment she thought that she had imagined the last few words. *The No. 1 Ladies' College of . . .* Surely not; the eye plays tricks on us; a few letters, seen quickly, might be made whole by the brain, but to completely misleading effect. The other day she had spotted a headline in the *Botswana Daily News* that read "Man Accused of Eating Neighbour's Children." She had been astonished, although nothing, she reflected, should astonish us any more; and then, going back a line, she had read it correctly as "Man Accused of Eating Neighbour's Chickens." She had mentioned this in the office, and Mma Makutsi had revealed that she knew the man in question — he had lived near her last house, the one she had occupied before she married Phuti Radiphuti, and nobody in the area had liked him much. "I am not surprised that he has been caught doing this," said Mma Makutsi. "It was only a question of time." But Mma Ramotswe had wondered about that; an unpopular man might well be accused of things he did not do, and could protest his innocence in vain. "It only says that he is *accused,* Mma," she had pointed out. "It does not say that anything has been proved."

Mma Makutsi was unconvinced. "Where there is smoke there's fire, Mma. I have always said that."

Mma Ramotswe could not let that pass. "But what does Clovis Andersen say in *The Principles of Private Detection,* Mma? Does he not say that you must be very careful to decide where the smoke is coming from? Smoke can drift, Mma. Those were his exact words, I think."

"Hah!" said Mma Makutsi. "There are more ways than one of looking at things."

The matter had been left there, with Mma Ramotswe asking herself whether Mma Makutsi was perhaps over-reaching in questioning — even if only indirectly — the authority of Clovis Andersen. Was she implying that she knew better? It did not bode well for her time at the helm of the agency if she were setting herself up as a greater authority than the author of *The Principles of Private Detection.* But she let things rest, and nothing more was said.

She put her foot on the brake, steering the van onto a rough track that led from the road to a strip of waste ground alongside it. By doubling back along this track she was able to draw level with the sign and read it properly. There was no reason why anybody should not call a business the No. 1 anything, but to combine No. 1 with Ladies' was without question taking matters too far. Perhaps she had misread it. Perhaps it was just the No. 1 something or other, without any mention of ladies. But no, it was as she had feared, painted in large, confident lettering, with quite breathtaking temerity.

Coming soon. The new headquarters of the No. 1 Ladies' College of Secretarial and Business Studies. A bright future awaits you! Enrolling now.

She read and reread it, and as she did so she remembered the conversation in the President Hotel. Then her gaze moved to something else. Depicted immediately below the wording there was a pointing hand, a neatly painted female hand . . . with long red fingernails. She gazed at the fingernails. There was something about them that disturbed her. It was bad enough that somebody was using the No. 1 description — and she supposed she could hardly stop that, even if it was derivative — but the

125

fingernails were something else altogether. Why should she worry about fingernails like that? Who had such fingernails? Long, sharp fingernails . . .

For a good few minutes Mma Ramotswe sat in her van, feeling vaguely uneasy. The engine was still running and the fan was doing its best to provide a current of air, but slowly the heat increased and discomfort stirred her. The painted hand pointed down a side road, one of those in between minor thoroughfares, tarred at some point but now largely forgotten by those responsible for maintaining it. Putting the van into gear, she turned down this road, thinking as the van bumped along its way of what she would say to Mma Makutsi. "Not just any school of secretarial studies, Mma, but the No. 1 Ladies' College . . ." Mma Makutsi would be indignant, of course; she was proud of the agency's name, and the thought that somebody should be using part of it in direct competition with her own alma mater, the Botswana Secretarial College, would undoubtedly distress her.

The building was only a short distance down the road. It was part of a small block that consisted of a bakery, an accountant's office, a paint depot, and there, at the end, a set of premises under renovation but already boasting a large, freshly painted sign identifying it as the No. 1 Ladies' College. Mma Ramotswe drew up directly outside the front door.

A man dressed in a painter's outfit appeared from round the side of the building. Getting out of the van, Mma Ramotswe approached him and greeted him in the traditional way.

"*Dumela,* Rra. Are you well?"

The man, who had been carrying a small ladder, rested the ladder against the wall. "*Dumela,* Mma. I am very well."

He looked at her expectantly.

"This is a new business, is it, Rra?"

The man nodded. "It will be opening next week, I think. I am just finishing some of the painting. Then it will be ready."

Mma Ramotswe smiled. "It will be very popular, I think. There are many people wanting this sort of qualification these days."

The man looked at her shrewdly. "Do you think so, Mma?"

She had not expected this. "Well, yes, I do. There is always a good demand for people who can do secretarial work. There are plenty of good office jobs going."

The man shrugged. "Maybe." He hesitated. "But who is going to do the teaching,

Mma? That is what I'd like to know. There is only one person running this place, I think."

Mma Ramotswe stiffened. It would be easy to ask directly, but she thought that it might be better to do so more tactfully. People could clam up if you appeared to be too interested in finding out something.

"Well, there are many one-man businesses, Rra . . . or one-lady businesses, should I say?"

The man shrugged again. "Everything done by her? By that one lady? I don't think so, Mma."

"Why do you say that, Rra?" She still had not asked the name. *Painted fingernails . . . painted fingernails . . .* These were common enough; just about everybody had painted fingernails. But long, scratchy ones . . .

"Because I do not think that one teacher can run a whole college."

Mma Ramotswe made a dismissive gesture. "But she won't run the whole college by herself. There will be other teachers, surely."

The man picked up his ladder. "I haven't seen any, Mma. When she comes round here, it's just her. And inside . . ." He tossed his head in the direction of the front door. "Inside there is only one desk in the office.

128

Just one. One desk and one chair." He gave Mma Ramotswe a challenging look. "Will the other teachers not sit down, Mma?"

"Maybe they'll come in and teach their lessons and then go. In many places like this the teachers are part-time."

He made a disbelieving sound. "And where are the seats for the students?"

"There are no seats at all, Rra?"

"Four chairs," he said. "Four chairs and one desk that isn't very big. That is all, Mma." He began to move away. "I think this college is a college for ghosts, Mma — that's what I think."

Mma Ramotswe took a step back towards her van, but then she half turned and said, "Oh, one thing, Rra . . . who is this lady?"

But at that moment, even as she uttered the question, the answer came to her. It came unheralded, but with complete certainty — so much so that she barely needed to listen to his response, which was audible, but only just, for there was at that moment a rumble of thunder. She looked up sharply, as did he, and they saw that the sky in the east had darkened slightly; the storm was as yet only a promise, but it might well come their way. She smiled at him, and he at her, as they were united in their relief that at last there was a sign of the rain that the country so thirsted for.

CHAPTER SEVEN:
SHE'S AT THE CONTROLS
NOW, NOT YOU

If there had been drama for Mma Ramotswe that day, then the same was true, she discovered, for Tlokweng Road Speedy Motors. Fanwell, the young mechanic, had lowered a car onto his foot, with the result that he'd had to be rushed to the emergency department at the Princess Marina Hospital.

"I warned him and warned him," said Mr. J.L.B. Matekoni as he came into the kitchen on his return from work. "I warned him, Mma Ramotswe. You probably even heard me — many, many times."

She nodded; she had heard him. He had a special voice for the issuing of warnings — the sort of voice that ministers sometimes used in church when they had something special to say. It was a voice that you felt you had to listen to — or you ignored at your peril.

"I've said it so many times," he continued. "You'd think they would remember. *When you're lowering anything — anything at all — always, always, always look at what you're lowering it onto.* Doesn't that make sense? Isn't it the sort of thing your great guru tells you in that book of his?"

"Clovis Andersen? *The Principles of Private Detection?*"

"Yes, that book."

Mma Ramotswe could tell that he was angry, which was an unusual state for him. Normally Mr. J.L.B. Matekoni was the most equable-tempered of men, but now there was a note of frustration in his voice.

"I know he's more careful than Charlie ever was," he continued. "He's in a different class altogether. But you'd think that he'd have more sense, you really would."

"He's still young," said Mma Ramotswe soothingly. "We have to remind ourselves of what we were like when we were Fanwell's age."

Mr. J.L.B. Matekoni made a visible effort to calm down. Mma Ramotswe always managed to put things into perspective. "Everything could always be worse," she would say, "and so be grateful that things are only as bad as they are." She was right; of course she was right. Fanwell could have been lying under the car and had the breath crushed out of him.

"What exactly happened?" asked Mma Ramotswe.

Mr. J.L.B. Matekoni sighed. "We had a car up on a pneumatic jack. He'd been doing something to the suspension. When he'd finished that, he began to lower the car, but didn't notice where his right foot was — directly below one of the front wheels. When it came to the last few inches, he let all the pressure out at once so that the car more or less fell that last little bit — onto his foot."

Mma Ramotswe winced. "Ow!"

"Ow indeed, Mma. He was yelling his head off. I thought he'd cut off a hand, or something like that. Mma Makutsi heard him too and came out of the office to see what was going on. We got the car up off his foot, but he was still howling. He said his foot was broken."

"Well, the weight of a car . . ."

"Oh, I know that. But when they X-rayed him at the hospital, they said only a tiny, tiny bone was broken. Nothing else. They didn't even put a plaster on."

"I don't think they have to do that for a tiny bone."

"No, that's what the doctor said. She said that he would get better but that he should be careful not to use his foot too much. She gave him a strong painkiller."

"And now he's all right?"

Mr. J.L.B. Matekoni nodded. "He seems fine. But we had a long wait at the hospital. Four hours. I couldn't really leave him there by himself."

Mma Ramotswe looked thoughtful. "You say Mma Makutsi went with you?"

"Yes, she was very good. She even held his hand while they were waiting for the X-ray."

Mma Ramotswe asked her question casually. "Did she speak much to you?"

"Of course. We were sitting in a corridor for a long time."

"What about?"

"What did she talk about? Oh, this and that. Phuti had a business trip over the border — to Johannesburg. She spoke about that a lot. Apparently, he bought a new vacuum cleaner while he was over there. She had a lot to say about that too."

"And anything else?"

He scratched his head. "You know how she is. She says all sorts of things. She said something about one of her uncles from Bobonong being bitten by a spider. Apparently, he almost lost a finger."

Mma Ramotswe smiled at that — not at the thought of the uncle's misfortune, but because the travails of Mma Makutsi's uncles were a frequent topic of conversation in the No. 1 Ladies' Detective Agency. It seemed that the Makutsi uncles led exceptionally accident-prone lives: one had recently been kicked by a mule, another had discovered that part of his savings — fortunately only a small part — had been eaten by termites, and now there was this uncle who had been bitten by a spider. But this was not what she wanted to find out. "Anything about work?" she asked. "Anything about the agency?"

Mr. J.L.B. Matekoni took a few moments to answer. "I think everything is all right," he said. "You mustn't worry about that, you know. Remember, you're on holiday."

"Oh, I'm not worried, Rra," said Mma Ramotswe. "I have complete faith in Mma Makutsi."

"Then you do not need to worry at all," said Mr. J.L.B. Matekoni. "For the next two weeks you can forget about work altogether. You can be like one of those pilots who put their planes on autopilot. They can read the newspaper if they like."

"But there is a pilot," said Mma Ramotswe. "There's Mma Makutsi."

Mr. J.L.B. Matekoni smiled. "Well, she's at the controls now, not you." He paused. "And you'll be pleased to hear that she's taken on a major case."

She spun round. "A major case? Did she say —"

He cut her short. "She didn't tell me what it was. But she did say that something big has turned up."

"That was all she said?"

"That was all she told me." He seemed to recollect something. "But then she said something else."

He looked at Mma Ramotswe as if he were assessing whether to pass on a piece of sensitive information. She was surprised; there were no secrets between them, but perhaps Mma Makutsi was trying to keep her in the dark and had asked him not to reveal whatever it was she had told him. She felt her face flush — really, it was too bad. Mma Makutsi had no business elbowing her out like this, even to the extent of recruiting Mr. J.L.B. Matekoni as an ally.

"I would not want you to break a confidence, Mr. J.L.B. Matekoni," said Mma Ramotswe. "If she told you not to tell me, then I would be the last person" — she paused for effect — "the very last person to persuade you to reveal something confidential."

His reaction reassured her. "But, Mma, there is nothing I wouldn't tell you. You

136

know that!"

Mr. J.L.B. Matekoni usually spoke in quiet, considered tones. Now there was an emotional edge to his voice.

She immediately felt guilty. "I'm very sorry, Rra. I wasn't thinking. I know that you would never keep anything from me."

As she spoke, she imagined what it would be like to live with somebody who had secrets. Instead of a comfortable atmosphere of trust there would be a nagging insecurity, like a corrosive crust, eating away at the fabric of the marriage. Doubts would spread like weeds, making it impossible to relax, spoiling everything. She stopped her train of thought right there. She had already experienced all that during her earlier, disastrous marriage to Note Mokoti, ladies' man, trumpeter, and bully. What had possessed her to marry that man? How could she have thought that she would be able to domesticate him? Of course she had been very young then, and when we are very young we think it will be different for us; we think the rules that apply to everything and everyone else do not apply to us.

She had closed her eyes while she thought of this, and she was brought back to the present moment by Mr. J.L.B. Matekoni's touch on her arm. It was something he did

137

at difficult moments — not that they had many of those — he touched her lightly on the arm as a hesitant child might do. It had always moved her, and it did so now.

"I know you think that, Mma Ramotswe," he said. "I know that, just as I know . . ." He searched around for the best way of putting it. "Just as I know that the sun will come up tomorrow morning."

She opened her eyes and smiled at him. "Sometimes I think things that I don't really think, Rra."

He laughed. "That sounds very odd, Mma. That sounds like something Mma Makutsi might say."

He was right. Mma Makutsi, for all her ninety-seven per cent from the Botswana Secretarial College, could at times say impenetrable things.

"What I meant to say is that . . . ," she began, but did not finish.

"This thing that Mma Makutsi told me," he said. "It is not very important, but she did say something that made me curious. She said that this new matter they are working on involves a very famous person."

"Did she say who it was?"

He shook his head. "I think she was going to tell me, but then the phone rang and she had to take the call. She did not finish."

The thoughts of trust were now forgotten. A very famous person? Mma Ramotswe was intrigued. There were different sorts of fame, of course, and it would be important to know what sort of fame Mma Makutsi had in mind. There was *big famous,* which was the sort of fame that surrounded the people one saw pictured in the magazines. She and Mma Makutsi had discussed this sort of thing on a number of occasions when Mma Makutsi had brought back a copy of *Drum* from the hair-braiding salon. "You see this man here, Mma — this one standing next to that woman? You see her shoes, Mma? I would never wear shoes like that — would you? But you see him and his big muscles making that shirt look as if the buttons are going to pop off at any moment? You see him? He thinks he's big famous, but you go over to America and you show them this photograph and they'll say, 'Who is this nobody man?' So he may think that he's big famous because they know about him in Johannesburg or Nairobi or somewhere like that, but he really isn't, you know, Mma."

That was *big famous.* Then there was *small famous,* which was famous in Gaborone. There were many small famous people. They were usually people who had money,

139

who drove large cars, and whose faces you saw in the *Botswana Daily News.* They were always there at the charity events; they were always there when there was some special party for this or that occasion. Sometimes they had done something special to deserve their fame, but usually it simply came with material possessions. If you had a big house, it seemed, then you were a big person.

Mma Ramotswe knew that was not true. The size of one's house might bear a relationship to the size of one's opinion of oneself, but it had nothing to do with one's real worth. But then fame had nothing to do with worth, anyway, except when . . . She paused. There were at least some cases where great deeds had been done and fame had been the result. Seretse Khama was an example. He was a great man, and a famous one. Martin Luther King was another. Winston Churchill. Gandhi. Nelson Mandela.

"I am very intrigued, Rra," she said at last. "We have not had many famous clients at the No. 1 Ladies' Detective Agency."

"Nor at the garage," mused Mr. J.L.B. Matekoni. "I have had some well-known cars, but nothing famous."

"I would like to find out, though," said Mma Ramotswe, thinking aloud. "It is very frustrating knowing that there is something important like that happening when I am on holiday."

"Should I ask her?" volunteered Mr. J.L.B. Matekoni.

She did not think this a good idea. She did not want Mma Makutsi thinking that she was breathing down her neck during her holiday, and she explained this to him. Mr. J.L.B. Matekoni understood, and the conversation turned to other things. She told him of her experience with the waif, and her encounter with the woman who was taking advantage of him. "He is happy now," she said. "He has Mma Potokwane to look after him. He is settled."

What she said amounted to so few words; so few words to describe what had happened at the Orphan Farm that morning when she had taken the boy out to Tlokweng and parked her van under the shade of the acacia tree beside the office. He had been silent for most of the trip and now she saw that he was shivering. She had reassured him that this was a good place and that he should not be frightened. "There is a very kind lady here," she said. "She will be your mother. She is waiting for you."

But this had not been enough to calm him, and when she went round to the other side of the van and opened the door for him to get out, he had remained cowering in his seat.

"You mustn't be afraid, Samuel. There is nothing bad that can happen to you here."

He had stared downwards, avoiding her eyes. After a moment she had reached out and taken his hand, and only then had he left the van, still reluctantly, and still shivering. And then she saw the wet patch on the front of the shorts he was wearing — the result of his fear — and her heart went out to him. He tried to cover this, but his little hands were inadequate to the task, and he began to sob. She took him to her, lifting him up, ignoring the damp against her skin, and began to carry him into the office. He seemed to weigh very little for his age, and she thought that this must be because he had not been given the food he needed. There was much that she wanted to say — angry words directed against that woman who had made such ill use of him — but she could not say these things, as now was not the time for recrimination. So instead she sang to him, a gentle, calming song that she remembered her aunt had sung to her in Mochudi when she had been a small girl and was frightened of something or other, as all children are from time to time. She felt the tension go out of him, and he clung to her tightly, his arms around her neck and his breath, the shallow breath of a frightened child, soft against her skin.

Mma Potokwane, of course, could tell immediately what was needed. On countless occasions over the years she had done just this, taking in a confused child, a child with nobody else to count upon, a child who had slipped through the mesh of that safety net of relatives, of aunts and grandparents that in Botswana, as elsewhere in Africa, had always coped with such circumstances. Recently she had been called upon to do this more and more, as disease stalked mercilessly through Africa and took from children all those who would normally provide them with the love and protection they needed. But Mma Potokwane did not flinch, and did what she needed to do, whatever the attendant difficulties.

"So," said Mma Potokwane. "Here we have another young man to join our family. This is a very happy day for us."

"This is Samuel," said Mma Ramotswe, turning round so that the boy could look at Mma Potokwane.

Mma Potokwane smiled and gestured to Mma Ramotswe to put the child down. "I have something special for you, Samuel," said Mma Potokwane. "I have some special cake here for you. It is just for you. A very big piece."

She gave him the cake and then took out of a drawer some clean khaki shorts. "You take these, Samuel. They are just your size. Go out onto the verandah and put them on there. Then come back and I will give you more cake."

With the boy out of the room, Mma Ramotswe looked apologetically at Mma Potokwane. "I know you're under pressure with numbers, Mma. But this is a special case."

Mma Potokwane wagged a finger playfully at her friend. "Everybody says that, Mma. I have never had somebody come in here and not say it." She paused, her face breaking into a smile. "And you know what, Mma Ramotswe, they're right. Every case *is* special."

"You are very kind, Mma," said Mma Ramotswe. Her eye had strayed to the tin from which Mma Potokwane had taken the slice of cake.

Mma Potokwane noticed. "Would you like a cup of tea, Mma?" she enquired.

Mma Ramotswe nodded. She continued to look at the tin.

"And perhaps a piece of cake?" continued Mma Potokwane.

It was not a question that required answering — looks, and body language, did it all.

CHAPTER EIGHT:
THE UNWISENESS OF DRIPPING

By the time Mma Ramotswe got out of bed the following day, Mr. J.L.B. Matekoni had already gone to work. Normally Mma Ramotswe would be up first and would make tea for her still somnolent husband. This she would place on the dresser at the side of the bed before going out into the garden to inspect the plants, savour the crisp morning air, and watch the sun float up over the horizon. So engrained was this routine that when she awoke that morning and found Mr. J.L.B. Matekoni no longer at her side her immediate reaction had been to assume that something terrible had happened. But then she had looked at the old Westclox alarm clock, with its shaky hands and its scratched dial, and it took only a moment or two to realise that she had slept in. Now she remembered that she was on holiday and could get up when she wished. Indeed, there was no need to get up at all: if she wished to stay in bed all day, nobody would have been any the wiser.

She thought of the children. With their growing independence, both Puso and Motholeli had been keen to show themselves capable of getting themselves off to school on their own. This had been particularly true of Puso, who almost two years earlier had mounted a successful campaign to be allowed to make his way to school without adult supervision. In pursuit of this goal he had agreed to help Motholeli with her wheelchair each morning, and he had been as good as his word. For her part, Mma Ramotswe was proud to see the boy managing to hold his own against one or two rather spoiled and unhelpful older boys who felt threatened by Puso's sporting prowess and his easy mastery of the curriculum. She had harboured some misgivings about sending such a young child off to school by himself, but she had been persuaded by a friend that refusing a child permission to stand on his own two feet could bring difficult consequences later on. "They do that in the villages," the friend had said. "The moment they learn to walk out there, they are ready to go."

Mma Ramotswe knew that was fundamentally true. The sight of tiny children by themselves was a familiar one in a village, but that, she thought, was only because there were many eyes in a village, and most of them, if not all, were watching out for other people. You were never alone in a village, even if you thought you were; somebody would notice if you tripped and fell down, somebody would see you if you needed help. But was that true of Gaborone, which had grown so much, and now looked so much like any bustling city? Obviously not, although there was still an intimacy to the place that marked it out from other towns: you did not change the soul of a place by simply making it bigger; you diluted its qualities, yes, but the heart of a country would still beat in this same way no matter how many new houses and shops and roads you chose to build.

She rose from her bed and went into the children's bedrooms to check that they had, in fact, left for school. Then, in the kitchen, with the kettle beginning to huff and puff itself to the boil, she saw the note that Motholeli had left her. *I have sent the Daddy to work. I made him sandwiches to take to the garage. I have made Puso change his socks. We shall not be back until five because I have garden club and Puso has to play football. He would not clean his teeth although I told him to six times. Love from Motholeli.*

She held the note to her. She thought she would keep it, putting it away in a box of papers she treasured, filing it alongside the deeds to the house, her marriage certificate, the words of a Setswana song her father had once written out for her — a haunting little song about the wedding of two baboons; the baboon bride and groom wear clothing they've stolen from humans — rags, really — but they are worn with pride. There would come a time when this crumpled piece of paper would remind her of what she would by then otherwise have forgotten — the innocent words of a child.

It seemed strange to be eating her breakfast by herself, and she did not linger long at the table. A bowl of meal porridge, drowned in milk and sweetened by a spoonful of syrup, was followed by a piece of toast spread with dripping and then sprinkled with salt and pepper. The toast was an indulgence — even by Mma Ramotswe's standards — but it was the one culinary treat she felt unable to give up, even in the face of evidence that it was really not very good for you.

"We must not eat dripping any more," warned Mma Makutsi from behind a healthy-living magazine. "We must give up

149

such things, Mma." This advice had been accompanied by a stern look in Mma Ramotswe's direction.

Mma Ramotswe had not taken that lying down. "Soon they will be telling us not to eat anything," she countered. "They will say that only air is good for you. Air and water."

Mma Makutsi had not approved. "You cannot fight science, Mma. Science is telling us that many of the things we like to eat in this country are not good for us. They say that these things are making us too large."

"I am not fighting science, Mma," replied Mma Ramotswe. "I am just saying that we have to have some things that we like, otherwise we shall be very unhappy. And if you are very unhappy you can die — we all know that." She allowed that to sink in before she continued. "There are many people who have been thinking a lot about science who are now late. It would have been better for them to spend more time being happy while they had the chance. That is well known, Mma — it is very well known."

Mma Makutsi had become silent. One could not argue against something that Mma Ramotswe claimed was well known, just as you could not argue against any view she attributed to the late Seretse Khama. She had learned that — indeed, it was well known — and so she had returned to her magazine with nothing more being said about the unwiseness of dripping.

Mma Ramotswe finished her piece of toast, licking the last of the dripping off her fingers. It was the most delicious foodstuff imaginable; there was nothing, she thought, to beat dripping. You could order the most expensive dish on the menu at the President Hotel and it would not taste anywhere near as delicious as dripping. Bread and dripping, preferably eaten outside, in the shade of an acacia tree, with the lowing of cattle not far away — what could be more perfect than that?

She stopped the reverie. I must get on, she thought. And then she asked herself: Get on where? She had nothing to do — unless, of course, she were to satisfy the curiosity that Mr. J.L.B. Matekoni had piqued the previous evening with his tantalising snippet of information about Mma Makutsi's new case. She deliberated, but not for long. She would find a pretext to drop into the office. It would not be a lengthy visit — she was not going to interfere — but if she timed her visit to coincide with the making of the mid-morning cup of tea, then she could stay for a chat and possibly find out what was going on.

The visit to the office would have another purpose too. Ever since she had seen the new college and spoken to the painter, she had been wondering what she should do about it. The realisation that had come to her outside the college was a starkly uncomfortable one: it was Violet Sephotho who was behind the new venture. That fact might have been of very little interest to most people, but to Mma Ramotswe and Mma Makutsi it was of considerable significance. Violet Sephotho was Mma Makutsi's archenemy, the enmity between them dating back to their time together at the Botswana Secretarial College, where Violet had been a half-hearted student, keener on men than on shorthand and typing, and arrogantly dismissive of the college and its staff. Thereafter their paths had crossed on a number of occasions, when Violet, bitterly envious of Mma Makutsi's marriage to a man as well off as Phuti Radiphuti, had not missed any opportunity to sow discord and disparage everything that Mma Makutsi stood for. The news that Violet Sephotho was planning to open a college of secretarial studies would infuriate Mma Makutsi and would probably distract her from other, more important issues. So she would have to raise the matter carefully, or perhaps leave it unmentioned altogether. No, she thought, I cannot do that. I shall have to tell her — gently.

Now that she had made up her mind to visit the office, she was able to enjoy the next couple of hours at home, cleaning and tidying — taking up where she had left off the previous morning when she had made such progress with the kitchen cupboard. She decided to sort out Mr. J.L.B. Matekoni's clothes. There were several shirts that had lost buttons, and she suspected that lurking in his sock drawer were socks that had long since lost their partner and could be thrown away. Men, she thought, were odd about their clothes: they liked to wear the same things until they became defeated and threadbare. For this reason, it was up to wives and girlfriends to weed out the old and outdated. The men would complain, of course, but they did not care enough about clothes to make too much of a fuss, and if you replaced a favourite item with something new, they would very quickly forget about the whole matter. Sometimes, Mma Ramotswe suspected, men did not even *see* clothes.

She timed her arrival perfectly, as they were all there when she reached the agency. She did not knock before she entered — and why should one knock at one's own door? — but went straight into the office.

The first thing she noticed was that Mma Makutsi was sitting at her desk — not her own, but Mma Ramotswe's. That was a shock, and it took her a moment or two to compose herself. Had she given her permission to occupy her place? She did not think she had, but on the other hand, if there was an unoccupied desk, then why should somebody not sit at it?

She struggled with her feelings. No, she would not say anything. Now she took in the rest of the scene. Mr. Polopetsi was sitting at Mma Makutsi's desk, engrossed in some stationery-related task, while Charlie was leaning against the filing cabinet on which Mma Makutsi kept the kettle. Three mugs were standing ready for tea.

Mma Makutsi looked up sharply. For a moment she looked blank, as if she had suddenly found herself in the wrong place, but then she pulled herself together and managed to reply to Mma Ramotswe's greeting.

"This is a big pleasure, Mma," she said. "Charlie is making tea and can make another cup for you, Mma. Your visit is very well timed."

"Oh," said Mma Ramotswe casually. "There was no timing, Mma. I have just dropped in to pick up my address book. I think I have left it in my drawer. I want to write some letters while I am on holiday."

"Very wise," said Mr. Polopetsi. "When you are on holiday you can do many things that you do not have time to do when you are working. But —"

"But you should not do too much," interjected Mma Makutsi. "When you take a holiday, it is important not to fill your time with all sorts of things because then you'll never have a real holiday."

"No," said Charlie. "When you are on holiday you must be careful not to do the things you normally do."

"Charlie is quite right," said Mma Makutsi. "You must be careful not to go into the office — for example."

When Mma Makutsi used the expression "for example" it was usually to make a strong point, and that was how Mma Ramotswe read her remark.

"I'm not intending to come in here every day," she said hurriedly. "Oh no, that would not be a very sensible thing to do."

"Good," said Mma Makutsi, looking at her watch — rather pointedly, thought Mma Ramotswe. She turned to address Charlie. "Now, then, Charlie, let's have this tea you've been talking about."

"Mma Makutsi says I make very good tea," said Charlie proudly.

Mma Ramotswe smiled. "I'm sure you do." Her eye moved to the three mugs already laid out on top of the filing cabinet. One of them was hers, and she wondered whether Mma Makutsi had been using it regularly in her absence; to take over somebody's desk *and* her cup was a bit much, she felt.

"I see my mug over there," she said. "I shall be able to have tea out of my own mug, which is very good — even when you are on holiday."

Mma Makutsi looked slightly shifty, which answered that question. "Get another one, Charlie."

Now Mma Makutsi said something about the desk. "I'm just using this while you are on holiday," she muttered. "Mr. Polopetsi over there needed somewhere to sit down. You cannot have a man like him not sitting down."

"Of course not," said Mma Ramotswe.

"And I do not mind if you use my desk, Mma — it is the sensible thing to do."

Charlie now poured the tea and passed a mug to each of them in turn. Then he dusted off the client's chair, inviting Mma Ramotswe to sit down. She noticed that Mma Makutsi shifted uncomfortably in her seat, occupying, as she was, Mma Ramotswe's rightful place, but she made no comment on that. She was not one to make another feel awkward, and so she said instead, "I'm glad that you are at my desk, Mma. It is good to think that there is somebody in your place when you are on holiday."

It was the right thing to say, as Mma Makutsi visibly relaxed. "You will be back before too long, Mma. You must enjoy your holiday."

"Yes," said Mr. Polopetsi from Mma Makutsi's desk. "If anyone deserves a holiday, Mma Ramotswe, it is you. Nobody would argue with that."

Mma Ramotswe took a sip of her tea. "So, what's going on?" she asked. "Anything important?"

There was complete silence. Then Charlie said, "Mr. J.L.B. Matekoni and Fanwell have gone out to Mokolodi to collect a truck. It has a broken axle. Big problem."

157

Mma Ramotswe digested this information. "That will keep them busy. But what about the agency?"

Mma Makutsi adopted a serious expression. "We are busy with the usual sort of thing, Mma. We have some new work, and some old work. We are doing both."

Mma Ramotswe seized her opportunity. "This new work — what exactly is it?"

Mma Makutsi put down her teacup. "It is very hot again. Do you think there will be rain?"

"There might be," said Mma Ramotswe. "But this new case — what is it, Mma?"

It was as direct a question as could be asked, and there was no escape for Mma Makutsi now. "We have been asked to look into a question of somebody's past."

"Ah," said Mma Ramotswe. "An employment case, then. That's a fairly common enquiry, isn't it?"

"Not employment," said Mr. Polopetsi. "A personal past."

Mma Ramotswe noticed that Mma Makutsi shot Mr. Polopetsi a glance, and she could tell what her message was. She did not want too much divulged.

"Is it matrimonial?" asked Mma Ramotswe. Very occasionally they had a client who wanted to find out something about the

intended spouse of a son or daughter —
usually a daughter. Those were difficult
cases, as the motive for the enquiry was
often simple dislike of the prospective
spouse rather than any real suspicion that
he (or she) may have something to hide.

Mma Makutsi frowned. "No, it isn't
matrimonial. It's a very straightforward
case, really. The client wants to find out
about her brother. It's curiosity, Mma —
that's all."

Mma Makutsi looked at her watch. It was
clear that she considered the matter closed
and that she did not want any further
discussion of the case. And Mma Ramotswe
understood: had she been in Mma Makutsi's shoes, then she too would have
wanted to handle things on her own —
anybody, particularly somebody who had
always been an employee rather than an
employer, would want a chance to do that.
And the actual case, she decided, was probably not all that important. The remark
made to Mr. J.L.B. Matekoni that a well-
known name was involved probably meant
that it was a footballer or a radio announcer
— nothing more glamorous than that.

She finished her tea. "Well, Mma," she
said to Mma Makutsi. "I must leave you to
get on with your work."

Mma Makutsi brightened. "Yes, of course. We must do that. We cannot sit about and drink tea all day, can we? We are not on holiday."

"No," said Mma Ramotswe wryly. "I am the one who is on holiday."

"I have never had a holiday," Charlie chimed in.

Mma Makutsi made a strange sound — a sound of disbelief mixed with scorn.

"But I work hard," protested Charlie. "You've seen me working hard, haven't you, Mma Ramotswe?"

Her tone was emollient. "Of course I have, Charlie. Everybody works hard."

"Not everybody," said Mr. Polopetsi. "There is a teacher at the school who certainly doesn't work hard. He is a man who knows nothing and therefore can't teach anything to the pupils. He gets them to read out from a book while he sits in his chair and looks out of the window. He is a very ignorant man and he is making all his pupils ignorant too." He paused. "There is a tidal wave of ignorance, Mma Ramotswe. It is a great tidal wave and it will drown all of us if we are not careful."

"You call a tidal wave a tsunami," said Charlie. "Did you know that, Rra?"

"Yes," said Mr. Polopetsi. "I have known

that for a long time, Charlie."

"People say there is no excuse for ignorance," observed Mma Ramotswe. "But I
don't think I agree with that. Not in every
case. There are some people who are ignorant because they have never had the chance
to find out what is what. That is not their
fault. Then there are people who have the
chance to be taught things but refuse to
learn. That is inexcusable ignorance, I
think."

"I agree with that," said Mma Makutsi.
"Those people have nothing in their heads."

"That is called a vacuum," said Charlie.

Mma Ramotswe remembered the other
matter she had to raise. "There's another
thing," she said. "I was driving in the van
yesterday and something caught my eye.
There's a new college."

Mma Makutsi did not seem particularly
interested. "There are new schools all over
the place. They're thinking of building one
near us. Phuti said that he saw the plans.
He thinks it looks as if it's been drawn
upside down. He is very rude about some
new buildings, you know."

"I don't think this one is a school," said
Mma Ramotswe. "Well, not a school for
children. I think this is a college for —"

"The thing I wonder about," interjected

Mma Makutsi, "is where they get the money to build all these new places. That's what I wonder about, Mma."

"I think that Violet Sephotho —"

Mma Ramotswe did not finish. Mma Makutsi had raised a hand. "Oh, don't talk to me about that woman. Please don't talk to me about her. I do not want to hear about her, Mma."

Mma Ramotswe frowned. "But this —"

"No, Mma, please. I have too much to think about and I cannot think about her too."

"But this is something that —"

"No, Mma, please. I cannot think about her. I am far too busy running the office while you are away."

Mma Ramotswe decided not to press the matter. She would have to try again, but she thought that this was clearly not the right time. "Very well, Mma," she said. "I must go now. You are obviously very busy."

Mma Makutsi smiled sweetly. "You go off and enjoy yourself, Mma Ramotswe. Put your feet up. Sit in your garden. Go to tea. There are many things you can do, Mma — many, many relaxing things."

Mr. Polopetsi accompanied Mma Ramotswe to her van. He was a very courteous man, and he opened the door for her. She liked that. People could say that such manners were a thing of the past, but even those who expressed such a view appreciated it if a door was opened for them; you could not go wrong, thought Mma Ramotswe, in opening a door for somebody.

"Thank you, Rra," she said. "You are very kind."

He acknowledged the compliment, but nonetheless seemed distracted. Mma Ramotswe had seen signs of that earlier on, and she sensed that he was under stress. "One thing, Mma Ramotswe," he said hesitantly.

She settled herself in the driving seat before she looked up at him. "Yes, Rra?"

He lowered his voice although they were alone. There were the two doves, of course, that had made their home in the acacia tree beside the garage, but there was no human ear to overhear what he had to say.

"Yes, Rra?" she repeated.

"That case Mma Makutsi referred to . . ."

She did not push him, but waited for him to continue.

"That case, Mma, is a very difficult one. She . . ." He inclined his head in the direction of the office behind them. "She has no idea how to deal with it."

Mma Ramotswe looked studiously ahead.

163

"Oh," she said, and then added, "I see."

"Yes," went on Mr. Polopetsi. "I am not being disloyal to Mma Makutsi, Mma. I have the greatest respect for that lady. You know that, I think."

"I do," said Mma Ramotswe. "I have always known that you admired Mma Makutsi, even if —" She stopped herself.

"Even if what, Mma?"

"Even if I think you may be a little bit worried about what she's going to say — or do. Not very worried, of course — just a little bit."

He bowed his head in acknowledgement of this truth. "Yes, maybe. She is very strong and she is very good at most things. But for some strange reason — and it is worrying me, Mma, this strange reason — she doesn't know what to do with this case."

"Oh dear," said Mma Ramotswe.

"Yes — oh dear. And now she has said that I must sort it out. She says that she has too much filing to do and that I should handle this case with Charlie. And Charlie doesn't have a clue, Mma. I do not want to be rude about Charlie, but there are very clear limits to what Charlie knows and can do."

"He is a good young man," said Mma Ramotswe. "But he has spent too much

time thinking about girls. That is his problem."

"Precisely," said Mr. Polopetsi. "I find the
same thing with the students I teach at the
secondary school. Teenage boys, in particular, will not concentrate on what they are
meant to be doing. They are always thinking of how they can impress girls."

"It is very sad," said Mma Ramotswe.
"But I think there must also be teenage girls
who can't stop thinking about boys."

Mr. Polopetsi agreed. "There are those
too," he said. "But be that as it may, Mma,
I have no idea either about how to deal with
this case. So I was wondering if you might
help me."

She had not expected this, and she
thought for a few moments before answering him. She did not want to undermine
Mma Makutsi, but this was a direct plea for
help from Mr. Polopetsi, who was, after all,
an unpaid volunteer and who therefore
deserved any help he wanted. "Come to my
house this evening," she said. "Come at six
o'clock and tell me all about it. Then I will
give you some advice — if I can think of
any to give."

"You are very kind, Mma."

"No, Rra, you are the kind one. You are
helping us out for nothing. That is a sign of

a kind man. That is well known, Rra."

He looked visibly relieved as he closed the van door. "I'll see you this evening, Mma."

She started the engine and began to make her way back to Zebra Drive. She was still resolved that she would not interfere with Mma Makutsi's affairs, but she could hardly turn down somebody like Mr. Polopetsi. She would do it tactfully, she thought, so that Mma Makutsi would never find out that there had been an intervention. That, she thought, was the best way to interfere in anything: if you did it in such a way that nobody noticed your interference, then no possible harm was done. That was what distinguished a successful meddler from an unsuccessful one, and she was determined that she would be one of the former rather than one of the latter. And who wouldn't?

CHAPTER NINE:
THE LATE
MR. GOVERNMENT KEBONENG

Mr. Polopetsi did not live very far from Zebra Drive and so he walked rather than drove to see Mma Ramotswe that evening. It had looked as if more rain was due, but the clouds that had built up over the horizon had dispersed, leaving the cloudless sky a soft shade of blue. A cushion of cool air had floated in from the south-west, refreshing the land, providing at least some relief from the heat of the afternoon. Mr. Polopetsi, who had embarked on a programme of exercise, was trying to take ten thousand steps a day; so far that day he calculated that he had walked only one thousand, and some of those, he thought, had been very small steps.

"I am walking for the sake of my heart," he said to Mma Ramotswe as he arrived. "It is a very good thing for the heart if you do a lot of walking."

She had been standing on the verandah

when she saw him arrive, and had gone out into the garden to greet him. "I should walk more," she said. "But in this hot weather it is very difficult. It may be good for your heart to walk, but if you die of heatstroke, then that is not too good. The doctors would say, 'A healthy heart, but now it has stopped because of heatstroke.' "

Mr. Polopetsi laughed. "If it is not one thing that will kill you, Mma, it is another. There is no way round it. We all become late some day."

"I am planning to become late in my bed," said Mma Ramotswe. "I shall be very old — I hope — and I shall be lying in my bed when they suddenly realise that I am late. Either that, or I shall be sitting under a tree and they will see that I have stopped moving. That is one of the best ways to become late, I think. You're sitting under a tree looking out at the cattle and suddenly — whoosh — you go up."

"I hope that is not for a long time yet," said Mr. Polopetsi. "I cannot imagine Botswana without you, Mma Ramotswe."

She was touched by his remark. Mr. Polopetsi was not a flatterer — what he said was sincerely meant — and this was an example of the kind things he said.

"You are very kind, Rra," she said. "I suppose the truth of the matter is that none of us can imagine the world without ourselves in it, but it always carries on, doesn't it, even after we've left?"

She gestured towards the verandah. "There is a place to sit there, Rra. And there is a pot of tea."

He followed her and sat down on one of the verandah chairs. "We do not have a verandah," he said. "I have often thought I would build one, but I have never got round to it."

"I am sorry that you have no verandah, Rra," she said as she poured him a cup of tea. It was time, though, to stop this talk of walking and becoming late and verandahs and get down to the real reason for his visit. "But now, Mr. Polopetsi, you might like to tell me what's going on."

He looked apologetic. "I'm sorry, Mma, I was not trying to conceal anything from you. It's just that Mma Makutsi is a bit . . ."

She held up a hand. "You don't need to apologise, Rra. I know that Mma Makutsi is a bit . . ." She paused. "Tell me: What's happening? Who is this client?"

He drained his teacup in a single swig. "I shall tell you, Mma, and I shall begin with that very first day of your holiday. We were in the office and a lady came in. She had not made an appointment, but we were all there — Mma Makutsi, me, and Charlie. I was sitting in Mma Makutsi's chair — at her desk."

She nodded politely, willing him to continue. "And Mma Makutsi at mine?"

"Yes, she was sitting at your desk. Charlie has no desk."

"No." And she thought: *Please, Rra, get to the point!*

"There is no room for a desk for him."

She sighed; she had not intended it, but a sigh escaped.

He looked at her with concern. "Are you all right, Mma Ramotswe?"

"I am perfectly all right, Rra. I just feel that it is as if we are walking around in the dark and not getting anywhere. You know those dreams we have — those dreams where we are trying to get somewhere and we can't get there because for some reason we can't move? It is a bit like that."

His expression brightened. "Oh, I have those dreams, Mma; I know what you're talking about. Last night, for instance, my wife woke me up and said that I was kicking about in the bed and she thought —"

She had to interrupt. "Mr. Polopetsi! We are not talking about dreams."

He was a picture of injured innocence.

"But you raised the subject, Mma. You're the one who mentioned dreams."

She sighed again. "Yes, you are right, Rra. I raised the subject of dreams. But I feel that we need to get back to what you were saying about the office. This woman came in . . . Carry on from there."

He became businesslike. "She came in. We were all there — as I have said. She came in and said: 'I am Mma Potokwane.' "

Mma Ramotswe gave a start. This was the last thing she had expected. She could not imagine Mma Potokwane as a client — it simply made no sense. And why would she need to introduce herself: even if Mr. Polopetsi had not come across Mma Potokwane, then Mma Makutsi and Charlie had; they knew exactly who Mma Potokwane was.

Mr. Polopetsi realised that an explanation was needed. "Oh no, Mma — not *that* Mma Potokwane. Not the Mma Potokwane who's a friend of yours. Not the matron at that place for orphans. That very big lady."

Mma Ramotswe did not think of Mma Potokwane as being particularly large; she was not small, of course, but then Mr. Polopetsi was a very slight man. She imagined that in his eyes just about everybody would look big, perhaps even intimidatingly so, and that might explain Mr. Polopetsi's rather diffident manner. "Another Poto-kwane?" she asked.

"Yes, precisely that, Mma. Another Poto-kwane."

She reached for the teapot. "So this Poto-kwane lady," she said, "this different Poto-kwane lady, came into the office. What then, Rra?"

Mr. Polopetsi leaned forward in his seat. "It is a very delicate story, Mma. Some of these matters, as you well know, are very delicate indeed."

She assured him that her years of experience as a private detective had already taught her that. "Ours is a very delicate profession, Rra. It really is."

Mr. Polopetsi appeared pleased by the reference to *our* profession. "Yes," he said, beaming with the pleasure that comes with inclusion in a club. "Yes, we have to be very careful. We have to tread like mice."

For a moment Mma Ramotswe saw Mr. Polopetsi as a mouse. He would suit the role, she thought, with his rather small nose and his dainty feet; he would be a very convincing mouse. She, by contrast, would not be much of a mouse; more of a cat, perhaps — a traditionally built cat.

Mr. Polopetsi continued with his story. "This Mma Potokwane explained that it was a family matter. She said that she is the wife of a man called Pound Potokwane. Her own name — before she got married — was Keboneng."

Mr. Polopetsi waited for her reaction.

"Ah," said Mma Ramotswe. "That is a well-known name, isn't it?"

Mr. Polopetsi nodded. "That man — the well-known Keboneng — was her brother. It was a small family, with just those two — Mma Potokwane, as she now is, and her brother, Government Keboneng."

"Of course he's late, isn't he? Government Keboneng was bitten by a snake, wasn't he? It was all over the papers."

Mr. Polopetsi recalled the story. "I remember it very well. I read all about it. It was a very shocking thing. He was at a church picnic out near the dam. He went into the bush to obey a call of nature and he was bitten by a mamba. They rushed him into the Princess Marina, but it was too late — those snakes are too poisonous. He was already late by the time they arrived in Gaborone."

"It was very sad," said Mma Ramotswe. "He was a very popular man. He was a politician, wasn't he?"

"He was." Mr. Polopetsi paused. "It was a good name for a politician. I wonder if it

173

was his real name or whether he just took it when he went into politics. Do you know, Mma Ramotswe?"

She did not. "It would not have suited him when he was a boy, I think. But I agree with you, Rra. If you have a name like that on the ballot paper — Government — then you surely are going to think, *This man is destined for power.* And if you think that, then you may well put your cross right there, opposite the good name."

"There are some very odd names," said Mr. Polopetsi. "People seem to like these odd names for some strange reason."

Mma Ramotswe smiled; she had encountered strange names on many occasions. "But this lady, Rra, this Mma Potokwane — what had brought her to the agency? Is she in trouble of some sort?"

Mr. Polopetsi thought for a moment. "I'm not sure that one would describe it as trouble, Mma."

Mma Ramotswe waited for him to continue, but he seemed to be expecting her to say something.

"Well," she said, "if she is not in trouble, then is somebody else in trouble?" Many people, she knew, felt too embarrassed to cross the threshold of the No. 1 Ladies' Detective Agency and sent friends or relatives in their stead. That could complicate matters, with a layer of misunderstanding, or sometimes embellishment, being added to the account of the facts.

But this was not the case. "No," said Mr. Polopetsi. "She is the one who wants our help. Her trouble, though, could be imagined rather than real."

"You must explain, Rra."

He drew a deep breath. "You see, Mma Ramotswe," he began, "this Mma Potokwane's brother, this Mr. Government Keboneng, had many people who were in his party. These people were very upset when he died, Mma — it was a very sad blow for them. Not only had they lost a friend — somebody they admired very much — but they had lost their leader. He was very good at making a speech."

Mma Ramotswe remembered that. "Oh yes, Rra, I can vouch for that. I went to hear him one day and we were laughing so much that we cried. He told some very funny stories and then, when we were all in a very good mood, he told us that there was bad economic news and we would all just have to accept it and pay more tax. But because we had been laughing so much, when he finished his speech we all felt very cheerful, and nobody mentioned the tax."

Mr. Polopetsi raised a finger in the air. "People do not like to pay too much tax," he said. "I have always said that, Mma. They like to hold on to their money."

"I think they do," said Mma Ramotswe.

"Yet they like the government to give them as much as possible," Mr. Polopetsi went on. "They think that the government has a big pot of money somewhere that is always full. That is what they think."

"Yes," agreed Mma Ramotswe. "People like to be given things."

"If I stood for election," said Mr. Polopetsi, "and I said, 'Free sunglasses for everybody, and free —' "

"— mobile phones," interrupted Mma Ramotswe. "And free sandwiches. If you said those things, then you would get many, many votes."

"It's called bribery," said Mr. Polopetsi, shaking his head sadly.

"Or politics," observed Mma Ramotswe. "You could call it politics. But let's get back to Mma Potokwane."

Mr. Polopetsi took another deep breath. "The people who liked this Keboneng, Mma, did not know what to do, we were told. They ran this way and that. They were looking for a man who was just like Government Keboneng, but the truth of the matter is that there was nobody else in Botswana who was at all like him. His shoes were empty, yes, but there was nobody to step into them."

Mma Ramotswe understood that. There were some empty shoes that she could never imagine being filled — the shoes of the late Seretse Khama, for instance: How could anyone ever occupy those? Or the shoes of her late daddy, Obed Ramotswe, that great judge of cattle who embodied everything that was finest in Botswana; there was not love or decency or compassion enough in all the land to fill that particular pair of shoes — there simply was not. And all those years ago, when she had said farewell to him on his final afternoon, when she knew that so much would die with him, she had thought there would never be enough tears to weep for him and what he stood for.

She looked at Mr. Polopetsi, who had known sadness in his life, and for a moment they were both silent. What had started as a straightforward account had suddenly become something else: a reflection on how we believe in people, how we need them, and how their loss diminishes us.

He broke the spell. "So these people — the supporters of Mr. Keboneng — were always writing to the newspapers to remind

177

people of what he had done and of how much Botswana owed to him. Some people said that they exaggerated, that, yes, he had been a good man, but there were many other good men whose followers were not always speaking about what they had done and were prepared to start talking about other people — people who were not yet late and who were anxious for people to vote for them and allow them to start doing good things for the benefit of the entire community."

She did not wish to break the flow, but she felt that she had to say something. So she said, "I see," and left it at that.

Mr. Polopetsi drew a deep breath. "These people — these Kebonengites, as some people called them — were very persistent, Mma. They were not the sort of people to give up, and they pestered and pestered the mayor. There were more letters to the papers — you probably saw them — and they even said that there should be some new building named after Mr. Government Keboneng. But the mayor said to them that he could do nothing about that, as it was up to the people who built buildings to choose what they called them and nobody had offered to give their new building this name. They even suggested that some new airport building might be called after him."

Mma Ramotswe raised an eyebrow. She thought that was going too far, as the airport already had a name, Sir Seretse Khama Airport, and to call one of its buildings something different would not only cause confusion, but could well be considered disrespectful.

"What about a bridge?" she asked. "Could they not call a bridge after him? They are always building bridges, these people, even if this is meant to be a dry country. Sometimes I think they are like little boys with a toy bulldozer."

"Or a new drain?" suggested Mr. Polopetsi, smirking at the suggestion. "Government Keboneng Drainpipe? How about that?"

"That would be a bit unkind," said Mma Ramotswe. "We must remember that Government Keboneng was a good man."

Mr. Polopetsi looked apologetic. "Of course," he said. "So, anyway, all this discussion went on and on, and then the city council said that they would name a street after him. The supporters were very pleased, although some of them were concerned that the new street was on the very edge of town and was not important enough for their hero. They wanted them to change the name of one of the streets in the middle of town and give him that."

Mma Ramotswe was not in favour of this. "You cannot change the name of a street," she said. "People would get very confused. They become used to a name for the place they live and they do not like to find that they are living in a new place." She imagined what would happen if Zebra Drive suddenly became Mr. Government Keboneng Drive or even The Late Mr. Government Keboneng Drive. She did not think that she would like to put "The Late" in her address. Of course they did change street names from time to time — she had seen a notice saying "formerly Wilson Road" or something like that. This happened when some of the names from the old Protectorate days were abandoned, which was understandable enough, as people wanted something that reflected themselves rather than those who had a less rooted connection with the country. But it should be done sparingly, she thought: some of the people from those very old days had a memory that should be cherished. There was more than one Moffat Road in Botswana, and rightly so, because Robert Moffat had been such a great man. He had been a friend of the Batswana people; he had been the first to put the

Setswana language into writing; and he had done so much to help those in need. And then there was Livingstone himself, who had married Moffat's daughter and been attacked by a lion out by Molelopole, not far away.

"Livingstone," she said to Mr. Polopetsi.

He looked at her blankly.

"I thought of Livingstone," she explained, "when I was thinking of changes in names. They have not changed the name of Livingstone up in Zambia, have they? That place is still called Livingstone."

Mr. Polopetsi prided himself on his knowledge of history. "He was a very good man," he said. "You would not want to change anything named after a man like Livingstone." He paused. "He was a very brave man, Mma Ramotswe. He was one of those who brought slavery to an end." He paused, and looked at her intently. "Many terrible things have happened in Africa, Mma."

She returned his gaze. So much had occurred, and so many of the things that had happened were bad. And yet there had been good things — acts of kindness, acts of loyalty and generosity of spirit; why did we forget these and remember only the bad? She had always preferred to remember the positive points in a person's life, but she knew that there were those who thought less of her for that. To dwell on such things was said by some to be a sign that you were not aware of how things really were; but she was, she was. She knew as well as anyone that the world could be a place of trial and sorrow, that there was injustice and suffering and heartlessness — there was enough of all that to fill the great Kalahari twice over, but what good did it do to ponder that and that alone? None, she thought.

Even Clovis Andersen, who was mostly concerned with practical matters of detection, referred to this in his great work. He wrote: *Do not allow the profession of which you are a member to induce you to take a bleak view of humanity. You will encounter all sorts of bad behavior but do not judge everybody by the standards of the lowest.* If you did that, he pointed out, you would misjudge humanity in general and that would be fatal to discerning judgement. *If everybody is a villain, then nobody is a villain,* he wrote. That simple expression had intrigued her, even if it was some time before its full meaning — and the wisdom that lay behind it — became apparent.

She returned to the subject of Mr. Government Keboneng. "So the city council said that they would have to be content with a new street?"

"Yes," said Mr. Polopetsi. "They said that they would not change the name of one of the streets in the middle of town because people would become confused."

"They would," said Mma Ramotswe. "They would wonder what was happening."

"And so Mr. Keboneng's supporters grumbled a bit, apparently, but they realised that they would have to make do with what they were offered. They felt that they had won a bit of a victory, even if not the full victory they would have liked."

"Very wise," said Mma Ramotswe. "Second prize is often better than first prize."

She was not sure why she said that, and she was not even sure that it was true. Why would second prize sometimes be preferable? Perhaps it was because being at the top brought unwelcome attention or onerous responsibilities. That must be it. It was surely better to be Deputy Chief than Chief. A disturbing thought came to her unbidden: Was it better to be Mma Makutsi rather than Mma Ramotswe? She thought that Mma Makutsi might perhaps take the view that being Head of the No. 1 Ladies' Detective Agency was better than being Deputy Head — the position that she currently occupied. Now, of course, she was Acting

Head, which had its compensations, as being "Acting" anything meant that there would come a time when you could simply hand the reins back to the permanent Head no matter how complicated and difficult the situation had become. She asked herself whether Mma Makutsi would do that. "Here is your desk back, Mma Ramotswe," she might say. "And here is a list of all the outstanding cases that we have been unable to solve during your absence. We are very sorry about those. You can solve them now, Mma." She could just hear that.

Mr. Polopetsi had said something that she missed. "I'm sorry, Rra," she said. "I was thinking about Mma Makutsi. What did you say just then?"

"I said that the supporters planned a party to celebrate the naming of the street. They even bought a large amount of food, which was a pity."

She asked him why.

"Because the council's decision was suspended."

She knew the ways of councillors. There was even one known popularly as Mma Stop-Start, and another as Mr. Green-Light-Red-Light. "They changed their minds?"

"They told the Keboneng people that

184

somebody had raised an issue with them confidentially. This issue, they said, was all to do with the suitability of Mr. Keboneng to have a road named after him." He paused, as if savouring the dramatic revelation. "There was a scandal in the background, they said. And because of this they were unwilling to go ahead."

"They said he was not quite the hero people thought he was? Was that it?"

Mma Ramotswe sighed. Nobody was perfect — every one of us, she thought, has done something of which we are ashamed. If that were not so, then we would hardly be human. And even if we had not done it, then we had at least thought of how we *might* do it if given half the chance. The important thing was that such things were few and far between in our lives, and kept that way. We could be weak, of course, but one would not want to be weak all the time.

Mma Ramotswe now guessed why it was that Mma Potokwane had sought the agency's help. "They want us to refute this allegation? Is that it?"

"Exactly," said Mr. Polopetsi. "Mma Potokwane had come on her own behalf, as his sister, but she was also representing his supporters. They all want to find out what this allegation is and prove that it is false. That is what they want, Mma."

That was reasonable enough, she felt: a reputation, even a posthumous one, was a precious thing and people could go to some lengths to protect it.

"Do they know anything about what is being said against him?" she asked.

He shook his head. "No. The council will not tell them. They said that it is confidential and that they cannot reveal what the issue is."

She understood why this should be so. Yet it would be extremely frustrating for the relatives and the friends of the late Mr. Government Keboneng to know that there was something besmirching his memory but not to be able to get to grips with it. It would be like wrestling with smoke.

"I can see that this must be a rather difficult case for Mma Makutsi," she said. "There's not much to go on, is there?"

Mr. Polopetsi suddenly looked morose. "That's why she's passed it over to me," he said. "She started to look into it and then she stopped — just like that, Mma — she stopped and said, 'You must take this case, Mr. Polopetsi. I am far too busy, I'm afraid. You must sort this out.' That is what she said to me, Mma. She said, 'You must sort this out.' "

Mma Ramotswe found herself at a loss. Why on earth should Mma Makutsi wash her hands of an important case like this? Surely this was exactly the sort of case that she would want to solve herself in a glare of publicity, incurring in the process the gratitude of the client. And yet here she was, passing it over to Mr. Polopetsi, who, although undoubtedly a good man, was only part-time — and a volunteer at that. It did not make sense.

"I can see how it must be very difficult for you, Rra."

He seemed relieved to know that his plight was understood. "It is very difficult, Mma Ramotswe," he said. "And that is why I've come to hand it over to you."

She had not expected this. "But Mma Makutsi is running the agency," she said. "I am on holiday. You know what she's like, Rra. She does not want me to interfere while she is running things. I must respect that."

"But she need not know," said Mr. Polopetsi. "I will do all the investigations. All I need is for you to tell me what to do." He hesitated, his morose expression now replaced by something much brighter.

"Oh, Rra, I don't know . . ."

"But you must help me, Mma. I do not

want to look stupid in Mma Makutsi's eyes, and that is how I'll look if I go to her and say that I cannot do this thing. She will laugh at me, Mma — you know what she's like. You have yourself just said that, I think. Those were your very words, Mma."

She talked to Mr. J.L.B. Matekoni about it because she felt that when one is faced with a problem quite so delicate there is nothing better than a heart-to-heart conversation with one's spouse, particularly if one's spouse knows the other parties involved.

She raised the subject that evening, when they were sitting opposite one another at the kitchen table, the evening meal ready on the plates before them.

"So," concluded Mma Ramotswe as she finished, "that is where matters stand at present. I have this request from Mr. Polopetsi — actually, it is more of a plea than a request — and frankly, Rra, I am torn. I do not know what to do."

Mr. J.L.B. Matekoni looked down at his plate. "I am worried that my food will get cold," he said. "This is such a big problem that my food will get cold if I try to deal with it straightaway."

"But of course," said Mma Ramotswe hurriedly. "You must eat your food, Rra.

First things first."

He picked up his fork. "While I am eating, I shall think. I find that it is sometimes easier to think when one is eating. Eating and thinking go together."

She reached for her own fork. "That is certainly true, Mr. J.L.B. Matekoni." She was not sure if that was really so; she felt that she did not do her best thinking while eating — that came, in her case, at least, when she was drinking a cup of tea. Had Mr. J.L.B. Matekoni said that drinking tea and thinking went hand in hand, then she would have been the first to agree; but he had not said that — he had said something quite different, as husbands and wives often will do: they say the opposite of what they should say.

But this was not the time for such reflections and so she waited — perhaps a little anxiously — until he had finished his beef and vegetables.

"So you have thought about it, Rra?" she asked.

He inclined his head gravely — as a judge might do before passing sentence. "I have thought about it very hard, Mma Ramotswe."

"And?"

"And it is very clear to me that you must

go and see Mma Makutsi," he said. "You must go and put your cards on the table." He looked at her for a moment or two before his gaze slipped back to his plate. "There wouldn't be any more, would there, Mma?"

She fetched a pot from the top of the stove. "There is definitely more, Rra," she said. "But before you eat, you must tell me why I should go to see Mma Makutsi."

He repeated himself. "You must go and see your friend."

"Yes, but why? Is there no other way of handling this?"

"No. You must go and see her and tell her that it is unfair to put Mr. Polopetsi under such strain. He is a thin man, that one, and he will not be able to bear much strain. That is why you must do it. He cannot deal with this — you can."

Mma Ramotswe was not sure that weight and emotional robustness were that closely linked, but she knew what Mr. J.L.B. Matekoni meant: Mr. Polopetsi was a vulnerable man who did not look as if he could tolerate a great deal of strain.

As she pondered, she found herself agreeing with him. "I think you are right, Rra. Although I must say that I'm a bit worried about her reaction: she will not be pleased.

She does not want me to interfere while she is in charge."

"But you're not questioning her authority," he parried. "All you are saying is that one of the agency staff appears to need help. That is quite different from saying that she is in any way rubbish. You are not saying that, Mma."

She began to falter; perhaps it was not all that clear. "I hope that she will not be awkward, but I cannot be sure of that. She is famous for being difficult. If she thinks that I am trying to take over this case, then . . ." She left the sentence unfinished. She knew that there would be a reaction from Mma Makutsi, but she could not be sure of what it would be.

Mr. J.L.B. Matekoni held up a finger — his signal for silence and a sign, too, that a good idea was in the offing.

"The point is, Mma," he began. "The point is that she will have no grounds to think you are trying to take the case away from her — in fact, quite the opposite. You will be encouraging her to fulfill her obligations rather than to try to offload them onto that poor, harmless Polopetsi." He paused. "Putting Mr. Polopetsi in charge of the investigation is like putting a rabbit in charge of the airport."

She was surprised by the analogy. Who would think of putting a rabbit in charge of the airport? And why was Mr. J.L.B. Matekoni so dismissive of Mr. Polopetsi? But she wanted to be sure. "I should tell her to carry out her promise to look after things?"

He looked at his plate again. "Of course, Mma. You tell her that — just that."

She ladled a helping of stew onto his plate.

"Very good stew," muttered Mr. J.L.B. Matekoni.

She did not hear the compliment — or not fully, as she was still thinking of his advice. Although she entirely understood the argument in favour of openness, there were limits to the extent to which one should speak frankly. She did not agree with the custom that was sometimes followed in Africa of avoiding direct confrontation with those with whom one disagreed — that led to all sorts of failures, she knew — but one should still be careful to avoid hurting feelings by challenging others too openly. Often it was better to be gentle — to say something in such a way that the person criticised did not feel too humiliated. It was all a question of face, she decided: you had to leave room for face to be saved.

She decided to speak to Mma Makutsi,

but she would be careful to be gentle. After all, an acting head of anything could well be upset if openly censured.

She sighed. "Being on holiday is not as easy as I imagined," she said, half to herself, half to Mr. J.L.B. Matekoni, should he be listening.

He looked up from his stew. "Mma Ramotswe," he said, "you can do anything. Nothing is too hard for a person like you — nothing. You are very good at doing everything, Mma, and anything you do, Mma — anything at all — will always be the right thing as far as I am concerned."

She gazed at her husband. Being loved and admired by a man like that — and she knew that this man, this mechanic, this fixer of machines with their broken hearts, did indeed love and admire her — was like walking in the sunshine; it gave the same feeling of warmth and pleasure to bask in the love of one who has promised it, publicly at a wedding ceremony, and who is constant in his promise that such love will be given for the rest of his days. What more could any woman ask? None of us, she thought, not one single one of us, could ask for anything more than that.

Chapter Ten:
Talking about Furniture

The next day was a Saturday, when businesses other than shops would be closed. That applied, at one end of the spectrum, to Tlokweng Road Speedy Motors and to the No. 1 Ladies' Detective Agency, and at the other to Debswana Diamonds, the Standard Bank, and the Office of the President of Botswana. For the Double Comfort Furniture Store, of which Mma Makutsi's husband, Phuti Radiphuti, was the owner and managing director, Saturday was an extremely important trading day, as it was then that young couples setting up home together, older couples thinking of home improvements, and even those who simply had nothing better to do would flock to the furniture showroom to view the displays of tables, chairs, sofas, cupboards, and beds.

Mma Ramotswe knew that Mma Makutsi often spent a large part of Saturday in the store, helping her husband with paperwork, or sometimes paging through catalogues and offering her advice on new lines they might order. She took with her the nursemaid she had employed to help with their baby, and this young woman would push Itumelang round the store in a small pram, encouraging and accepting admiring comments from shoppers.

"She is very happy for people to think he is her baby," Mma Makutsi had confided in Mma Ramotswe. "But I don't mind, Mma. It gives her pleasure and she has no children of her own. I can share."

Mma Ramotswe thought it would be easier to speak to Mma Makutsi about Mr. Polopetsi on the neutral ground of the Double Comfort Furniture Store. She could have waited until Monday, of course, and called in at the office of the No. 1 Ladies' Detective Agency, but this could have been far more likely to result in an accusation of interference. To raise the issue on a casual visit to the store would be a different matter altogether.

It was almost midday when she arrived at the store. The car park to the front of the large yellow building was already almost full and such shady parking places as there were had long been filled. A vacant spot appeared near the door, and she took that, leaving her window open to prevent heat building up in the cab. There was nothing of any value inside and no thief with any ambition would think of stealing the van itself. Indeed, when she had last filled in the insurance form, she had been asked to declare the van's value, and had simply written "Sentimental value" in the relevant box. And that was true, she thought; she loved that van, but she knew nobody else would — to others it was just a rather tired, now dented, piece of increasingly ancient machinery, capable of getting from A to B, but not much further, and not with any dispatch. But to her it was a friend, her faithful companion on more adventures than she could readily remember, the mute witness to hours spent watching some place of interest, to long conversations between herself and Mma Makutsi, to periods of quiet reflection on long drives through the country. All of that was part of the tiny white van's history, and that was why she would never replace it and, when it would finally go no more, would ask for it to be left somewhere in the bush, some private place, where it might return in due course to the earth from which it had once been created — metal to metal, glass to glass . . .

As she entered the building she felt, with

some relief, the cool touch of the air-conditioning on her skin. Phuti Radiphuti had recently installed a new system that had proved very popular with the customers in the hot season and inclined them, he claimed, to make larger purchases.

She looked about her. The store was busier than she had ever seen it, even in the few days before Christmas, when shopping fever seemed to grip the nation. Immediately in front of her a young couple was inspecting a bedside table, opening each of its three drawers and whispering comments to one another. Beyond them a family was trying out the chairs around a large and highly polished dining-room table. The three children sat at the table wide-eyed with wonder at the momentous nature of the anticipated purchase — could such a table really be for *them*? The mother ran her fingers over the glossy surface, as one might touch an object of great religious or artistic significance, while the father examined the mechanism by which the table might be extended or folded in upon itself.

She smiled at the sight, remembering how proud she had once been of her father's purchase of a fine white Brahmin bull. A bull was not a table, but the feeling of satisfaction that a parent could buy some-

197

thing big like that was surely the same. She did not linger, though, and made her way towards the office at the back of the showroom, where Mma Makutsi, if she was in the shop, might be found.

The office door was slightly ajar, allowing Mma Ramotswe to see Phuti Radiphuti standing inside. As she approached, the door opened wider and Mma Makutsi appeared, a clipboard in her hand. She gave a start when she saw Mma Ramotswe, frowned in momentary confusion, but then gave her visitor a welcoming smile.

She spoke warmly. "I did not expect you, Mma, but this is very good timing on your part. I was just about to make tea, and here you are."

"I can always tell when there is a possibility of tea," said Mma Ramotswe. "It is a very odd thing, but there it is. I can *feel* the onset of tea."

Mma Makutsi beckoned her into the office, but as she did so her smile faded. "Oh, Mma, there is a big problem — a very big problem."

Mma Ramotswe was quick to say that if they were busy she could return later on. "I know that Saturday is your busy day," she said. "I can come back, Mma, when you have finished selling sofas and whatnot. It will be no trouble."

"Oh, it's not that," Mma Makutsi reassured her. "There are plenty of assistants to do the selling. It's just that . . ."

Phuti Radiphuti, who had been standing beside his desk, now came forward. "I think I can guess what the trouble is," he said. "There is no red bush tea. Is that the problem, Grace?"

Mma Makutsi nodded. "We did have it, but one of the people in the office drank it all and I forgot to get some more. It is my fault entirely, Mma."

Mma Ramotswe laughed. "That is no problem, Mma Makutsi. I am perfectly happy to drink ordinary tea. Five Roses tea? That will be fine with me."

"There!" exclaimed Phuti Radiphuti. "That is one problem solved. *Nobody makes better tea than you and Five Roses!*" He sang the line of the advertising jingle in a slightly croaky voice, causing Mma Makutsi to look at him with undisguised embarrassment.

"Phuti would like to be a singer," she said to Mma Ramotswe. "But unfortunately . . ."

"He has a fine voice," said Mma Ramotswe. "Perhaps he will teach Mr. J.L.B. Matekoni to sing a bit better. He is always trying to sing something, but I cannot tell what it is. Perhaps it is the national anthem.

Perhaps it is a hymn. Perhaps it is just something he heard on the radio. It is a very great mystery, this unknown song of his."

Mma Makutsi gestured for Mma Ramotswe to sit down. With the kettle switched on, she joined her guest round a table on which a selection of trade catalogues was stacked. "So," she began, "what brings you to the store, Mma? Are you thinking of new furniture?"

"I was driving past," said Mma Ramotswe. That was, strictly speaking, true; she had inadvertently driven past the turning into the Double Comfort Furniture Store and had been obliged to go back. "I was driving past and I thought I might pop in and say hello."

"That is very kind of you," said Phuti Radiphuti.

Mma Makutsi said nothing, and for a moment Mma Ramotswe entertained the disturbing thought that she had seen through her claim. "Actually," she said, "I had been thinking of coming to see you." This, too, was true — as far as it went. But then she thought: I must be honest with my friend; and, after she had told herself that, the further thought occurred: I must be honest with *everybody*.

She sighed. There were arguments against

200

having that voice within you that told you what to do. That voice had many forms: it could be the voice of a teacher or a parent; it could be the voice of an old friend; it could be the voice of an aunt or an uncle; or it could be a voice that one knew was oneself — one's own inner voice. And it knew how to choose its words: *Really? Do you really think you should do that? Aren't you being just a little bit selfish?* If you had no such voice, or if you knew how to ignore it, you would have no moments like this when you realised that what you said was not absolutely true and you had to retract your words.

Taking a deep breath, she began afresh. She had not heard the voice, but she knew what it would say. "Actually, Mma, the truth of the matter is that I need to talk to you about Mr. Polopetsi."

Mma Makutsi waited for her to continue.

"He came to see me," Mma Ramotswe said. "He came to Zebra Drive yesterday and told me about this Potokwane case."

Mma Makutsi's eyes narrowed with disapproval. "But you are on holiday, Mma. Mr. Polopetsi has no business disturbing you like that."

Mma Ramotswe was quick to say that she did not mind. "It was not a disturbance at

201

all, Mma. I was not doing anything at the time."

"But that is what a holiday is for," interjected Phuti Radiphuti. "So if you stop a person on holiday from doing nothing, then that is a disturbance — I would have thought."

Mma Ramotswe needed a moment to work out the meaning of this. But then she said briskly, "It did not matter. I was pleased to see Mr. Polopetsi — I always am."

Mma Makutsi looked impatient. "Leaving all that aside, Mma, the question is: Why did he come to speak to you about the Potokwane case?"

There was a short silence before Mma Ramotswe answered. "He was concerned, Mma. He said that you had asked him to take over the investigation —"

Mma Makutsi interrupted her. "Yes, I did. I decided to give him some responsibility." She paused, looking challengingly at Mma Ramotswe. "What is the point of having an assistant like Mr. Polopetsi if you give him no responsibility?"

It occurred to Mma Ramotswe that there might be a further barb behind this question — a suggestion that Mma Makutsi, in her days as assistant, had not been given enough responsibility. But this was not the time to rake over those ancient coals.

"Responsibility is a good thing," Mma Ramotswe said evenly. "I would never say that it was a bad thing to give others the chance to prove their ability."

"Well, then," said Mma Makutsi. "That answers that, I think."

She rose to her feet to make the tea.

"I am not sure," said Mma Ramotswe hesitantly. "There is a difference between a challenge and a burden. One is something you can carry on your shoulders easily enough — the other is something, a big sack, that bends you double."

Mma Makutsi poured the hot water into the teapot. She did not look at Mma Ramotswe as she replied. "There is no heavy sack here. It is a simple case that even Charlie could handle, if we gave it to him. Do you think I should hand it over to Charlie, Mma? Is that what you're suggesting?"

"I'm not suggesting anything," said Mma Ramotswe. "All I'm saying is that Mr. Polopetsi feels out of his depth. I thought that perhaps you did not know that, and that is why I'm telling you now. He needs help."

Mma Makutsi returned with two mugs of tea. She handed one to Mma Ramotswe and put the other one down on the table. "We all need help, Mma. We could all do with a hand."

"But some more than others," Mma Ramotswe said quickly. "Especially if, like Mr. Polopetsi, you are a bit rusty when it comes to the work we do."

She watched for the effect of her words, but Mma Makutsi seemed unmoved, even if Phuti Radiphuti had started to nod enthusiastically. Now was the time to draw on whatever wells of courage she possessed. "I think you should take the weight off him," she went on. "Take over the case once more. You are very experienced, Mma — you are a director of the agency . . ."

Flattery had worked with Mma Makutsi before; indeed, she seemed particularly susceptible to a compliment. With that in mind, Mma Ramotswe now threw caution to the wind. "After all, Mma, remember that you are . . . how shall I put it? Remember that you are confident — with your ninety-seven per cent behind you — whereas Mr. Polopetsi, well, his confidence was destroyed by that unfortunate business with the prescription."

It did not work. "Mr. Polopetsi has had a long time to recover from all that," said Mma Makutsi dismissively. "And you should remember, Mma, that his wife is an important lady these days. He is quite capable of looking after himself."

Mma Ramotswe decided to try again. "Yes, he is better these days, Mma. But just because he is feeling better, that does not mean he will know much more. And that's the problem, I think. He just doesn't know what to do."

"Oh, I think he does, Mma Ramotswe," said Mma Makutsi. "He can easily make the necessary enquiries in this Potokwane business. I cannot treat him as if he were a small boy."

"I'm not asking you to do that."

"But you are, Mma. You're asking me to tell him that he doesn't know what he's doing. You're asking me to hold his hand. That sounds as if he is being treated as a small boy."

Phuti Radiphuti came to her defence. "I don't think she's doing that, Grace," he began. "Mr. Polopetsi asked her, after all . . ."

He did not finish. A glance from Mma Makutsi, as eloquent as it was unambiguous, brought his intervention to an end. Noticing this, Mma Ramotswe decided to desist. She had no desire to provoke an argument between husband and wife, especially where the wife, as was the case here, was a woman of some mettle; Mma Makutsi was not one to cede ground easily.

"Well," she said breezily, "we don't need to talk about this any more, Mma Makutsi. I am on holiday, as you know, and you are —"

"Acting Head of the agency," supplied Mma Makutsi.

"Yes, that is what you are. So I won't discuss it any further. You are the one to decide, and then —"

Again she was interrupted. "Exactly, Mma. We shall leave Mr. Polopetsi to deal with this. He will do very well, I'm sure."

Mma Ramotswe bit her tongue. It really was too bad; Mma Makutsi owed her position as Acting Head — owed everything, in fact — to her, as she had admitted more than once, and here she was refusing even to consider a perfectly reasonable request to relieve Mr. Polopetsi of his anxiety. Could she not remember what it was like to be in a new job and out of one's depth? Some people, it seemed, forgot that feeling rather quickly.

"There's just one thing," Mma Ramotswe ventured. "The client in this case . . . I was very surprised when I heard that she was called Potokwane. At first I thought it was our Mma Potokwane looking for help."

206

Mma Makutsi laughed. "That would be the day, Mma. No, it's not our Mma Potokwane at all — it is the wife of her husband's cousin. He has the same name — Potokwane."

Mma Ramotswe wondered whether Mma Potokwane — the matron — knew that a relative of her husband's had approached the agency. "I would have expected her to be in touch with me about it if she knew," she said. "Even just a telephone call — something like that."

Mma Makutsi agreed. "I think that she doesn't know," she said. "They are keeping the whole thing quiet, I think. And I can see why they should do this. People do not like it when rumours begin to spread. You know how it is, Mma. One person says one thing and then the next person adds a little bit — just to make it a bit more interesting. And soon the story is all over town and everybody is shaking their heads."

Mma Ramotswe knew what Mma Makutsi meant. For all that it had grown, Gaborone was still an intimate place where people were aware of the business of others. Such a town was fertile territory for gossip and the spread of rumours.

"Fortunately," continued Mma Makutsi, "there has not been any talk about this matter. So far, nothing about the council's change of mind has been in the papers. I imagine that they want it to remain like that."

Mma Makutsi now became silent, but only for a very short time. It seemed to Mma Ramotswe that the other woman was weighing up something, and now, with a rather abrupt change of tone, she announced her decision. "I do not think that anything will be discovered," she said. "So even if Mr. Polopetsi gets nowhere — and I think you may be right, Mma: he will get nowhere — even if that happens, then that will not matter too much. The whole thing will go away."

Mma Ramotswe hesitated. She found it difficult to grasp what was happening. This was not the Mma Makutsi whom she knew. This was not the tenacious, sometimes prickly, often argumentative, but ultimately determined person she had employed when the No. 1 Ladies' Detective Agency first opened its doors.

"I'm not sure . . . ," she began, but did not finish. Mma Makutsi had put down her mug and reached for one of the trade catalogues.

"I need your advice, Mma Ramotswe," she said. "It is on a furniture matter."

Phuti Radiphuti had been listening to their conversation but had not joined in. Mma Ramotswe had watched him, and had decided that he was unhappy about something; now he looked at his watch and made an apologetic gesture. "I hope you won't mind if I leave you, Mma Ramotswe. We have taken on some new members of staff, and I have to check up on them."

Mma Ramotswe replied that she would not take offence. "Your wife has things to discuss with me," she said, adding mentally, *even if she won't talk about the things that need to be talked about.*

Mma Makutsi nodded to Phuti Radiphuti and then turned back to the catalogue. "We are thinking of taking a new line in sofas," she said. "These are for what we call the larger market."

"What is that, Mma?"

Mma Makutsi licked a finger to turn the pages of the catalogue. "I'll show you, Mma. The larger market is for larger people. Some furniture is too small for these people. So we need to have a section of furniture for traditionally built customers." She paused. "Perhaps for people like yourself, Mma."

Mma Ramotswe did not take offence. There were those who would resent being described as traditionally built, but she was not one of them. She was proud of her build, which was in accordance with the old Botswana ideas of beauty, and she would not pander to the modern idea of slenderness. That was an importation from elsewhere, and it was simply wrong. How could a very thin woman do all the things that women needed to do: to carry children on their backs, to pound maize into flour out at the lands or the cattle post, to cart around the things of the household — the pots and pans and buckets of water? And how could a thin woman comfort a man? It would be very awkward for a man to share his bed with a person who was all angles and bone, whereas a traditionally built lady would be like an extra pillow on which a man coming home tired from his work might rest his weary head. To do all that you needed a bit of bulk, and thin people simply did not have that.

Mma Makutsi found the relevant section of the catalogue and pointed out to Mma Ramotswe pictures of sofas spread across two pages. "You see all these, Mma? This is what they call the Karoo Range. The sofas here are named after that place they have down south."

Mma Ramotswe knew about the Karoo. "It is like our Kalahari," she said. "But it has sheep."

"Yes," said Mma Makutsi. "There are many sheep." She put a finger on one of the photographs. "I think that sofa would be good," she said. "What do you think, Mma? Would you want to sit on that one?"

Mma Ramotswe studied the picture. "I am not sure," she said. "It is a bit close to the ground. You see there? Its legs are very short."

"That is to save space," said Mma Makutsi. "These days they're making furniture with short legs to save space. And materials too. If you have short legs on furniture, then you save wood."

Mma Ramotswe saw difficulties with that. "But then if you sit on a sofa like that, Mma, your knees will go up in the air because you are so low down. And there will be some traditionally built people — not all, but some — who will find it difficult to get up if they are at that angle. They may have to call for help." She peered at the picture again. "Perhaps a sofa like that should have some sort of alarm button, Mma. If you got stuck, then you could press it and an alarm would sound."

Mma Makutsi looked at her disapprovingly. "They do not make such things, Mma."

211

"I was just thinking aloud," said Mma Ramotswe.

Mma Makutsi closed the catalogue. "I think that I should get back to work, Mma."

Mma Ramotswe took the hint. "And I must get over to the supermarket. We have very little food in the house and I need to stock up."

"That is because you have a man in the house," said Mma Makutsi. "We women buy food, but men just come along and eat it. That is happening all the time. Women buy food and men eat it."

"Very true," mused Mma Ramotswe. "Now that one comes to think about it."

But she was not thinking about the purchase and consumption of food. She was not thinking about men and their little ways. Rather she was thinking of why Mma Makutsi was behaving so strangely. Was something wrong? She remembered Clovis Andersen saying something about this in *The Principles of Private Detection,* and as she left the store his words came back to her. *If a person acts out of character, then there's one thing you can be sure of: there is something wrong. I have seen this so many times I have lost count.*

CHAPTER ELEVEN:
IT IS A COMPLICATED STORY.
WE SHALL NEED MORE TEA

She did not spend long in the supermarket at Riverwalk, confining her purchases to supplies she would need for the next few days. There was beef for a stew, a large pumpkin, a packet of beans, a dozen eggs, and two loaves of bread. The pumpkin looked delicious — almost perfectly round and deep yellow in colour, it sat on the passenger seat beside her so comfortably as she drove out of the car park, so pleased to be what it was, that she imagined conducting a conversation with it, telling it about the Orphan Farm and Mma Potokwane and her concerns over Mma Makutsi. And the pumpkin would remain silent, of course, but would somehow indicate that it knew what she was talking about, that there were similar issues in the world of pumpkins.

She smiled. There was no harm, she thought, in allowing your imagination to run away with you, as a child's will do, because the thoughts that came in that way could be a comfort, a relief in a world that could be both sad and serious. Why not imagine a talk with a pumpkin? Why not imagine going off for a drive with a friendly pumpkin, a companion who would not, after all, answer back; who would agree with everything you said, and would at the end of the day appear on your plate as a final gesture of friendship? Why not allow yourself a few minutes of imaginative silliness so that you could remember what it was like when you believed such things, when you were a child at the feet of your grandmother, listening to the old Setswana tales of talking trees and clever baboons and all the things that made up that world that lay just on the other side of the world we knew, the world of the real Botswana.

She did not drive home, but joined the flow of traffic going east on the Tlokweng Road, her destination the Orphan Farm and her friend Mma Potokwane. It being a Saturday, she did not expect to find Mma Potokwane in her office, but her house was on the premises and she would almost certainly be there.

The road was busy, with cars going in both directions. Mma Ramotswe wondered where everybody was going, but then remembered that there was a football match on at the stadium, where the Zebras were playing against a team from Zambia. Charlie would be there, she imagined, and Fanwell too. Over the years she and Mma Makutsi had been obliged to listen to so much chatter about the Zebras and their doings, none of which had meant very much, and very little of which had remained in her memory. Last year, she recalled, the Zebras had scored an important goal in a crucial game against a traditional rival, and that had brought great pleasure to both young men. Charlie had breathlessly explained how one of their players, a man with a ridiculous nickname she could not remember, picked up the ball in his own half and dribbled past half the opposition, before placing it in the top corner from twenty-five yards. The keeper, he said, had had no chance at all. She and Mma Makutsi had just smiled indulgently at this account, but Charlie and Fanwell had performed a spontaneous dance of joy, although Mma Makutsi had somewhat spoiled the celebration by remarking, "Those poor people who lost — I wonder what they're doing now."

By the time she had to turn off the Tlokweng Road the traffic had thinned to the point where there was now just the occasional car. The last section of the road was untarred, and vehicles would throw up a cloud of red dust, like the vapour trail of an aircraft. One of these red clouds came towards her now, enveloped her, and then passed, and shortly thereafter she was at the gate. The sign at the entrance portrayed a smiling child protected by two encircling adult hands, and underneath this picture were the words *This is an abode of love.* The letters were hard to read now because the paint had blistered from years of exposure to the sun; but the love was still there, she thought, like the sun.

Mma Potokwane's house was a short walk from her office, not far from the acacia tree under which Mma Ramotswe usually parked her van. It was not a large house, or a particularly attractive one, but it had about it that indefinable quality marking out places that are loved by those who live in them and that, in return, provide more than mere shelter. On one side there was a rain tank, painted green, and linked to the gutters of the house by a sloping pipe; on the other was a makeshift lean-to garage, sheltering the old blue minibus Mma Potokwane had been given by a local hotel company, a steadfast supporter of the children's home. This vehicle had been used to transport hotel employees to and from work before it was eventually replaced by something newer and smarter. When it had come to the Orphan Farm, the age and experience of the minibus had begun to show; it had been a poor starter and, indeed, a poor runner, and displayed a tendency to cut out at speeds above forty miles an hour. None of these weaknesses had been a match for Mr. J.L.B. Matekoni, though, who had spent the best part of three days renewing and revitalising the vehicle until it ran smoothly and reasonably reliably.

Mma Potokwane's husband was a keen gardener, and his touch was very much in evidence. Surrounding the house was a four-strand goat-proof fence, creating a protected yard in which he had planted vegetables, flowering shrubs, and the waxy desert plants that thrived so well in Botswana's climate. The visual interest provided by these plants was complemented here and there by small concrete ornaments, painted in white and blue, the national colours of Botswana — a kingfisher perching on one concrete leg, a hippo the size of a small dog, an indeterminate crouching creature that might have been a lion or a domestic cat, or something in between.

She made her way up to the front door,

pausing briefly to examine the flowers on a round, cactus-like plant. The plant itself was ugly — like a turnip into which needles had been placed — but the flowers were tiny, delicate things, as beautiful as any expensive and exotic orchid.

She was disturbed by a voice from within the house. "That's very pretty, that one, Mma Ramotswe. If it has any children, I shall give you one or two for your own garden."

She looked up to see Mma Potokwane standing in her doorway. It was a surprise to see her dressed in the way she was — not in the matron's outfit she always seemed to wear but in a pair of blue jeans and a white muslin top. The jeans were sufficiently voluminous — Mma Potokwane, like Mma Ramotswe, was traditionally built — but seemed to be fighting a losing battle against the pressures of the flesh, looking as if they might at any moment be shed like a snake's skin.

"They are very beautiful," said Mma Ramotswe. "What are they called, Mma?"

Mma Potokwane shrugged. "I have forgotten, Mma. My husband knows their Setswana name, but he is probably the only one who does. Those names are going, Mma. We are all forgetting them. Soon we shall look about us and not be able to identify anything. Even the sky will have lost its name."

"That will not happen. The sky will always be . . ." And for a dreadful moment, Mma Ramotswe forgot the name of the sky, until Mma Potokwane, laughing, came to her rescue.

They went inside, where Mma Potokwane said a pot of tea had just been brewed. Mma Ramotswe realised that she had been in Mma Potokwane's house only once before, and that had been some years ago. The two friends invariably met in the matron's office, which meant that it was there that Mma Ramotswe always imagined her. It was the same with her bank manager, her dressmaker, and the women who taught Puso and Motholeli. All of these people must have houses, but she could not envisage them in a domestic setting. Nor could she imagine the President in his house, although she had driven past its high white walls on many occasions and knew the colour of its roof. Even the greatest in the land must have a room that was just for them, where they kept personal things, where they could go barefoot or put their feet on the chairs.

Mma Potokwane's house was furnished simply. There were no shiny surfaces, no glass tables or expensive sitting-room suites; none of the furniture, she noticed, matched. But it was homely, and from the kitchen, and pervading the whole house, came a delicious smell of baking — a smell that was redolent of rich fruit, of molasses, of roasted almonds.

Mma Potokwane invited Mma Ramotswe into the sitting room. "I was baking," she began, and then paused, waiting for her friend's reaction.

Mma Ramotswe laughed. "It is my job, Mma, to put two and two together. That is what I do."

Mma Potokwane was already making for the kitchen. Over her shoulder she called, "So the only question is one slice or two?"

"There are some questions," said Mma Ramotswe, "that do not really need to be asked."

There were several framed photographs on the walls of the living room. Mma Ramotswe rose from her chair to study these while Mma Potokwane was out of the room. She felt justified in doing this: photographs on a wall were there for people to see and to examine if interested; an album is a different thing, and she would never have opened a photograph album without Mma Potokwane's permission, tempting though that might have been.

There was a wedding photograph: a slimmer, and younger, Mma Potokwane stood with a good-looking man in front of a doorway, a group of older people to the side. That was the family, she imagined, but she could not tell whose side it was. Sometimes physical appearance made that quite clear, but not in this case. Then there was a photograph of Mma Potokwane, again a younger version, in a nurse's uniform, smiling broadly. That must have been taken when she finished her training, Mma Ramotswe thought, perhaps on her first day as a fully qualified nurse, as there was a look of pride on her face and the uniform looked so pristine. And now that she came to examine the background, she could see that it was a hospital and, yes, it was the Princess Marina in Gaborone, as she could make out one of the buildings in the background, a ward with some patients looking out of the window. That building was still there, though now it was used as an office block for the hospital administration.

Then there was a photograph of a small group of children, with a middle-aged woman standing beside them. She recognised the surroundings as being the Orphan Farm, but she did not recognise the woman.

"That is one of the housemothers," said Mma Potokwane, who had reappeared from the kitchen and was standing behind her. "She retired shortly after I came here, but she was very good to me when I was appointed. She showed me everything."

"That must have been very helpful," said Mma Ramotswe. "A new job can be very confusing."

"Who did you have to help you?" asked Mma Potokwane, placing a low tray on the table in the middle of the room.

"I only had a book," said Mma Ramotswe. "There is a book by a man called Mr. Clovis Andersen. I found a copy of that."

"Then that would have helped," said Mma Potokwane, pouring tea from a teapot.

"It did. And then, you know, I met him. Mr. Andersen came to Botswana. He called in at the office."

Mma Potokwane looked impressed. "I have never met a person like that, although I did know Professor Tlou. He wrote a book on the history of Botswana. He was a very good man. He is late now, but many people remember him very fondly."

"Yes," said Mma Ramotswe. "We have had some very good people in this country . . ." She stopped, realising that the conversation had taken her naturally, and without any forcing, to precisely that point where she could talk about what she wanted to talk about. "I have come to see you, Mma . . ."

"Yes, Mma. I was wondering. You're always welcome to drop in any time — you know that — but I was wondering."

Mma Ramotswe took a sip of her tea. "It is a delicate matter."

Mma Potokwane made an expansive gesture. "I am used to delicate matters, Mma Ramotswe; they do not worry me one little bit. Not one little bit. All these children . . . their young lives are full of delicate matters."

"Of course, of course. A matron knows about such things."

"So, Mma?"

Mma Ramotswe looked at Mma Potokwane. She knew that she could be as direct as she liked with her, and that anything she said would be treated confidentially. There were very few people, apart from her friend, of whom she could say that: Mr. J.L.B. Matekoni, of course, who was always very discreet, and . . . The list petered out at that point.

"As you know, Mma, I am on holiday."

"Well deserved, I must say."

"Thank you. But of course business has to go on as usual, and I have left Mma

Makutsi in charge of the office." She paused. "This is very good cake, Mma."

Mma Potokwane passed Mma Ramotswe her second slice. "She'll be quite capable, I should think."

"Oh, she is certainly capable. We also have Mr. Polopetsi working with us — on a part-time basis, of course — and we have young Charlie."

The mention of Charlie's name brought a smile to Mma Potokwane's face. "That young man will go far," she said. "I don't know in what direction, but he will go far."

They both laughed. Then Mma Ramotswe continued, "Now the problem is this, Mma. I have been dragged into a case they took on. I did not want to be involved, because I have not wanted Mma Makutsi to think that I am interfering, but Mr. Polopetsi came to talk to me, you see, and I did not really have much choice in the matter."

"She's pushing him too hard?"

Mma Ramotswe was taken aback at the insight. "You're right. Yes."

"And he feels he's out of his depth?"

"Yes."

Mma Potokwane sat back in her chair. "I've seen that sort of thing. We've had it out here. You appoint a new foreman or whatever and then a few days later the first of the junior staff comes knocking at your door. It's a very familiar thing."

Mma Ramotswe asked how Mma Potokwane handled such situations. The explanation was simple. "A quiet talk with the senior person. Not a dressing-down. Lots of compliments on efficiency and so on. Then you mention that the junior staff are so impressed that they are trying too hard to please their new superior. They are becoming exhausted, and they need to conserve their strength. Perhaps a little bit less pressure?"

Mma Ramotswe listened carefully, nodding her agreement at the solution. "That is very helpful," she said. "I have tried to talk to her, though, and I got nowhere. She has put him in charge of a particular case and she will not listen."

Mma Potokwane had crossed swords with Mma Makutsi before. "She can be a very stubborn lady. She is famous for that, I think."

"The case, though, is an interesting one," Mma Ramotswe continued. "The agency had a visit from a Mma Potokwane."

This brought silence — and puzzlement.

"Not you, of course," continued Mma Ramotswe. "This Mma Potokwane is the sister of the late Mr. Government Keboneng."

"Ah," said Mma Potokwane. "For a moment I was confused, Mma. That is another Potokwane. I do not know that lady very well, but I do know her slightly. We do not see one another very much, but there is a connection. We meet at baptisms and funerals — that sort of thing."

"Can you tell me about that family?" asked Mma Ramotswe.

"It is a complicated story. We shall need more tea."

Their cups refilled, Mma Potokwane began. "As you said, that woman was the sister of Government Keboneng. She is quite a bit older than me. She worked as a teacher, although I do not know exactly where. I think it was small children — maybe even nursery school. She met my husband's cousin, who was also quite a bit older. He is late now. He was called Pound Potokwane."

"Tell me about him," said Mma Ramotswe.

"Pound? He was one of three brothers. I'm not absolutely sure if I've got it right, but I think the other two were called Saint and Saviour. Yes, that's right. Saint was the youngest, I think, and then there was Pound and then Saviour. Saviour is late too. He was killed in a tractor accident. It rolled right over him, I think. That can happen, you know. He drove into a donga, they said, and the tractor toppled over."

"I am sorry to hear that."

"Yes, it was very sad. He was a popular man."

"And Saint? Is he still alive?"

"Yes, he is. He lives off the Lobatse Road. He is looked after by a cousin on his mother's side. They have a small place there."

"Looked after? Is he not well?"

Mma Potokwane sucked in a cheek. "He is not ill, if that's what you mean, Mma. He is not any worse than he was before. No, I would not say that he is not well."

Mma Ramotswe waited for her to continue; she was unsure how to interpret the look that Mma Potokwane was giving her, a look that seemed to be asking, *Do I have to spell it out, Mma?* "Of course, I do not mean to pry . . ."

Mma Potokwane smiled. "But that is what you do, Mma. You're a private detective and I am a matron. You pry . . . on behalf of other people, I know, who cannot do their own prying. And I look after children . . ."

". . . and the kitchens, and the housemothers, and the gardens, and your husband, and . . ."

They both laughed, and the slight tension that had built up dissipated. Not only had Mma Ramotswe paid tribute to her friend's abilities, but she had also summed up the lot of women everywhere. *There are broad shoulders,* the saying went, *even where there are no broad shoulders.* Or Mma Ramotswe thought that somebody had said that; she was not quite sure. Usually, if she thought of an apt aphorism she would attribute it to the late Sir Seretse Khama, on the grounds that he'd said many wise things and even if he had not made that particular remark, then he might well have done — had he thought about it.

Mma Potokwane sipped at her tea. Her sips were large ones, Mma Ramotswe had noted; a cup of tea would be drained in two sips, if she had things to do, whereas Mma Makutsi could make a cup of tea last for almost half an hour, and even then there would be a small amount of tea left at the bottom of the cup. She had learned to leave cups like that when she first came down to Gaborone from Bobonong; Mma Ramotswe, with great tact, had told her that one should not drain one's cup immediately and in one swig. "It is just one of these things," she had said. "Down here we don't drink the full cup immediately. That is considered a bit rude — not that I'm saying that people are rude up in Bobonong; I am definitely not saying that, Mma. It's just that sometimes people do things differently in town, and this, I think, is one of those cases, Mma. It just is."

The phrase "It just is" tends to bring any discussion to an end. There are some things that "just are," and any amount of time spent questioning these will get you nowhere. If something "just is," it needs no justification. It was, thought Mma Ramotswe, like the old Botswana morality: it was pointless to discuss the tenets of that; the ancestors knew what they were doing when they decided what that morality should be, and it was not for us to come along and disturb that settled expression of the will of so many generations. You respected those rules because they were like the sun and moon: they were always there. Of course if one really looked into what those rules said, you would find behind them the simple idea that people should be treated with respect. That was Rule Number One, if one liked to put it that way. And what was wrong with that rule? There were other rules, of course, right down to the rules about not putting one's dusty shoes up on the chairs. You might look in vain for a precise statement of that rule, but there was no doubt that the old Botswana morality would disapprove of such conduct.

And it would disapprove, too, of the habit that men had of leaving their dirty clothes lying on the bathroom floor. Mr. J.L.B. Matekoni tended to do that, as did Puso. And no amount of reminding them of the existence of the washing basket seemed to make any difference — the clothes were still thrown down. An enquiry to Mma Makutsi had revealed that Phuti Radiphuti, although considered a house-trained husband in so many other respects, did the same thing; perhaps, thought Mma Ramotswe, the government of Botswana should pass a law about it. It would be a novel piece of legislation that could provide a lead to the rest of the world. She imagined the wording: *It shall be an offence for any man, either a husband or other person of the male sex, married or otherwise, being over the age of twelve years, to throw any item of clothing, having been worn by the said person for whatever length of time, upon the floor of any bathroom or any room adjacent to and connected to a bathroom, without good cause.* There would be difficulties of proof, of course, and the police might get tired of being called to people's bathrooms, but it might be sufficient for the government just to pass the law in order to provide wives with a threat. *If you don't stop leaving your clothes in a pile on the bathroom floor I am going to have to call the police . . .*

This thought occurred to her as she was waiting for Mma Potokwane to speak, and since Mma Potokwane had clearly not yet decided what to say, Mma Ramotswe asked her, "Does Rra Potokwane throw his clothes down on the bathroom floor, Mma? I do not wish to pry — as you know — but I have just been thinking about that problem."

Mma Potokwane put down her teacup. "It's funny you should ask, Mma, but only yesterday I had to talk to him about that. I told him about what happened to the husband of one of the housemothers. Her husband left his clothes in a pile on the floor and then decided to put them on again. There was a scorpion hiding under the bath — you know how they like those dark places, Mma."

Mma Ramotswe winced. "I think I can see what's coming."

"Yes," said Mma Potokwane. "But he didn't. He got out of the bath, dried himself, and then started to put on his clothes. He had his shirt on first and then he started to put on his pants, which was where the scorpion was hiding."

"Ow, Mma! Ow!"

"Yes, Mma — I believe that is what he said." Mma Potokwane wagged a finger for emphasis. "A scorpion sting is very, very painful. It made him swell up, Mma — very badly."

"That is very bad, Mma. One does not want men to swell up."

"No."

They were silent for a moment while they contemplated the misfortune of what had occurred. Then Mma Potokwane said, "Going back to Saint Potokwane, the brother of Saviour. You asked whether he was ill, and I said that he was not. What I have to tell you, Mma, is that he is not quite right in the head."

"I am very sorry to hear that, Mma."

"Thank you, Mma. You see, he was like that from the beginning. They never found out why, but he was one of these unfortunate children whose brains don't develop normally. He was a very nice little boy, apparently, but he could not be taught anything and he would often just sit there and say nothing for hours on end. He smiled a lot, though, and he never caused any trouble, but he would never be able to be taught how to do a job or anything like that."

Mma Ramotswe shook her head in sympathy. "I have known children like that. It usually seems hard for the family, doesn't it? But yet the child may be quite happy — and the family too."

Mma Potokwane agreed. "In most cases," she said, "there is enough love to go round. There is enough love for everybody."

Mma Ramotswe thought about what her friend had said. *In most cases there is enough love to go round.* Yes, it was true, as many unexpected things were true. It was easy to imagine the worst about people; it was easy to imagine that they would be selfish or unfeeling, or that they would abandon those who needed their love and their help. But that was not the way that people really were. Time and time again people showed better qualities than we might dare to hope for, sometimes against all expectation.

"What age is Saint now?" asked Mma Ramotswe.

Mma Potokwane shrugged. "I have not seen him for many years. I think that he must be about fifty. Maybe a bit more."

"And the other brother — the one who died — was he married, Mma?"

Mma Potokwane looked at her fingers. "Now, Mma, let me remind myself of who's who. We have Mma Potokwane, the one who came to see you — no, who came to see Mma Makutsi." She held up her thumb. "That is her. And she was married to my husband's cousin" — the thumb touched the forefinger — "who was called Pound and he had two brothers, Saint and then Saviour, who is late" — the middle and the ring finger were raised — "but was married to a lady called . . . called . . ." Memory was wracked until it came up with the answer. "Naledi. Yes, that is her name. Star, in English, of course."

"And where is she, Mma? Where is this Naledi?"

"Oh, she lives in Gaborone. She remarried after Saviour became late. I forget the name of her second husband, but I know where he works. He has a suitcase shop."

"I know that place," said Mma Ramotswe.

"It's called Big Suitcases."

Mma Ramotswe nodded. "I have been there. I bought a suitcase from them a few years ago, but I have never used it."

Mma Potokwane looked concerned. "Is something wrong with it?"

"No, the suitcase is all right. I have just not been anywhere."

Mma Potokwane understood. "We are too busy, Mma. That is why we cannot go anywhere. At least you have had a holi-

234

day . . . even if you have not gone anywhere. That is a start, Mma. Maybe next time you have a holiday you will go somewhere."

"You wouldn't know where she lives, would you, Mma?"

"No, Mma. But I could find out, if you like."

Mma Ramotswe declined the offer. "It isn't important, Mma. I was just wondering." She paused. "Do you know anything about her?"

"Not really. I never see her, even at family funerals. She is no longer a Potokwane, I suppose. She does not have to come."

"No, but . . ." It was a difficult subject; the obligation to be present at a funeral was a strong one in Botswana, with even the remotest relatives attending, but modern life sometimes made it more difficult for people to be there.

Mma Potokwane seemed to be weighing something up; it was as if she was about to say something else, but then thought better of it. Mma Ramotswe knew that look; it was the look of one who knew something that could harm another, so refrained from revealing it because they knew what hurt it might cause.

There was a final question. "And that place down on the Lobatse Road where

Saint lives — where exactly is that, Mma?"

Mma Potokwane explained. Saint was looked after by a relative who owned a small farm. It was past the Mokolodi turnoff, on the right as one drove down. There was a sign that said *Eggs*, and it was along that track. "There are no eggs any more," said Mma Potokwane. "I suppose that there must have been a chicken farm there some time ago, but not now."

"There are so many old notices," said Mma Ramotswe. She rather liked these abandoned signs, even if they made promises that could no longer be kept; they were a reminder of the Botswana that had been there before, linking people to a past that, although recent, might otherwise so easily be lost. Those bonds were important — however much we proclaimed our present self-sufficiency, however much we professed to believe only in those things that could still be seen and touched.

But now it was Mma Potokwane's turn to ask a question. "I know it is no business of mine, Mma," she said, "but why did this Mma Potokwane come to the agency?"

Mma Ramotswe hesitated. She never talked about the private affairs of clients, and yet Mma Potokwane was a matron, and she fully understood the importance of keeping confidences. And you had to be able to talk to someone, after all, or you would find the job impossibly stressful. It was therefore in the interests of the client to sound out somebody like Mma Potokwane; indeed, it was probably her *duty* to speak to her.

She told her about the council's plans to name a road in honour of Government Keboneng and about the suspension of these plans after the unspecified allegations. Mma Potokwane listened carefully and then held up her hands in a distancing gesture. "I don't want to get involved in any of that," she said. "That man is late. His memory should be left undisturbed."

"So you don't think there can be any truth in what they're saying?"

This question was followed by a moment of hesitation — only a moment, admittedly, but a longish one. "I don't think we should even think about all that," she said at last.

And with that she looked at her watch in such a way that Mma Ramotswe was in no doubt that their discussion was at an end. Watches may be looked at in a number of different ways. There is the look of regret — a glance that conveys the message that if there were more time, then the wearer of the watch would be only too happy to spend it on you; then there is the look of concern suggesting that time is really very short and that the conversation, appreciated though it may be, should be concluded as soon as possible; and then there is the look of determination, which is what Mma Ramotswe now witnessed. This indicates that the subject is closed and there is nothing more to be said. That look has nothing to do with time, but has everything to do with the marking of that which is out of bounds.

As she made her way back to her van, Mma Ramotswe asked Mma Potokwane about the small boy, Samuel.

Mma Potokwane sucked air through her teeth as she considered her reply. Mma Ramotswe knew this sign, and it was not a good one. Children took time to settle down, though; she should not be surprised to hear he was finding it hard.

It was worse than that. "He is very unhappy," said Mma Potokwane. "We get children here who are very sad, but that boy is inconsolable, Mma."

"His mother?" Mma Ramotswe had reported to Mma Potokwane her conversation with the woman from whom she had taken Samuel. She had mentioned the fact that Samuel's mother had died; she assumed he would have to be told sooner or later. "You broke the news, Mma?"

Mma Potokwane inclined her head. "It was not easy, Mma. It is not an easy thing to tell a child." She paused. "It is not an easy thing to tell anybody, is it? Even when you have been on this earth for a long, long time, it is not something that you wish to hear. It is not easy to take the news that a parent is late."

Mma Ramotswe looked up at the sky. What could one say about a child's grief? What could one say about that small boy to whom the world had been so unwelcoming? So she said nothing, knowing that Mma Potokwane would understand exactly how she felt.

CHAPTER TWELVE:
I WORRY ABOUT YOU TOO . . .

Mma Ramotswe's mind was now made up. In conversation with Mma Potokwane she had sensed that there was something her friend did not wish to discuss. It could be that this had nothing to do with the unsubstantiated allegations against Mr. Government Keboneng, but she was still concerned. Wherever the truth lay, there was an unresolved issue here — a mystery, so to speak — that needed to be resolved. Mma Makutsi seemed uninterested in following it up, assigning it to Mr. Polopetsi, who would not get very far with it. Mma Potokwane — the client Mma Potokwane — had come to the agency for help, and it was a fundamental article of faith in the No. 1 Ladies' Detective Agency that one did one's best for the client. If Mma Makutsi was not going to do that — for whatever reason — then it was incumbent upon Mma Ramotswe to take responsibility for the matter, holiday or no holiday.

"I am going to bring my holiday to an end," she announced to Mr. J.L.B. Matekoni that evening. "I have had enough."

He raised a hand in protest. "But, Mma Ramotswe, you've only been on holiday for a few days. This is ridiculous —"

She cut him short. "A short holiday is as good as a long holiday, Rra. I was reading about that in a magazine only yesterday. They said that even if you only have a few days off, you will feel the benefit. I have had a few days and I am definitely feeling the benefit. I am very relaxed — I've probably even put on weight."

He looked at her reproachfully. "Mma Makutsi will be in a very bad mood," he said. "She is enjoying being in charge. If you come back now, she'll feel that she has not had enough time as managing director." He paused, and then added those words so often uttered when Mma Makutsi was spoken about: "You know what she's like, Mma."

"I do know what she's like. And for that reason, although I am ending my holiday, I am not going back to the office. Mma Makutsi need not know that my holiday has come to an end."

He asked her how she could work on a

case without all the papers she would need. In answer, she tapped her head. "There is a lot of paperwork up here, Rra. It is very efficiently stored — even Mma Makutsi could not file this information better. I am telling you, Mr. J.L.B. Matekoni, there will be no problem."

He shrugged. "It is your business, Mma. And it's your life too."

Her tone became conciliatory. "I know that you worry about me, Rra. I know that."

He nodded — rather miserably, she thought. "I worry about you a great deal, Mma. I worry that you will take all the cares of the world on your shoulders and that you will collapse under the weight. I worry that you will open your heart to so many people that eventually it will be full — crowded — and it will stop because there is no room for the blood to go round. I am worried that you will look after so many people that you will forget that there is one person who also needs looking after, and that person is you, Mma. I am worried about all these things."

She was touched by what he had said. "And I worry about you, too, Rra. I worry that you will be taken advantage of by people who say, 'Here is a kind man coming, we will take advantage of him.' I am worried that people will get you to fix their

cars for them for too little money because
you feel sorry for them, or for the car too. I
am worried that you will not eat enough
lunch and that you will become thin and
people will say, 'That Mma Ramotswe
doesn't know how to look after a husband.'
And I'm worried by all sorts of other things
— ridiculous things, Rra. That you will be
struck by lightning one day, or that you will
drive off the road and hit a tree, or that a
wheel will fall off your truck and it will crash
into a ditch. All of these are ridiculous worries, Rra, but they still come to me, especially at night when you are asleep beside
me and I am awake, looking up at the ceiling, which is like an empty sky with no
stars."

They looked at one another, surprised by
what each had said, but reassured, too, by
the love that lay behind their confessions of
anxiety. Then, after a further few moments,
Mma Ramotswe's face broke into a grin.
"We are very silly, Rra. There is no point in
worrying."

"No," he said. "There is no point. And
you, Mma Ramotswe, must do whatever you
think is the right thing. If you think it is the
right thing to go and sort out all this Keboneng business, then that is what you must
do."

"It is," said Mma Ramotswe.

"Then that is what you must do," he reaffirmed.

She felt unable to telephone Mr. Polopetsi at the agency, as that would have made Mma Makutsi suspicious. So instead she passed a message to him through Mr. J.L.B. Matekoni, who relayed it the following morning. The message was that he was to meet Mma Ramotswe that lunch time at her favourite café at Riverwalk. It was important that he should say nothing about this meeting, for reasons she was sure he would understand. Furthermore, if at all possible, he should make sure he was free that afternoon — unless, of course, he had teaching duties at the school.

He was there before her, sitting at a table near the steps to the Portuguese restaurant on the floor above. When she approached the table, he sprang to his feet and extended a hand to shake hers. Mma Ramotswe approved of this — Mr. Polopetsi's manners were impeccable, and in an age of increasing casualness, old-fashioned politeness was always reassuring.

"So, Mma," he said. "I am here — as you requested. And I am at your disposal until five o'clock, when I have to go home."

She sat down and ordered tea; he already had a cup of coffee before him.

"Now, Rra," she began. "This Keboneng business. I have been to see Mma Potokwane — not the one who is our client, but the one who is our friend. I gave her the broad details of the case and asked her about the family. She was able to give me information about the Potokwane side — I do not know anything about the Keboneng people."

"So she told you about Saviour, and Saviour's wife?"

Mma Ramotswe was taken aback. How did Mr. Polopetsi know about them if, as he had said, he had been unable to make any progress with the enquiry? She asked him to explain.

"You see," he said, "at the beginning of this case I went with Mma Makutsi to speak to that lady — the one who was married to Saviour Potokwane. Mma Makutsi hoped that she would be able to tell us about Mr. Government Keboneng. We saw her at that shop of theirs . . ."

"Big Suitcases?"

"Yes, it was that place."

Mma Ramotswe was puzzled. Mma Makutsi had not disclosed that she had taken an active part in the investigation, but here was Mr. Polopetsi saying that she had got as far as questioning Saviour's widow. This was very strange.

"What did that lady say?" asked Mma Ramotswe. "Was she prepared to talk to you and Mma Makutsi?"

"She was polite enough," said Mr. Polopetsi. "She asked us why we wanted to talk to her, and Mma Makutsi explained that it was to do with Mr. Government Keboneng and some enquiries about him. She did not say exactly who was making these enquiries and why they were interested in a man who is now late."

"And what was her reaction to that?"

"She changed, Mma. You know what is meant by saying that a cloud may pass over somebody's face? You know that expression? That is what I saw. There was a cloud."

"And she stopped talking?"

"No, she still talked, but she was much more guarded. I wouldn't say that she was friendly after that. She was not rude, but she was not friendly."

Mma Ramotswe asked whether Mma Makutsi had persisted.

Mr. Polopetsi looked thoughtful. "Yes, she did persist. As I recall it, Mma, she said something about being able to tell that there was some problem. She said it would probably be better to talk about whatever it was that was worrying her, because if she talked, the matter could be handled more sensitively."

"And?"

"And then she asked me to leave."

"Who asked you to leave, Rra? Mma Makutsi?"

Mr. Polopetsi shook his head. "No, Mma. It was that lady — that Naledi — who said that she wanted to talk privately to Mma Makutsi. Sometimes ladies do not like men to be present when they say private things — I've often noticed that, Mma. Have you?"

"I have seen that happen," said Mma Ramotswe.

"So I went out of the shop — there was nobody in it at the time, apart from Naledi and Mma Makutsi — and I stood outside. But . . ." He trailed off, looking slightly embarrassed.

"But you were able to hear what was said?"

"No, I did not hear, but I was able to look through the window, past the display of suitcases, and I saw Naledi talking to Mma Makutsi in a very . . . well, in a very concerned way, I should say. She was wagging her finger at her, a bit like this, Mma. See? Like this."

He demonstrated, using a forefinger.

"As if she was telling her off?" suggested Mma Ramotswe.

"Precisely," said Mr. Polopetsi.

"And then what happened, Rra?"

He explained that the two women talked for about ten minutes. Then Mma Makutsi came out of the shop and told him that they were going back to the office. She also told him that Naledi had had nothing to say. "She said to me that that lady knew nothing about the Keboneng family. She told me that she had nothing to say about anything."

"But she was shaking a finger at her," pointed out Mma Ramotswe. "Do we shake our finger at people when we have nothing to tell them? Are we saying *nothing, nothing, nothing* and then underlining it with a finger?"

Mr. Polopetsi raised an eyebrow. "I do not think so," he said.

"And neither do I," said Mma Ramotswe.

They were both silent for a while. Then Mr. Polopetsi asked, "Do you think we should go and speak to her again?"

Mma Ramotswe hesitated. Then she said, "I do not think there would be any point. I think that something has passed between Mma Makutsi and Naledi that has brought

248

that line of enquiry to a conclusion.

"Do you think Naledi threatened her?" asked Mr. Polopetsi.

"I'm not sure," replied Mma Ramotswe. "Sometimes it's difficult to tell the difference between a request, a threat, and a warning. This could be any of those, but I think that lady would not welcome a visit from us."

"So what are we to do, Mma?"

"We shall go and see somebody else, Rra," said Mma Ramotswe. "We shall go to see somebody whom nobody would think it worth speaking to. Such people often have the most to say, you know."

"When?" asked Mr. Polopetsi.

"Now," said Mma Ramotswe.

"Who?"

"A man who may see more than people think he sees," said Mma Ramotswe, and then, sensing Mr. Polopetsi's frustration at her opaque answer, she added mischievously, "A saint."

He laughed. "This is why I like working with you, Mma Ramotswe. This is much more fun than teaching chemistry."

"Although we have no explosions, Rra?"

He looked serious once more. "Explosions are not the real point of chemistry, Mma Ramotswe. The real point of chemistry is reactions."

"We have reactions too in this business, Rra."

He smiled again. "You're right, Mma Ramotswe, but then you're right about everything, I think."

Such a remark might be seen as flattery were it to come from any different quarter, but not from Mr. Polopetsi, whose admiration for Mma Ramotswe was genuine and unforced. He looked at her as they rose from their table and he found himself thinking how wonderful it would be to be married to Mma Ramotswe — to be in the shoes of Mr. J.L.B. Matekoni. But he hastily suppressed the thought: he was very happily married to a woman, and it was wrong to think thoughts like that about other men's wives. But he could at least allow himself to think this: What if Mma Ramotswe were his mother? Now, that was a thought one could think without guilt, although, on balance, it might be best not to speak too openly about such a longing.

Driving down the Lobatse Road with Mma Ramotswe, Mr. Polopetsi looked out of the window in the direction of Kgali Hill, a great towering mound of rock, split across its vastness with zig-zag cracks in which trees grew — those trees that grew as well from rock, it seemed, as from soil; a home for baboons and vultures and, from time to time, a prowling, secretive leopard. Mr. Polopetsi was not gazing at the hill, though, but at the sky behind it, which was darkening with rain.

"Good," he said. "There will be some more rain, I think. We need it badly."

Mma Ramotswe took her eyes off the road briefly and glanced at the rain clouds. "That is a good place for it to fall," she said. "Over there — in that direction. It can get very dry there and any rain they get will help to fill the dam."

She thought of her friend Gwythie, who lived with her husband at Mokolodi, off to the right of the road on which they were now travelling, and of the difficulties they had encountered when they had first tried to get water for the house they had built. They had drilled a borehole, but it had been dry, and so they tried another borehole, deeper this time and in a different place, and that one had been dry too. They had then engaged a water diviner, and he had come onto their land and walked about, silent in his solemn purpose, with his twist of copper wire held out before him — an antenna to pick up the radio signals from the water deep down below; but there had been nothing, as if the radio stations were all abandoned, their signals ceased; and only later, much later, had they found an elusive underground stream in a place where nobody thought it would be.

"Have you ever watched a water diviner working, Rra?" she asked Mr. Polopetsi.

He looked at her with amusement. "That is all nonsense, Mma. It is like witchcraft. It is not something that scientific people like me can be bothered with."

"And yet they find water," Mma Ramotswe pointed out.

"The water is there already," retorted Mr. Polopetsi. "If you or I got hold of one of those bent twigs and stood on top of some water we would get the same results. We would push the stick down and say, 'Oh, there is some water here,' and people would say, 'Look at that! You see — it works!' "

"I don't know, Rra . . ."

The normally mild Mr. Polopetsi now became animated. "I'm telling you, Mma Ramotswe, people don't ask themselves enough questions about what causes what. That is what scientists do. I keep telling the students in the school, 'You must ask yourself why things happen. You must not think that because one thing happens after another thing, then it is the first thing that causes the second thing. You must not think that, because it might not be true.' That is what I say to them, Mma."

"And do they agree, Rra?"

He sighed. "They look at me for a very short time. They stare at me as if they've seen a ghost. Then they turn away and start chewing a piece of gum or something. Young people are very stupid these days, Mma. Their heads are full of all sorts of nonsense. They should be thinking of chemistry, but they are secretly thinking of loud music. That loud music is going on in their heads, I think, while I am talking about chemistry. I say, 'Take a clean, dry test tube and pour in twenty-five mils of hydrochloric acid,' and inside their heads what they hear is not about hydrochloric acid and test tubes but *la, la, la, boom, bang, boom . . .* That is what their music sounds like, Mma."

Mma Ramotswe grinned. It was a vivid picture that Mr. Polopetsi painted, and she could imagine the scene. There would be the small, neat chemistry teacher in his white shirt and his dark blue tie with the serious expression that he always seemed to wear — the expression that Mma Makutsi described as being a little bit like that which one sees on the face of a rabbit — and there would be the teenagers with *la, la, la, boom, bang, boom* going on in their heads.

"But I think we were all a bit like that when we were their age," she said.

Mr. Polopetsi shook his head vigorously. "I wasn't," he said. "I certainly was not like that, Mma."

She said nothing. He was probably right — about himself, at least; but for most of us it was *la, la, la, boom, bang, boom* in one form or another. We forget, she thought. We think that we were always the way we are now, but we were not.

She saw the sign that said *Eggs* from some distance away, although she did not make out the lettering until they were much closer. She had already deciphered it and was preparing to turn when Mr. Polopetsi, who was somewhat short-sighted, peered over the dashboard and said, with an air of triumph, "*Eggs,* Mma! There it is. That says *Eggs.* Can you see it, Mma? Right over there — look."

"Yes, I think I can, Mr. Polopetsi. That was well spotted — thank you."

He was pleased with the compliment. "My wife says I have a good sense of direction," he said. "I may not be like those San trackers, but I can still tell which direction is east and which is west and so on." He began to point, to demonstrate, but hesitated and dropped his hand furtively.

Mma Ramotswe covered his embarrassment. "There are some people who are lucky that way," she said. "Mr. J.L.B. Matekoni can find his way about with his eyes shut. And my late daddy could do the same, you know. He could walk through thick bush and know exactly where he was going."

"Like a bird," said Mr. Polopetsi. "A bird always knows where it is going."

Mma Ramotswe began to swing the van across the road and onto the narrow track that promised eggs. "Do you know why that is, Rra? Why do you think a bird knows where it is going?"

Mr. Polopetsi shrugged. "I think there is some special part of their brain. I think there is a sort of biological compass."

Her father, the late Obed Ramotswe, had asked her that very question when she was a small girl. She could hear him now, bending down to speak to her, as he always did during her childhood. "And how do the birds know where they're going, my Precious? Do you know the answer to that big question?" And she had not known, but when he told her it made perfect sense.

255

She wrested herself back from Mochudi, and from the memory. She only half tuned to Mr. Polopetsi; the road was bumpy and she needed to concentrate. "Perhaps it is because they are up in the air," she said. "Perhaps it's because they have a good view."

Mr. Polopetsi weighed up this answer. "Perhaps it is that," he said, "but then there might still be a biological compass. Look at those birds that fly from here to Europe, Mma. How do they get there? They can't see all that way just because they're up high, can they?"

The discussion was broken off by the appearance of a large hole in the road ahead. It did not prevent their further progress, but it called for careful negotiation. Soon afterwards the farmhouse appeared a short distance away — a rambling building under a low-eaved red tin roof. It was typical of farmhouses of a particular period — that time before the Bechuanaland Protectorate became Botswana, a time when the land was quiet and dreamy, when nothing of much note happened; a time when nobody knew of the diamonds beneath the soil and cattle were all that mattered.

In the dry climate people might age quickly, desiccated by the heat and the warm wind on their skin, but with buildings change came more gradually. Human structures survived as long as they were unattractive to termites, and so this house, like so many others of its type, was largely untouched by the decades that had passed since its construction. Its paint had flaked, of course, and had been touched up, in a slightly different shade of cream, lending to the whole a slightly patchy complexion; and the garden that somebody a long time ago had tried to create had all but disappeared.

"A very nice place," said Mr. Polopetsi. "And there are some good cattle over there, Mma. Look."

She followed his gaze. He was right about the quality of the cattle, she thought: they were fine beasts.

They parked a short distance from the house. To drive right up to it in the van would have been impolite: you cannot knock or call out *"Ko! Ko!"* when you are in a vehicle. As they alighted, a woman appeared on the verandah and stared in their direction.

Mma Ramotswe led the way, and greeted the woman once she was close enough to call out. Her greeting was returned equally politely and they were invited in.

"My name is Precious Ramotswe," Mma

Ramotswe began. "I am from the No. 1 Ladies' Detective Agency in Gaborone. This is my assistant, whose name is Polopetsi. He is fully certified."

The woman glanced at Mr. Polopetsi. Then she addressed Mma Ramotswe. "He is actually my granddaughter's chemistry teacher," she said.

There was an awkward silence.

"Yes," said Mma Ramotswe at last. "He is very good at teaching chemistry. But he is only part-time. For the rest he works with me in my detective agency. That is why he is with me now."

The woman seemed to be happy enough with this explanation. "My granddaughter's name is Monica Malatsi," she said to Mr. Polopetsi. "Do you know that child, Rra?"

Mr. Polopetsi gave an exclamation of delight. "But she is a very bright child, Mma. She is very good at chemistry."

The woman's face broke into a broad smile. "Yes, she is very bright, Rra. She gets her brains from my side of the family, you see. We have some very bright people on my side."

"I can tell that," said Mr. Polopetsi. "She often gets one hundred per cent in the tests I set the children. She is the only student who gets that. The others are all down in

258

the seventy per cent range. Monica is exceptional, Mma."

The atmosphere was now not only cordial, but warm.

"I am glad that you have come to see me," said the woman. "I must tell you who I am. I am Mma Comfort Potokwane."

Mma Ramotswe could not contain her gasp of surprise. "Another Mma Potokwane! I am a great friend of Mma Sylvia Potokwane, who runs the Orphan Farm at Tlokweng. She and I have been friends for many, many years."

"I know that lady," said Mma Potokwane. "I have not seen her for many years, but her husband is a distant relative of my husband, who is now late."

"I am sorry to hear that, Mma," said Mma Ramotswe.

"It was a wisdom-tooth operation," said Mma Potokwane. "There was too much bleeding and they couldn't save him. But it was many years ago now and he is with the Lord." She paused. "I will make you tea if you would like some."

"And then we can tell you why we have come to see you," Mma Ramotswe said.

The woman looked disappointed. "You have not come to discuss Monica?"

"No," said Mr. Polopetsi. "Monica is doing very well. There is nothing to discuss in that department."

Mma Potokwane went into the kitchen, leaving her two guests in a rather sparsely furnished sitting room. On the walls there were pictures cut out from magazines, stuck up with tape or pinned with drawing pins. Mma Ramotswe moved over to examine one of them, a picture of Nelson Mandela, under which the printed legend ran: *World's Greatest Hero.* Next to it was a picture of the late king of Lesotho, King Moshoeshoe II. A line of type under that read: *He presided over his mountain kingdom, but now . . .* The line ran out. She knew the ending, though, and the photograph saddened her. There was a photograph of the President of Botswana taking the salute from soldiers of the Botswana Defence Force.

Mma Potokwane returned. "These photographs are not mine," she said, nodding at the pictures. "I look after a man here. They are his photographs. He cuts them out of magazines."

Mma Ramotswe seized her opportunity. "That is Mr. Saint Potokwane?"

Mma Potokwane confirmed this with a gesture of her hand. "He is a relative of my late husband. We took him on many years ago because he is unable to look after himself, Mma. He is a very gentle person, but there are many things he cannot do."

"Every family has somebody like that somewhere," said Mr. Polopetsi. "It is part of being human."

"You are very kind, Rra," said Mma Potokwane. "There are some people who do not understand that, you know.

"There are many more kind people than not-so-kind people," said Mma Ramotswe. "That is well known, Mma."

Mma Potokwane poured the tea. "May I ask why you are here?"

Mma Ramotswe explained about Government Keboneng and the road. Mma Potokwane listened, and when Mma Ramotswe had finished, she said, "I am sure there is nothing in any of that. You know how people are always inventing stories about other people, especially people who are late. They cannot stand up and say, 'That is not true,' because they are late."

"Indeed," said Mma Ramotswe. "That is why I think Government Keboneng's sister wants to put these stories — whatever they are — to rest."

"That is quite understandable," said Mma Potokwane.

"So I am speaking to all the members of that family," explained Mma Ramotswe.

"They might have nothing to say about it all, but I need to speak to everybody so that I can say to our client that we have left no stone unturned."

"I am one who has nothing to say," said Mma Potokwane. "Other than to add that I think such stories will be nothing more than idle gossip."

"Thank you," said Mma Ramotswe. "I shall note that down later. But I wondered about Saint Potokwane . . ."

Mma Potokwane smiled. "Saint will not be able to help you."

"But could I speak to him?"

"Yes, of course you may. He has been listening to you, you see. He is always listening."

Mma Potokwane rose to her feet. Crossing the room, she opened a door that had been left half ajar. "Saint," she said, "these people would like to say hello to you."

There was a darkened corridor beyond the door and Mma Ramotswe and Mr. Polopetsi could see only a few shapes. But one of these was a man, who stepped out into the living room and positioned himself close to Mma Potokwane — so close as to be almost leaning against her, as a child will do with an adult for security.

Saint was a middle-aged man, dressed in

a curious khaki outfit, rather like a military uniform. On the chest of his tunic, strips of brightly coloured cloth had been sewn in lines, to resemble campaign medals, while onto plain epaulettes three brass buttons had been attached on either side. The overall effect was eccentric in the extreme, and Mr. Polopetsi's astonishment was scarcely concealed; Mma Ramotswe was more prepared, and gave no sign of surprise.

"This is Saint," said Mma Potokwane. And to Saint she said, "Greet our visitors, Saint."

Saint brought his heels together and lifted his hand to give a military salute. The salute, though, seemed to have been lowered, from eye to chin level, which created an overall comic effect. After he had done this, he looked to Mma Potokwane for approbation.

"Very good, Saint," said Mma Potokwane. She looked at Mma Ramotswe. "Would you like to talk to Saint, Mma?"

"Yes, Mma, I would."

"Well, in that case, I think your colleague and I should leave the room. Saint prefers not to have others in the room when he talks. It will be best if we leave you to it." Picking up Mma Ramotswe's anxiety, she went on to say, "Saint is very gentle, Mma.

You will be fine."

Left by herself with Saint, Mma Ramotswe gestured for him to sit next to her on the sofa. He said nothing but stepped forward and brushed one of the cushions for a minute or so, as if removing dirt. Then he sat down.

She looked into his eyes. There was no focus. It was as if he were not quite there.

"I like your medals," she said encouragingly, speaking Setswana now. "You must be very brave to get all those medals."

He was silent.

"Botswana Defence Force?" said Mma Ramotswe. "They are very fine soldiers, I think."

Suddenly he spoke. "They have a helicopter."

The voice was rather high — not unlike the voice of a child.

"Yes," said Mma Ramotswe. "They have several helicopters, I think."

"A big helicopter," said Saint.

"Yes, I think I've seen it," said Mma Ramotswe.

"And a gun," said Saint. "They have a gun."

"They have quite a number of guns," said Mma Ramotswe.

"And blankets," said Saint. "The soldiers

have blankets."

"Those are for the night," said Mma Ramotswe. "They need blankets for the winter nights. Not for now, as it's so hot. But in the winter, yes, they have blankets."

She looked at him again, trying to fathom something from his eyes, but it was impossible. It was as if he had no pupils.

"Botswana Defence Force," Saint suddenly said.

"Yes," said Mma Ramotswe.

"They have a helicopter," said Saint.

She smiled at him. "Do you remember your brothers?"

He frowned, as if plumbing the depths of his memory. And then he said, "Pound. He is my brother."

"Yes," said Mma Ramotswe. "Pound is your brother."

"And Saviour too. He is my brother. He flies in helicopter. Up there."

"I see."

"Saviour has a gun."

"Does he?"

Saint looked at his hands, as if looking for stains. "He has no gun any more."

"I see."

"He makes children with that one, that other one. She is Naledi. She makes children with that man and with other men. All Potokwane men! From all over. From here. From there. From Gaborone. From Lobatse. From Tlokweng. Hah! Many children. Making children all the time."

Mma Ramotswe waited for more, but he seemed to have completed what he had to say.

"Naledi? She makes children with another man, not just with Saviour?"

At first it was as if he had not heard the question. Then he replied. "Naledi makes children with Government. Government is a big man. A big car. The big car comes to the house. They make children and then he goes in helicopter."

"They go in the helicopter after he has made children with Naledi? Is that what happened, Saint?"

The question hung in the air, unanswered. She watched him, noting his growing confusion. "Government and Naledi," he said at last. "Then he stole my cattle. Government took them. He took my cattle. All gone. No helicopter. Yes, a helicopter."

Mma Ramotswe was listening so intently that she did not notice Mma Potokwane re-enter the room. Her presence, though, registered with Saint, who immediately stiffened.

"I think that Saint is getting a bit upset,

266

Mma," said Mma Potokwane. "He becomes tired very quickly."

"Of course," said Mma Ramotswe. She turned to Saint. "Thank you for talking to me, Saint."

"You can go now, Saint," said Mma Potokwane. "You can go and water the vegetables. Not too much water — just a little."

Saint left the room, looking over his shoulder at Mma Ramotswe when he was halfway through the door. Mma Ramotswe raised a hand in a gesture of farewell, and he did the same.

"Poor man," said Mma Potokwane. "It is very sad."

Because she was preoccupied with thoughts of her unsettling encounter with Saint, Mma Ramotswe drove back along the track rather too fast. For most of the short journey back to the main Lobatse Road that would not have mattered too much: the track, although in a bad state of repair — or in no state of repair at all — was well within the capacity of the tiny white van's specially strengthened suspension. That suspension had been fortified by Mr. J.L.B. Matekoni, who had observed the way in which the van listed to starboard — the driver's side — and had tactfully corrected the matter by installing new and stronger springs all round. But no van, no matter how doctored by the best mechanic in Botswana, could cope with its near-side front wheel dropping at speed into a substantial hole in the ground at the same time as its off-side partner hit a small termite mound. Those mounds, painstakingly constructed by countless tiny pincers, can achieve the consistency and strength of concrete, which that one had. And the result was inevitable: although the wheel that had dropped into the hole somehow managed to emerge at the other side, there was a bone-juddering bump, an almost uncontrollable swerve, and, thereafter, a disturbing sound not unlike the kind made by an animal in pain. They were still on the road, though, and they appeared to be heading in the right direction.

"That was close," muttered Mma Ramotswe, as she regained control of the vehicle. "This is a very bad road, Rra."

"I think something's broken, Mma," said Mr. Polopetsi nervously.

Mma Ramotswe had regained her calm. "Oh, things break in cars pretty regularly," she said. "That's why we have garages, Mr. Polopetsi. That's what keeps Mr. J.L.B. Matekoni in business."

268

"He'll fix this?"

"Of course he'll fix this. It's probably just a few nuts and bolts." She wiped a thin layer of dust off the inside of the windscreen before continuing, "I may not even trouble him over this one. I may get Charlie to fix it in his spare time. He has done that for me before."

They completed their journey along the track at a lower speed and in silence — apart from the protesting noise emanating from the compromised suspension. They passed the sign that said *Eggs* and turned onto the Lobatse Road. The noise was less obvious now, and Mma Ramotswe suggested that the van was perhaps getting better by itself. "Sometimes that happens," she said. "A car recovers."

Mr. Polopetsi said nothing, and it was not until they were almost on the edge of the town that they spoke again.

"He was a very unusual man," said Mma Ramotswe.

"That man back there? Saint?"

"Yes. He said some very strange things to me when you were out of the room."

Mr. Polopetsi shrugged. "I think some of these poor people live in a different world. They see things that we don't see."

Mma Ramotswe agreed, but pointed out

that the reason they saw things we did not see was because we did not know they were watching. "People think somebody like that doesn't observe what's happening," she said. "But all the time, such a person will be seeing everything." She paused. "And that, I think, is what has happened here."

They were nearing the first of the traffic circles, and Mma Ramotswe slowed down. A line of cars was building up, drawn onto the main highway from a number of tributary roads. "I think that the answer is this," Mma Ramotswe continued. "This Government Keboneng was probably not perfect — no man is, I suspect. I think that he was seeing that woman, Naledi, who was Saviour's wife. And I think she was seeing other men too."

"So that is the scandal they were talking about?"

"Probably," answered Mma Ramotswe.

Mr. Polopetsi looked out of the van's window. He had spotted a large bird, a kite of some sort, soaring on a thermal current in the air. The rain clouds they had seen earlier on seemed to have disappeared, and the sky had returned to a faded and empty blue.

"So you have solved the whole thing, Mma? Is it at an end?"

She took her time with her answer. "No," she said. "I don't think so. What do you feel, Mr. Polopetsi?"

"There is more to it than meets the eye, Mma."

"That is exactly the problem, Rra. There is more to this than meets the eye."

Mma Ramotswe drove on, taking the road that led past the Water Affairs Office. That route would take them close to Mr. Polopetsi's house on the edge of the area known as the Village, and she could drop him off at his gate.

"That will be very convenient, Mma," he said. "I think my wife —"

He stopped suddenly. They had drawn up at an intersection, alongside a car and a truck. The drivers of all three vehicles happened to look at one another, as sometimes happens in traffic. The truck driver looked at Mma Ramotswe, and Mma Ramotswe — and Mr. Polopetsi — glanced at the car beside them. Mma Makutsi, sitting behind the wheel of one of Phuti's cars from the Double Comfort Furniture Store, returned their glance.

"Oh no," muttered Mma Ramotswe.

The traffic began to move again, and the driver behind her sounded his horn impatiently. They drove off.

271

CHAPTER THIRTEEN: SHE THOUGHT SHE WAS A BIT FAST

So much for the restful effects of being on holiday: Mma Ramotswe lay in bed that night, unable to sleep, watching the shadows thrown by the moonlight. On the ceiling directly above her was what appeared to be the pattern of a bush, perhaps a tree, and beside it, moving slightly, was a waving hand — both shadows made by the bougainvillea framing their window. She closed her eyes, hoping that sleep would come, but that only seemed to make her more alert. Now she seemed to see the white van moving along a track, and the track suddenly opened up into a great hole the size of Kgali Hill itself. The van plunged into the hole, and beside her Mr. Polopetsi was shouting, "There is a great hole, Mma — be careful!"

She opened her eyes. On his side of the bed, Mr. J.L.B. Matekoni, covered only with a sheet because of the heat, breathed quietly in the depth of sleep; he never suffered from

272

insomnia and would remain in that state of utterly peaceful oblivion until the first cock-crow of dawn. It was easier for men, she thought; they did not have to worry about kitchens and children and doing the shopping . . . These were things that could interrupt the sleep of anyone, and when you added to it the cares of other people, of Government Keboneng's sister and his political supporters, then nobody could be expected to drop off to sleep with all that around her neck.

As quietly as she could, she got out of bed, felt for her slippers in the darkness, and made her way into the kitchen. Mr. J.L.B. Matekoni was not a light sleeper, but the children were, and once roused they were difficult to settle again. Once away from the sleeping quarters, she switched on a light and looked at her watch. It was four in the morning. She had retired to bed at nine, and she knew that she had dropped off to sleep for the first part of the night — perhaps until shortly after two, when she had woken up and had lain there thinking. That meant that she had enjoyed five hours of sleep, which was enough, she felt, to see her through the day. There was no point in going back to bed now, as she would merely lie awake until dawn, which at this time of the year would begin not long after five-thirty. It would be far better to stay up and get some of her morning chores done before the day began in earnest.

And then she thought: Am I on holiday, or am I back at work? She had told Mr. J.L.B. Matekoni that her holiday was over, but this did not mean that she would be returning to her usual routine. So there would be no going into the office, no awaiting — with pleasure — the first cup of office red bush tea, no leisurely perusal of the mail, no listening to Mma Makutsi telling her about Itumelang's latest achievements, no patient questioning of clients to find out what they really wanted . . . The thought of all this made her feel nostalgic. She still had ten days of the original holiday left to run, and she was missing the office so much.

She sat down at the kitchen table, a blank piece of lined paper in front of her. At the top of this she wrote: *The Troublesome Keboneng Case.* Then she underlined this, to make it clear that this was a heading, and on the line below she wrote: *(1) Mma Potokwane, sister of Government Keboneng, thinks Government was above reproach — and wants that to be established. Our duty? To help her in that quest. (2) Was Government Keboneng a good man? Yes. Did he do anything to be ashamed of? Yes. What was it? See (3).*

She paused. The practice of writing out a summary of a complicated case was one that she had learned from the pages of Clovis Andersen's *The Principles of Private Detection*. He said: *Make a list of what you know, what you don't know, and what you'd like to know. Make a list of possible outcomes. Choose the outcome you think is best, then go for that!*

This, she thought, was sage advice — as was all the advice that Clovis Andersen gave his readers. There were times, though, when advising something was easier than doing it, and this, she suspected, was one such time. But she would persist.

(3) Government Keboneng became involved with Naledi Potokwane, the wife of Saviour Potokwane, the brother of Pound Potokwane, who was the husband of the Mma Potokwane who is our client, and of Saint Potokwane. Saint Potokwane is a simple man, but he was probably telling the truth because it would not occur to him to lie. He said that Naledi was involved with all the men in the family — shameless woman! — including Potokwanes from Gaborone, Lobatse, and . . .

She sat quite still, her pencil poised above the page. She had not thought before this of his exact words, but now they came back to her. He had talked about Gaborone, Lobatse, and Tlokweng. There was, she thought, only one family of Potokwanes in Tlokweng, and that was the family of her friend Mma Potokwane, the matron. She drew in her breath in horror. Naledi had been involved with her own friend's husband. She had not thought of this before, but now the uncomfortable truth was staring her in the face.

For a good few minutes Mma Ramotswe sat at the kitchen table, her head sunk in her hands. Of all the information she might wish to come across, this was the very last thing she wanted to know. As far as she knew, Mma Potokwane's marriage was a sound one, and she had never heard of anything that suggested otherwise. But men had their little ways and they sometimes strayed. In her view, this did not in every case make the man wicked, it simply made him thoughtless — and weak. Sometimes the slip was a very short-lived one — something to do with the male menopause you read about — and on these occasions all could return to normal quite quickly. On other occasions even a single act of infidelity could be the end — something never to be forgiven, a deep rent in the fabric of the

276

marriage, sundering all those bonds of trust marriage required.

Mma Ramotswe sat up straight. She had started to make her list, and now she would finish it. It was painful, but it had to be done.

(4) Saint said something about his cattle being taken from him. Who inherited the cattle from the father of Pound, Saviour, and Saint? They would each get an equal share of the family's assets, but it is possible that somebody took advantage of Saint's lack of understanding and embezzled his cattle from him. He said that was Government Keboneng; that might have been the case, but how can we prove it? We cannot.

(5) What should we tell Mma Potokwane (the client)? If it becomes generally known that Government was involved with his relative's wife, then that will not be viewed well by the public. You do not seduce your relative's wife. You just do not do that. So what do we do? Nothing? But we owe it to the client to tell her what we have found out — unless, of course, we realise that this knowledge will make her unhappy, and there is no point in adding to all the unhappiness there already is in this world. If anything, we should try to make that mountain of unhappiness a bit smaller — if we can.

(6) If we start talking about Government's indiscretion, then that will lead to our talking about Naledi's bad behaviour, and one of the people she behaved badly with might be the husband of our good friend Mma Potokwane (the matron).

She paused in her writing. That was a dreadful conclusion, and it was one that she would have to think about long and hard. Could it be true? If so, then she would be in a very difficult position, as she would have to decide whether to look further into the matter or to keep that knowledge from her friend. We did not always need to know the whole truth about things, and it may be that Mma Potokwane should be protected from facts that might ruin her happiness. There were times when the past should be put to rest, and this might be one of them.

(7) So we do nothing, or . . . or we tell the client that we have found some bad thing that it is best for her not to know about. We then point out to her that it is not such a bad thing that it should make her feel too ashamed. Her brother was weak, but then all men are weak. That is well known (except, perhaps, by the men themselves). In this case he fell for a woman who liked to tempt men. Those are very bad women, but men cannot see it. Forget about the past and stop talking about

278

it. Let Government Keboneng be remembered in the hearts of those whom he has helped. That is the best memorial there is.

She put down her pencil, folded the piece of paper, and closed her eyes. She would make a pot of tea, then she would go and sit on the verandah until the sun began to rise. She knew what she had to do.

Mma Ramotswe decided that the agency was no place for the sort of meeting that she must have with Mma Makutsi. There were too many distractions in the office, and there would also be the presence of Mr. Polopetsi and Charlie to be taken into account. Mma Makutsi was very conscious of her own dignity and would be loath to discuss anything sensitive in front of Charlie. The relationship that those two had was a curious one: Charlie had always taken pleasure in baiting Mma Makutsi, and for her part she had frequently been quite dismissive of him. Yet Mma Ramotswe was sure that beneath the badinage, behind the exchange of barbed comments and asides, there was affection between them. This had shown itself on numerous occasions when Charlie had been in trouble; even as she huffed and puffed about the fecklessness of young men, Mma Makutsi's expression

279

betrayed her true feelings of concern for the young man. And even as Charlie poured scorn on Mma Makutsi's ninety-seven per cent, it was clear that he admired not only this result but her general capabilities, and would defend her against criticism from any external quarter.

Mr. Polopetsi was another matter altogether. He stood in awe of Mma Makutsi, and whenever she expressed a view on any issue — which of course happened regularly — he would nod his head in automatic, unconditional agreement, like an ally bound by an unbreakable treaty. He would also quote her — a rather touching habit — referring to her pronouncements as if they had the authority of the statements of Clovis Andersen himself. Indeed, he had recently said that in his view there was little to distinguish the opinions of Mma Makutsi and those of Mr. Andersen. "They are like two tomatoes," he began, and then faltered. "Or is it like two peas in a pod? Which is it, Mma Ramotswe?"

"People say 'two peas in a pod,' Rra. That is what people say."

"Well, Mma Makutsi and that man who wrote that book you have — Mr. Clovis Andersen from New York . . ."

"Not New York, Rra," Mma Ramotswe

corrected him. "Muncie, Indiana. That is another American place, just like New York, I think."

Mr. Polopetsi acknowledged the correction. "Yes, Mr. Clovis Andersen from Muncie, Indiana. When you hear what he says and then you listen to Mma Makutsi, it is almost the same thing, Mma. They think the same way. That is why they say the same sorts of things."

This generous comparison had been overheard by Mma Makutsi, who beamed with pleasure. "He is a very good man, that Mr. Polopetsi," she later confided to Mma Ramotswe. "People look at him and think, *Who is that funny little man?* They think he is a nobody person; they think he is just some downtrodden husband with a wife who is much bigger than he is . . ."

"She is," said Mma Ramotswe, in a matter-of-fact way. "She is a very large lady, Mma. I have seen her. You could lose Mr. Polopetsi under her skirts. You could be talking to her and suddenly you would realise that there is a husband under there. And then his head would pop out and you would get a big surprise."

"But you would be wrong if you wrote him off," continued Mma Makutsi. "He has a way of saying things that are very true, I think."

Even if a warm relationship existed between Mma Makutsi and Mr. Polopetsi, it would still be awkward if Mma Ramotswe aired what had to be aired in the presence of both of them. No, the conversation she was planning to have with Mma Makutsi needed to take place in private. It was not going to be easy, though, nor could it be put off. It would have to be that morning — before Mma Makutsi left for work. It would have to be in the Radiphuti house, on her own ground.

Now that her mind was made up, Mma Ramotswe was able to tackle her morning tasks with equanimity and efficiency. By the time the household awoke that morning, packed lunches had been prepared for Mr. J.L.B. Matekoni and the two children, the table had been laid, and on the stove there was simmering a pot of meal porridge, the breakfast that Mma Ramotswe had eaten as a girl and that was the morning meal of all traditional people. Not only that, but the kitchen, the living room, and the verandah — the *stoep,* as she called it — had been vigorously and comprehensively swept, while in the garden Mr. J.L.B. Matekoni's rows of beans, his pride and joy, had been carefully provided with water saved from the kitchen sink.

Mma Ramotswe looked at her watch as the other three members of the family sat down. "I am going to have to go out early," she said. "I have a meeting first thing."

"But you are on holiday," protested Puso. "You must not go to the office when you are on holiday."

"I used to be on holiday," she said. "But now I am working again — not in the office but —"

Puso did not let her finish. "You cannot work if you are not in the office," he said. "How can you work . . . just in the air?"

"Many people do work in the air," said Motholeli. "You do not need an office to work. People work here and there. In their cars. In their houses. There are many different ways of working these days, Puso."

"I'm going to do some work at Mma Makutsi's house," explained Mma Ramotswe. "She and I have things to talk about."

Mr. J.L.B. Matekoni gave her a meaningful glance. "Be careful, Mma."

She tried to reassure him. "I am always careful in the way I treat Mma Makutsi, Rra. I have known her for many, many years now. I know how to deal with her."

"Good," said Mr. J.L.B. Matekoni. "Because sometimes, Mma, I feel that I do not know that. I say something to her — something very simple — and she goes off like a . . . like a BMW."

It was, thought Mma Ramotswe, a very good expression. We all say the things that make sense to us, and mechanics said things just like that. *Goes off like a BMW.* That was a very suitable thing for a mechanic to say.

"I shall be very careful not to make her go off like a BMW," she said.

"Good," said Mr. J.L.B. Matekoni again, and returned to his bowl of porridge.

She sat in silence at the table. She was sure that she was doing the right thing in going to speak directly to Mma Makutsi, but there was something else that was worrying her. How was she going to explain to Mma Makutsi about being in the van with Mr. Polopetsi? It must have been apparent to Mma Makutsi that they were engaged in some sort of investigation together, and she felt a hot flush of shame at the thought of being found out in such an obvious and compromising way. Now, when she went to speak to her, Mma Makutsi would probably think that the only reason for her doing so was because she felt that she had been found out. She would be like a child caught doing something wrong who tries to fend off the consequences by getting in first with an apology or justification. That sort of thing could avert recrimination, but one hardly came out of it with any credit.

It was Phuti Radiphuti who greeted her at the front door.

"Mma Ramotswe," he said, "I am very surprised that it is you." Then he hastily added, "And pleased, of course. Sometimes it is just people wanting to sell things who come to the door this early. They are so impatient to get you to buy something that they will even wake you up."

She looked at her watch. She was early — deliberately so — but had she come just a little bit too early? She was from a household that was accustomed to an early start, but there were houses where a very different philosophy held sway. In such places, she had heard, people could still be in bed at eight o'clock, difficult though it was to believe.

"I hope that I have not woken you up, Rra," she said.

Phuti laughed. "Mma, when you have a small child in the house, then you are always up early. Five o'clock today — wanting something to eat. Wanting to talk to us."

She tried to remember exactly how old

Itumelang was. "But . . ."

"Oh, I don't mean to talk with words — he is not speaking in that way just yet." Phuti looked proud. "He can communicate very well, though. He uses strange sounds, but we know what they mean. There is one for 'I want food.' There is one for 'I am tired of being in bed.' There is one for 'I am happy.' " Phuti paused. "Actually, that is a very strange sound, that one."

Mma Ramotswe knew what Phuti was speaking about, as she had heard Itumelang Clovis Radiphuti purring. There was no other word for it: he was a baby who purred — perhaps the only purring baby in all Botswana.

Phuti gestured for her to enter the house.

"Grace is busy with Itumelang at the moment," he explained. "She is changing him and washing his face, I think. She won't be long."

"I will wait," said Mma Ramotswe. "I am not in any hurry."

Phuti Radiphuti took her into the living room. As Mma Ramotswe expected of the living room of the proprietor of the Double Comfort Furniture Store, the chairs and the sofa were new and luxurious. What a change for Mma Makutsi, she thought. When she had first come to Gaborone from

Bobonong, she had lived in one small room, with a window so small as to admit only the slightest chink of light, and furnished with a single chair, a mattress on the floor, and a small cupboard. Now she lived in a house with four bedrooms, a large verandah, and a shaded place at the side to park a car — not to mention a good husband, of course, and a purring baby. Mma Ramotswe was glad that Mma Makutsi had found all this, and often reflected on how it had all come from that singular chance of going to a dance lesson at the Botswana Academy of Dance and Movement and meeting a man unable to dance a step and who had, at the time, a bad speech impediment. That was Phuti Radiphuti, who, unknown to Mma Makutsi, also had a large family herd of cattle and a prosperous furniture store. It had all worked out so well, and yet had she had a headache that evening and not gone to the dance class, it would never have happened. On those little chance events, thought Mma Ramotswe, hung our entire lives.

Phuti left her in the living room for a few minutes while he went to fetch her a cup of tea. She sat there and closed her eyes. It was not going to be an easy conversation with Mma Makutsi, but it was a necessary one. Mma Ramotswe did not believe in allowing anything to fester: if there was an issue with somebody, then it was always better to bring it out into the open. Doing that was like looking at something outside, under the open sky, for things looked less frightening in the sunlight.

Phuti came back, carrying a tray with two cups of tea.

"I'm drinking red bush tea too," he said. "I am getting used to it now, and it is making me feel very well."

"There are many things it does," said Mma Ramotswe. "It is good for the skin too. I have heard of people who put it on their skin."

Phuti smiled. "Although you would not expect — if you went to somebody's house and they asked you if you wanted some tea — you would not expect that if you said yes, then they would go off and fetch a teapot and pour it all over you! You would not expect that, Mma Ramotswe, would you?"

He laughed loudly at his own joke. Mma Ramotswe laughed too, less uproariously, perhaps, but then she had not been the one to crack the joke in the first place. Phuti Radiphuti, she thought, had many fine points, but his sense of humour was at times rather juvenile . . . mind you, many men had a sense of humour like that, when one came to think of it. Look at Charlie: he had once found it amusing to put an empty oil can on the top of the door so that it fell on Fanwell's head when he came in for his morning tea. Charlie had doubled up with mirth, so much so that his eyes had filled with tears, while Mma Ramotswe and Mma Makutsi, who had witnessed the prank, simply stared at one another in mute disbelief that anybody could think such a thing so amusing.

And even Mr. J.L.B. Matekoni, who was such a cautious and deliberate man, had narrated the story of how, as a boy, he had gone on a scout camp and they had sewn up the leg of the scout leader's pyjamas so that he found it difficult to get into them. That, he said, was the funniest thing he had ever seen, but again Mma Ramotswe and Mma Makutsi had looked at one another with that look that women keep in reserve for the peculiarities of men. It was a very special look: a look that combined pity with resignation. It was a look that said: we know that this is what you men like to do, and we understand, but do not expect us to look at things in quite the same way.

When he stopped laughing, there was a

marked change in Phuti Radiphuti's expression. Now he became grave.

"I'm glad you dropped by, Mma Ramotswe," he said. "There is something I need to talk to you about."

She took a sip of her tea. "I am listening, Rra."

"It is about Grace."

"I hope that she is well, Rra."

Phuti clasped his hands together. He looked uncomfortable. "Oh, there's nothing wrong with her health. Grace is a very fit person, you know. No, it is just that she's very worried about something. She came home yesterday and hardly spoke. And I know what that means, Mma. When you live with somebody, you know when there is something worrying them. They don't need to spell it out, do they?"

"They do not, Rra. I can always tell when Mr. J.L.B. Matekoni is brooding about something. He sits there and looks worried. It is very easy to tell."

Phuti understood. "There are many things that could be worrying him, I suppose. He's a businessman, after all, and those people always have one hundred things to worry about. He may be a mechanic, but he's running a business with people to pay and taxes and everything. That is not easy."

"He copes with most of that," said Mma Ramotswe. "What he worries about is gearboxes and such things. He worries about people's brakes. He worries about how much it is going to cost them to fix their suspension after they have driven into one of those holes . . ." She thought suddenly of her van; she had done nothing about the suspension and would have to deal with that before too long.

"There is something happening at work, I think," said Phuti. "I fear that there must be a big problem. I asked her, but she would not talk about it. She just said that she had been concerned about something and that she did not want to discuss it."

Mma Ramotswe felt her heart sink. It was as she had feared: Mma Makutsi had seen her in the van with Mr. Polopetsi and had concluded, quite correctly, that things were being done behind her back. Of course she would be disappointed by that — who would not?

Phuti Radiphuti was looking at her anxiously.

"You see," he said, "on the subject of your holiday, Mma: the fact that you are out of the office has perhaps placed a very big burden on her. She has Itumelang, she has the house, she has her position on the committee of that home for bad girls — she has all these things to worry her now, and maybe it's too much."

"I can imagine all that must be very hard," said Mma Ramotswe.

"So I wondered, Mma, whether your holiday needs to be quite as long as you planned. I hesitate to say that, Mma. You should not tell somebody that they do not deserve a holiday — you obviously do. But I wondered whether you might be thinking now of coming back just for a few hours each day, Mma, to take the pressure off Grace. Do you think that might be possible, Mma Ramotswe?"

Mma Ramotswe winced. What he was asking her to do would, she feared, only make things worse.

"It's very difficult, Rra," she said. "I would like to come back and help her, but that might just make matters worse. She will think that I don't believe she is capable of handling things herself."

"But perhaps she isn't," said Phuti. "Grace is a very intelligent woman and she is good at many things. But perhaps the agency is too much work for one lady. After all, it is the No. 1 Ladies' — in the plural — Detective Agency, not the No. 1 Lady's — just one lady's — Detective Agency."

"I know, Rra, but . . ."

A door opened behind her, and she turned round to see Mma Makutsi framed in the doorway, the light from the window reflecting off the large lenses of her spectacles. It was never a good sign when the light did that, and for a moment Mma Ramotswe regretted her visit.

"Ah," said Grace, making her way towards a seat opposite Mma Ramotswe's. "I thought I heard a familiar voice."

She turned to Phuti. "Phuti, would you be so kind as to go and settle Itumelang? He is getting tired now after being up so early. He needs a sleep."

That was another bad sign. When Mma Makutsi asked anybody if they would be "so kind" as to do anything, it meant that she was cross.

Mma Ramotswe reached for her cup, seeking the protection of tea, but it was empty. She replaced the cup on the table, hoping that this might prompt Mma Makutsi to offer to make more. That would defuse the situation, at least to some extent. But Mma Makutsi ignored the hint; yet another bad sign.

They sat in an awkward silence that was eventually broken by Mma Ramotswe. "I've come because of some complications," she began.

Mma Makutsi had fixed her with a stare that showed no sign of wavering. "Some complications, Mma? What sort of complications? Some holiday complications, perhaps?"

Mma Ramotswe drew in her breath. "You saw me, I think, Mma."

Mma Makutsi pursed her lips before speaking. "I believe I've seen you many times, Mma Ramotswe. I saw you when you came into the office to fetch something. I've seen you at the supermarket — although you did not see me — and I've seen you driving all over the place . . ." She left the sentence unfinished.

"With Mr. Polopetsi," added Mma Ramotswe. "At that intersection. I looked and suddenly I saw you, Mma. Mr. Polopetsi saw you too. He said, 'Oh, look, there's Mma Makutsi,' or something like that — I cannot remember his exact words."

There was ice in Mma Makutsi's voice. "I hope you had a good drive together. In this hot weather I think it can be very pleasant to go for a drive and get some cool air coming in through the window. One does not need air-conditioning in a car if you have a window open, I find."

Mma Ramotswe looked down at her shoes, her flat work shoes that were so broad and unglamorous and comfortable. She imagined Mma Makutsi's shoes engaged in a slanging match with her own shoes, pouring scorn on their breadth and outdatedness. It would be a war of the shoes — a war she would most certainly lose.

She drew in her breath again. "I was working with Mr. Polopetsi, Mma," she said quietly. "He and I were working on the Government Keboneng case."

Mma Makutsi said nothing.

"We went down to see a man called Saint Potokwane," Mma Ramotswe continued. "I had a very interesting conversation with him, and I think now that I have an idea of what lies behind all that business."

She heard Mma Makutsi's breathing, like the sound of an angry horse. It was a strange sound, and Mma Ramotswe thought at that moment that she knew where Itumelang got his ability to purr. But then, quite without warning, Mma Makutsi seemed to deflate. The angry breathing stopped, to be replaced by tears — a wail of heartfelt, harrowing tears.

"Oh, Mma," she stuttered. "How can you do this to me? How can you go on holiday and tell me that I will be the boss and then you turn round and take it away from me — just like that, Mma, as if I am some person who can do nothing? How can you do that, Mma?"

Mma Ramotswe rose to comfort her, but she could tell from Mma Makutsi's sudden stiffening that she should keep away. She returned to her seat.

"I am very sorry, Mma," she said. "Mr. Polopetsi came to see me. He did not know what to do."

"But I told you to leave him," said Mma Makutsi, her voice rising. "I told you, Mma — leave it up to him."

"But I couldn't do that, Mma Makutsi. We have our duty to the client."

This brought a strange sound from Mma Makutsi — a mixture of a snort and a sigh. "The client, Mma? The client?"

"Yes. We owe a duty to our clients. We have to do our best by them."

Mma Makutsi's glasses flashed another signal — this time of outrage. "But the client, Mma . . ." She faltered, and then, making a visible effort to calm down, she said, "Just tell me what you have found out, Mma."

Mma Ramotswe was relieved that the outburst was over. Speaking carefully, so as not to reignite Mma Makutsi, she gave an account of their visit to Saint Potokwane. She repeated their conversation and then added an account of her subsequent listing of possibilities. Mma Makutsi listened intently, but Mma Ramotswe noticed that with each major point in her account, the other woman shook her head. This she did with sadness, almost as if she were commenting on the fact that somebody could get something so wrong. At the end, Mma Ramotswe asked her if she thought her conclusions were reasonable.

"No," said Mma Makutsi. "You are one hundred per cent wrong, Mma. One hundred per cent wrong."

Not even ninety-seven per cent, thought Mma Ramotswe.

"I'm sorry, Mma Makutsi, I just do not see how you can say I am wrong." She paused. "Do you have another explanation?"

"Yes," said Mma Makutsi. "I do. You see, Mma, you are assuming that our client is telling the truth. What if the client is lying? Don't you remember that Mr. Andersen himself said something about that — in chapter six, I think it was. He says that you should not always believe your client, because he or she may be concealing something or even telling complete untruths.

Those were his words, Mma Ramotswe —
complete untruths."

Mma Ramotswe did not know what to say.
She stared at Mma Makutsi in disbelief.
Why would Mr. Government Keboneng's
sister lie about anything to do with this
case? Her objective was simple enough,
surely; it was to protect the reputation of a
late brother who could not defend himself.
She brought this up now, challenging Mma
Makutsi to refute it.

"Because she never liked her brother,"
said Mma Makutsi. "She was always in his
shadow. People were always saying that she
was the sister of Mr. Government Keboneng rather than saying that he was her
brother. That can be very hard for people.
They do not like to be in the shadow. I'm
afraid she hated him, Mma. That is a terrible thing, but it is true."

It took Mma Ramotswe a few moments to
absorb this. "But why would a sister want
to stop the naming of a street for her own
brother, even if she did not have friendly
feelings towards him?"

"Because it was the last straw," answered
Mma Makutsi. "Because all her life she had
heard people saying what a great man he
was. When she was a little girl, he was
described as a great boy. Then he became a

great man. She could not bear it."

"And so she told the council about a scandal? Did she know of anything?"

Mma Makutsi shook her head. "I don't think so. I think she told them about it and then she decided that she would try to find something real — some real scandal — to back up her allegations. That is why she came to us. She did not want us to prove that there was nothing, as she claimed when she first consulted the agency; on the contrary — she wanted us to find something, on the grounds that if you dig deep enough around any politician, you will find something. And then, I'm afraid, after I put in a preliminary report that we were not uncovering anything, she set up the scandal herself."

"And how did she do that, Mma?" Mma Ramotswe posed this question not as a challenge, in the spirit of disbelief, but to receive an explanation.

"Well," Mma Makutsi continued, "she was never very fond of Naledi Potokwane. She thought she was a bit fast — and she may be, but only a little, I think. So she decided to create a story that Government had had an affair with Naledi, and that Naledi had had an affair with virtually everybody else. She put this idea into the head of Saint

Potokwane, knowing that he would always talk about something without worrying about its effect. She imagined that we would find out about him and speak to him. So she put all that nonsense in his head."

There was something that Mma Ramotswe did not understand. "But how do you know that she told Saint this?"

Mma Makutsi smiled. It was the first smile of the morning, and there was a ring of triumph to it.

"As it happens, Mma," she said, "I know somebody who goes to the same church as Saint and that woman who looks after him. So I went there on Sunday and while everybody was drinking tea outside, as they do at that place, I went up to Saint. He was standing about and nobody was with him. So I went up and asked him about the family and whether he knew Government Keboneng well and so on. He spoke quite freely. A lot of it was about the Defence Force and helicopters, but when I asked him about Government he said that Mma Potokwane — the client Mma Potokwane — had told him to say that Government was seeing Naledi and Naledi was seeing other men. He told me all this in a very matter-of-fact way, because these people who are like that often speak very openly. And that, Mma, is how I discovered what our client was up to."

Mma Ramotswe listened in silence. She thought: *Did I teach this woman to do all this?*

"And then," continued Mma Makutsi, "I went to see Naledi and put the whole thing to her, and she was incensed. She said that it was all lies. She said that she had never had any affairs while she was married to Saviour and now she was happily married again to a very respectable man. She was very cross."

"I see."

There was still resentment in Mma Makutsi's voice. "Yes, Mma, I'm glad that you see."

Mma Ramotswe closed her eyes, allowing her feelings of relief to wash over her. Not only was she pleased that the case had been resolved, but she could now put out of her mind any possibility that Mma Sylvia Potokwane's husband had been involved with Naledi. That had been an uncomfortable possibility, and it was now firmly disposed of. Good.

But there remained something that had not been cleared up, which she now raised with Mma Makutsi. "May I ask you, Mma, why you haven't tackled the client over this?

Are you proposing to let her get away with it?"

Mma Makutsi seemed prepared for this. "I did not speak to her, Mma. When I found out what I found out, I realised that it might be difficult to prove any allegation I made against her. So what I did was to go to the council and tell them that we had made a full investigation and that we had discovered nothing. We told them that Mr. Government Keboneng's reputation was sound, and that any charge to the contrary was motivated by malice and came, moreover, from a source we knew about but were not at liberty to divulge." She paused, savouring this last phrase. "Not at liberty to divulge, Mma."

"Why did you do that, Mma?"

"Because it achieved everything necessary. It meant that Mr. Government Keboneng's reputation was restored and the whole issue could be put to bed. And that, Mma Ramotswe, was very important because it saves poor Saint from being drawn further into something he can't understand."

Mma Ramotswe understood that — and thought that it was exactly the right thing to do. "There was something about cattle, though — something about Saint's cattle having been taken away from him."

302

"There is no truth in that, Mma. I think she put him up to saying that."

"Perhaps."

"Not perhaps, Mma — definitely. I made further enquiries, you see. And his cattle are down at that place where he lives — they are very fine cattle."

Mma Ramotswe realised these were the cattle she had seen — and they were indeed fine beasts.

Mma Makutsi was now fully composed. "But our client does not get away with it altogether," she said. "I did what you have always done, Mma. I decided to give her a second chance -- along with a warning."

"What did you do, Mma?"

"I told her that I had discovered that she was the informant who had gone to the council. I had not discovered this, of course, but her reaction to it confirmed that it was true. Then I told her that she should go to Naledi and apologise. She should ask for her forgiveness and she should promise not to spread any more rumours. If she did not, then people might just discover that she had tried to destroy her own brother's reputation. And there are many followers of Mr. Government Keboneng who would be very angry if they were to hear that."

"So she agreed."

"She agreed, Mma — people usually agree to do what they really have to do. And I said something else to her, Mma Ramotswe. I told her that she would need to forgive her brother — to forgive him for being a good man."

Mma Makutsi looked intently at Mma Ramotswe. "At first she didn't know what I meant, Mma, but then, after a while, I think she did."

Mma Ramotswe sat back in her chair. She looked at Mma Makutsi. "Mma," she said, "I should never have doubted that you were on top of this case. I am very, very sorry, Mma. I have done you a great injustice."

Mma Makutsi shook her head. "If you have done me an injustice, Mma, you did it for a good reason. And I know how hard it is to let go of things. I know how hard it is for you to realise that I am fully capable."

"It is not hard now, Mma Makutsi," said Mma Ramotswe. "You are the most capable lady I have ever met."

"Oh, Mma, you are very kind . . ." The coldness and the anger had all gone; Mma Makutsi, the familiar Mma Makutsi, was back. And that familiar Mma Makutsi seemed to be thinking about something, as there came a flash of light from her glasses — a coincidence, of course, the sun can catch glasses at all sorts of times, but it so often seemed to catch Mma Makutsi's just at the point where she was thinking about something. "Mr. Polopetsi . . . ," she said.

Mma Ramotswe looked up. "Yes. What about him, Mma?"

"I think that I might have been unfair to him. I think that it was a bit unkind to throw him into the middle of the river."

Mma Ramotswe suppressed a smile as she imagined the scene: Mma Makutsi, who was considerably bigger than Mr. Polopetsi, picking him up, tottering to the bank of the Limpopo River, and then tossing him, arms flailing, into the middle of it. Then Mma Makutsi would adjust her glasses, rub her hands together, and stand there as poor Mr. Polopetsi floundered in the water. Of course, there were people who really did throw others into rivers — it had happened a few years ago in the Okavango Delta when one person had thrown another into a river, but had slipped and fallen in as well. And then the person who had thrown the other person in was bitten by a crocodile, while the first person (the person thrown in by the second person) had clambered out in time and avoided being bitten. That had been widely reported in the newspaper because it somehow made a point about justice.

Mma Makutsi continued with her self-examination. "It was wrong, I think. I shouldn't have left him to make enquiries that I knew would get nowhere."

Mma Ramotswe was glad that Mma Makutsi had raised this, because it was something that had been worrying her. She could not see why Mma Makutsi should have used Mr. Polopetsi in this way: What was the point of wasting his time in the investigation of an issue she had already solved? She chose her words carefully. "I have been wondering about that, Mma," she said. "I have tried to figure out why you should think you needed to mislead him" — and here she hesitated, but decided to go ahead anyway — "and I was wondering why you told me that everything was in hand. You might have brought me into your confidence, Mma."

There was reproach in that final sentence; she had not intended it, but reproach came through.

Mma Makutsi looked at her with an intensity that took Mma Ramotswe slightly by surprise. "Oh, Mma . . . ," she began, but then her voice trailed off.

Fearing another emotional moment, Mma

Ramotswe was quick to reassure her. "It was just a thought, Mma, just a thought."

"No," said Mma Makutsi. "It is a very good question. It is just the question that anybody would ask. And you have asked it, I think."

Mma Ramotswe nodded — and waited.

"It is all to do with Mma Potokwane," Mma Makutsi pronounced.

"Which Mma Potokwane?" asked Mma Ramotswe. "There are many, many Mma Potokwanes."

"Our Mma Potokwane. Mma Sylvia Potokwane. The matron. Her."

There was a further pause, and then Mma Makutsi continued, "You see, I found out that one of the people that Naledi was said to have been involved with was her husband — Mma Sylvia Potokwane's husband, that is. Yes, Mma: that is what that poor man, Saint Potokwane, said to me."

Mma Ramotswe shook her head. "But I do not understand, Mma. You said that Saint told you that he had been instructed to relate that story about Naledi and her affairs."

"That was on our second meeting," explained Mma Makutsi. "We had two meetings, you see. The first meeting had been set up by the client. She told me that as it

307

happened there was a family member I might like to talk to. She was looking after him for a couple of days while the woman who normally did that was away. I met him at the client's house. She left us alone together but told me that I could ask him about the family. Out it all came — obviously, just as she had intended. I was suspicious, but at that stage I could not put my finger on anything. So I worked out a way of seeing him again — when the client would not be around. That was the meeting at the church, the one that I've told you about. He forgot that I had spoken to him earlier — and out came the truth. He said that he had been told to tell a story."

Mma Makutsi watched as Mma Ramotswe thought about this. "Do you see, Mma Ramotswe?" she asked.

Mma Ramotswe nodded. "I see. At least, I think I see."

"I wanted to keep you from finding out about Mma Sylvia Potokwane's husband. I wanted to protect you from this information about your friend's husband. I wanted to protect Mma Sylvia Potokwane too. Even when I realised that it was a lie, I didn't want anybody to hear about it. Lies can sometimes be as powerful as the truth, Mma. A lie about somebody can hurt that person even if everybody knows it's a lie."

"So you thought you could keep the whole thing from coming out into the open?"

"Yes. I thought that I would deal with it myself. I would keep the client Potokwane quiet. I would protect the reputation of an innocent man. And nobody would be upset."

Now Mma Ramotswe understood. If Mma Makutsi had concealed things from her, it had been done for the very best of reasons: to protect her — and her close friend too — from distress. It had been selfless; it had been kind.

"It was very difficult for me," Mma Makutsi continued. "I was very stressed by the knowledge that I was hiding things from you. That is why I haven't been myself, Mma."

Mma Ramotswe made a gesture of reassurance. "I noticed that. Now I understand. And I can see why you felt you needed to use Mr. Polopetsi in all this."

"I had to, Mma, but I shall apologise to him. I shall tell him that he did very well — which I think he did."

"He is a very good man," said Mma Ramotswe. "If I were ever to make a list of the good men in Botswana, then he would be on it, I think."

Mma Makutsi liked the idea of a list of good men. "We could publish an annual list, Mma: 'The No. 1 Ladies' Detective Agency Official List of Good Men in Botswana.' It would be a very important list."

Mma Ramotswe laughed. "And it would be led by two names," she said. "Mr. J.L.B. Matekoni and Mr. Phuti Radiphuti."

"Naturally, Mma. Then the other names would come."

Mma Ramotswe continued the fantasy. "And Charlie?"

Mma Makutsi made a face. "Poor Charlie. He would have to work to get on that list. Perhaps there would be a secondary list of young men who might grow up to be good men but who are not there quite yet."

That, thought Mma Ramotswe, was a very sound idea. "It is always helpful to give people something to aim for," she said, and then added, "But here's another thing, Mma. I am going to take a proper holiday now. I am going to go up to Mochudi for a few days, just by myself. I promise that I shall not interfere with the agency." She shook her head, as if in incredulity that she could ever have done anything to the contrary. "I promise you that."

Mma Makutsi now got up and crossed the room to sit beside Mma Ramotswe. She put her arm on her friend's shoulder briefly, and squeezed it in a gesture of wordless but unambiguous reconciliation.

They sat together in silence for a while. In the background, somewhere deep within the house, they heard a baby's cry.

"That's Itumelang," said Mma Makutsi. "He's sometimes difficult to settle once he has been up. He is tired, but he does not want to get back to sleep."

Mma Ramotswe smiled. "It is good that you have such a hands-on husband, Mma. Some men just walk away when the child cries."

"Not Phuti," said Mma Makutsi. "He's so . . ." She waved a hand in the air. "He's so . . ." She dropped her hand. "What is the time, Mma?"

Mma Ramotswe, glancing at her watch, told her.

Mma Makutsi rose to her feet. "I have an appointment, Mma," she said. "And I think you might like to come with me. I know you're meant to be on holiday, but this is a very tricky issue and I would like to have you with me."

Mma Ramotswe indicated that she was willing. "I take it that it's a client, Mma; but who is it?"

Mma Makutsi hesitated for a moment.

Then she smiled as she answered the question. "In a sense it is you, Mma."

Mma Makutsi seemed to take pleasure in keeping Mma Ramotswe on tenterhooks. Rather than reveal where she was going, she merely told her friend to follow her in the white van. Mma Makutsi had a newish car, a white car with a red stripe down the side, and it was considerably more powerful than Mma Ramotswe's van; she drove slowly, though, to allow Mma Ramotswe to keep up with her as they made their way along the road leading from the block of plots around the Radiphuti house. Mma Ramotswe was vaguely irritated by Mma Makutsi's reticence, but any feelings of this sort were outweighed by her surprise — and, to an extent, relief — over the resolution of the Keboneng affair. She felt real pleasure that the other woman had managed to deal with what could otherwise have been an unusually messy investigation.

Yes, she thought, everything had worked out as Mma Makutsi had hoped, but even so there had been an extraordinary number of misunderstandings. She had misunderstood what Mma Makutsi had been up to, and Mma Makutsi had not only misinterpreted what she herself had been trying to do but had also been unaware of what she knew. Mr. Polopetsi had likewise been under a misapprehension about Mma Makutsi's inability to handle things. It was a web of misunderstanding and deceit, but ultimately it was truth that had come to the fore. Which so often happened, thought Mma Ramotswe. Truth had a way of coming out on top — and it was just as well for everybody that it did. If there ever came a day when truth was so soundly defeated that it never emerged, but sank, instead, under the sheer volume of untruth that the world produced, then that would be a sad day for Botswana, and for the people who lived in Botswana. It would be a sad day for the whole world, that day.

At first she thought that they were going to the office, but instead of turning off as Mma Ramotswe expected her to do, Mma Makutsi continued along the Tlokweng Road before taking a right turn into the area of the town known as the Village. Perhaps, thought Mma Ramotswe, the mysterious appointment was with somebody who lived in one of the older houses there, but if it was, why should Mma Makutsi have been so coy about telling her? And what did she mean by the tantalising remark that she —

Mma Ramotswe herself — was, in a sense, the client?

For a moment she allowed herself to imagine that Mma Makutsi was preparing a surprise present for her. It was her birthday in a few days and Mma Makutsi always gave her a present. In the days when she had been a secretary pure and simple, the present had of necessity been modest, but it had always been chosen with thought and worked with love — a crocheted cover to keep flies out of her teacup, a set of table napkins made from salvaged squares of material, a shoe horn fashioned from a cow's horn. After her marriage to Phuti Radiphuti, it had been possible for her to buy rather than make presents, and these had sometimes been so generous as to cause Mma Ramotswe a tinge of anxiety. Now she looked down the road on which they were travelling — there was a dressmaker who lived in one of the flats round the corner; Mma Makutsi knew that she occasionally had dresses made by this woman, and she wondered if perhaps her birthday surprise was a fitting. It was just the sort of gift that Mma Makutsi liked to give, she thought; yes, that was where they were heading. And what a pleasant surprise it would be; she did not think she was entitled to a new dress, and to get it as a present would remove all the guilt that a fresh outfit would otherwise have spawned.

But no, they passed the turning to the three-storey block in which the dressmaker lived and were now headed for the university and the golf club. And that route, of course, took them past the sign that had caught Mma Ramotswe's attention a few days earlier but that had been forgotten about with everything else that was happening.

When Mma Makutsi slowed down and turned on her indicator, Mma Ramotswe caught her breath. Of course it was possible that there was something else altogether taking her down that particular road, but it now occurred to Mma Ramotswe that their destination was, indeed, the so-called No. 1 Ladies' College of Secretarial and Business Studies.

They parked a short distance from the building housing the college. Mma Makutsi stopped her car, climbed out of the driver's seat, and waited for Mma Ramotswe to finish parking and emerge from her van.

"This is where you have your appointment, Mma?" asked Mma Ramotswe, nodding in the direction of the college building, now with a freshly painted sign.

Mma Makutsi took off her glasses and

polished them as she replied. "Do you know about this place?" she asked.

Mma Ramotswe frowned. "I was going to talk to you about it, Mma. I saw it a few days ago. I spoke to a man who was doing some painting. He said that —"

Mma Makutsi cut her short. "Violet Sephotho," she said. "It's her, you know."

"I'd worked that out. My suspicions were aroused and I thought, *There can be only one person who would do this sort of thing.*"

"Your suspicions were right," said Mma Makutsi, grimly. "I have made further enquiries and it is all confirmed, Mma. This is Violet Sephotho's place."

They looked at one another, unspoken thoughts of disapproval going through their minds. What could anyone expect of somebody like Violet Sephotho? To what depths would she not sink? And although Mma Makutsi did not think this, Mma Ramotswe did: *Poor woman — what unhappiness must Violet have felt to want to share it with others . . .*

Mma Ramotswe glanced in the direction of the college; a door was open and she could make out a light on somewhere inside in spite of the brightness of the morning. "Is your appointment in there, Mma?" she asked.

316

"Yes, it is with her, Mma."

Mma Ramotswe's eyes widened. "Are you sure, Mma?"

"I am very sure, Mma Ramotswe."

Mma Ramotswe drew in her breath. She had seen Mma Makutsi on the warpath several times before, and she wondered whether she was about to witness another such confrontation. Mma Ramotswe did not like conflict, and would avoid direct, head-to-head arguments if she could, but there was something irresistible about the thought of a Violet Sephotho–Grace Makutsi match; it would be not unlike that famous boxing match of all those years ago that she remembered her father talking about, when those two great boxers met for the Rumble in the Jungle and one of them — now, which one was it? — knocked the other out, against all expectation.

She saw Mma Makutsi looking at her quizzically.

"Why are you smiling, Mma Ramotswe?"

She pulled herself together. "I am just thinking, Mma. I was thinking of a famous boxing match a long time ago. My late daddy talked about it."

Mma Makutsi looked over her shoulder in the direction of the college. "I did not give her my name," she said. "I made the appointment without telling her who I was. I said that I wanted to discuss a course with her. She was very helpful."

"Because she thought you were a potential student?"

"Yes. I could hear her thinking about the fees." Mma Makutsi paused. "Sometimes, you know, Mma, you can hear what people are thinking. Don't you find that?"

As they walked towards the building, Mma Ramotswe asked Mma Makutsi what she planned to say to Violet.

"I am going to tell her that I am watching her," Mma Makutsi replied. "I am going to tell her that if she is up to any tricks, she can expect me to find out. I shall be giving her a warning, Mma."

Mma Ramotswe looked thoughtful. "She will not like that, Mma."

"I know."

They reached the door of the college. Immediately inside was the main classroom, a large space furnished with the desks that the painter had discussed. A portable blackboard, resting on an easel, had been placed at the head of the room, some sentences in white chalk written on it and underlined in blue. Beyond the classroom, through an open door, could be made out an office of some sort — the edge of a desk, a filing cabinet, a chair or two.

They walked through the empty classroom and knocked at the office door.

"Please come right in," called a voice from within.

The effect of their entry was immediate. Seated behind her desk, Violet Sephotho, dressed in a low-cut purple dress, looked up sharply and, for a few moments, was clearly confused. She quickly regained her composure, though, and a forced smile appeared on her lips.

"Grace Makutsi . . . Well, well, what a pleasant surprise. And Mma . . . Mma . . ."

"Ramotswe," supplied Mma Ramotswe. She knew that Violet was perfectly well aware of who she was — of course she was.

"Mma Ramotswe," said Violet smoothly. "Of course; silly me for not remembering. You're the woman married to that man who works for that garage, aren't you?"

Mma Makutsi corrected her. "He is the owner of that garage, Mma. He is not just a mechanic."

Violet made a dismissive gesture. "I'll remember that, Mma. Thank you for telling me about it. I shall remember — if anybody ever asks me who owns that place, I shall know what to reply." She looked down at her desk, where a diary was open before her.

"I have an appointment, I'm afraid. So I shall not be able to spend much time talking to you ladies."

"The appointment is with me," said Mma Makutsi. "I'm the one who made it."

Violet Sephotho was unprepared for this, and faltered. "You did not . . . You didn't say that . . ."

"I didn't say anything," said Mma Makutsi. "But I am here now, and we can have the talk for which I made that appointment. That is why I am here."

Violet was marshalling her resources. "Impossible," she said sharply. "I cannot sit around and talk about the old days. I have very important things to do."

"But you told me on the phone," countered Mma Makutsi, "that you would not be busy and that we would have plenty of time to talk."

Violet's annoyance showed; as she replied, her voice rose noticeably. "I thought that you were a client," she said. "Of course I have time to talk to clients — that is quite different from talking to any old person who comes in off the street for a chat." She paused. "Even you should understand that, Grace Makutsi."

Mma Ramotswe sensed that battle was about to be joined. She thought that perhaps she should intervene before things were said that could never be retracted, but now it was too late — Mma Makutsi had taken a deep breath and was ready to begin.

"Oh, so I am just any old person," said Mma Makutsi, and, turning to Mma Ramotswe, repeated, "any old person — that is who we are, apparently, Mma Ramotswe. Any old person."

"Oh, I don't think that Mma Sephotho meant it like that, Mma —"

Mma Ramotswe was not allowed to finish. "I can tell what you mean, Mma," said Mma Makutsi, addressing Violet. "I am not so stupid. And I can read too, Mma. I can read that sign that says the No. 1 Ladies' College. I know that that is meant to exploit the goodwill that goes with the name of Mma Ramotswe's business. I can see that, you know. I may be any old person, but I am not any old stupid person."

"You're talking nonsense," snapped Violet. "You are talking big nonsense. You cannot claim words in the English language and say those are yours. You cannot stop other people using the words *number* or *one* or *ladies* because those are your private words. You cannot lock words up in the safe, you know."

Mma Makutsi ignored this point. "I

wanted to tell you something as a friend, Mma. I wanted to tell you that we are watching you. I'm going to go and speak to the Botswana Secretarial College people and tell them to watch you too. We do not need another college like this — we have a perfectly good one already, and you know the name of that."

Violet Sephotho's nostrils flared. "Oh, Mma? Oh, do I? The Botswana Secretarial College — that old-fashioned dump. That place that thinks it's so special, but is only for failures and . . . and for people from Bobonong and places like that."

Had she spent hours preparing her insults, had she brooded over them, burnished them, and then brought them out as weapons are brought out before cheering crowds at military parades, Violet Sephotho could not have chosen her words with more devastating effect. For a good minute or so, Mma Makutsi said nothing, but stood where she was, her mouth agape, glaring at the woman in the purple dress seated behind her desk. Then, very slowly, as if muscles that had previously been in a spasm of shock were restored to normal, she inched closer to her adversary.

"You are a very wicked woman," Mma Makutsi hissed. "You have no loyalty to the college that took you in and made a secretary of you. You clearly have no gratitude for that — no feeling of loyalty; nothing, Mma, nothing. You are full of nothing. There is nothing in your head and nothing inside that heart of yours. Nothing, Mma."

"Oh, don't be so ridiculous," said Violet. "The Botswana Secretarial College is irrelevant to the new Botswana. People are looking for better training. They want ideas. They want modern views."

Mma Makutsi's breathing was now quite audible; laboured and irregular, it was the breathing of one whose heart was pounding wildly within her as adrenaline raced through her system. "Fifty per cent," she hissed. "That's what you got, isn't it? Fifty per cent. The bare pass mark. Maybe that's a modern result. Hah!"

"Those things mean nothing," said Violet. "Those things are for children."

"Oh, do they?" responded Mma Makutsi, now almost shouting. "If they mean nothing, why do they have them, then?"

"To impress people from places like Bobonong," said Violet. "They are clearly very easily impressed."

Oh dear, thought Mma Ramotswe. *Not even the Secretary-General of the UN, not even the Pope, could do much to defuse this crisis,* but she would try. "Perhaps we should think about all this," she began. "Perhaps we should . . ."

She did not finish; a young woman had appeared at the door of the office and was clearing her throat. "Excuse me," said the young woman politely. "Excuse me, but I need to talk to you, Mma Sephotho."

Mma Makutsi and Mma Ramotswe fell silent.

"I can come back later if you wish," said the young woman.

Something, some inner voice, seemed to tell Mma Ramotswe that this was important. Perhaps it was Mma Makutsi's shoes — and perhaps Mma Makutsi heard them too, because she looked down at that precise moment.

Those fancy-looking shoes have got something to say, Boss. We'd listen if we were you.

Mma Ramotswe glanced at the young woman's shoes. They were indeed fancy. But surely the voice was illusory; surely it was all in the mind and the voice apparently coming from the shoes was merely an expression of what one was thinking.

Mma Ramotswe acted. "No, don't worry about us," she said to the young woman. "We have plenty of time. You can speak to Mma Sephotho."

The young woman did not notice Violet Sephotho stiffen. "Thank you, Mma," she said. "I mustn't stay too long because I am expected at my work. I just wanted to check up on how often you needed me to come and sign in — for the regulations. Was it once a week, or was it once a month?"

Mma Makutsi exchanged a glance with Mma Ramotswe. For her part, Violet looked flustered. "We can talk about this some other time," Violet said.

But it was too late. Mma Makutsi turned to the young woman and smiled. "I think I'm in the same position, Mma. I don't want to be caught."

It worked. It was a stratagem that she had found in Clovis Andersen's *The Principles of Private Detection.* The author of that seminal work had written that if you suspected that somebody was doing something wrong, then one way of eliciting information was simply to suggest that you yourself were engaged in the same wrong. *They'll fill in all the details you need,* he wrote.

"No," said the young woman. "That's the last thing I want. I don't want them to think that I'm not a proper student."

"Of course not," said Mma Makutsi quickly.

"Because then you have big problems with

work permits and tax and so on," continued the young woman. "This sorts all of that out — as long as we do it right."

There was a strange sound from Violet, but it did not interrupt the exchange.

"Have you found a job?" asked Mma Makutsi.

Violet opened her mouth to protest, but the young woman seemed unaware of her discomfort. "I've found a great job. The pay is really good and the hours not bad at all. I'm very happy with it."

Mma Makutsi looked pleased. "And no problem with a work permit?"

The young woman shook her head. "None. If you're a student you're allowed to take on a part-time job. You know that, don't you?"

Mma Makutsi nodded. "I know that," she said, and then looked directly at Violet Sephotho. "This is very interesting, Mma."

Violet rose to her feet. "You get out of here, Grace Makutsi!" she shouted. "You just get out!"

"Oh, I'll leave, all right, Mma. But where shall I go once I'm out of this office — this so-called office, should I say? Shall I go straight to the police? Or shall I go to the Labour Department? What do you think, Violet?"

Mma Ramotswe stepped forward. "There is no need to go to the police," she said.

Mma Makutsi shot her a reproachful look. "But this whole thing is a criminal operation, Mma."

This was the signal for Violet to scream. "You're calling me a criminal? You're calling me a criminal, Grace Makutsi?"

"As a matter of fact, I am," said Mma Makutsi.

Mma Ramotswe intervened again. "I think we should all calm down," she said.

"I'm very calm," hissed Mma Makutsi. "I am as calm as a currant."

As calm as a currant? Mma Ramotswe looked perplexed. But this was not the time for a discussion of words and what they mean. "I have a proposal to make," she said softly. "If this college is a sham . . ."

"It is a sham, Mma," said Mma Makutsi. "It is a big sham. One hundred per cent sham."

"If it is a sham," Mma Ramotswe went on, "then it should be closed. That is very clear."

"And money refunded," added Mma Makutsi.

"It is not your money," said Violet. "It's my money. It is legitimately charged for courses."

"For rubbish," said Mma Makutsi. "How can you teach these subjects when you got only fifty per cent in the finals? Answer that, Violet Sephotho!"

The young woman had been silent in the face of this exchange, but now she joined in. "Fifty per cent? A teacher with fifty per cent? The principal of a college with fifty per cent?"

"You shut up," snapped Violet. "You're just an ignorant student. You know nothing about nothing."

This was not a wise remark. Drawing herself up to her full height, the young woman fixed Violet with a steely gaze. "You call me ignorant, Mma? Well, I am going to go and discuss that with the other students and see what they think. I shall also tell them that you are a person who has only fifty per cent, and they will say, 'Oh, this is very sad that we have been hoodwinked by such an ignorant woman.' That is what they will say, Mma."

"You shut up!" screamed Violet. "You shut up, shut up, shut up!"

"No, Mma," said Mma Ramotswe. "You are the one who must shut up, Violet. You must shut up and then you must close this place down. There must be no more fooling of our immigration and labour people. Do you understand that, Violet?"

Violet had been listening carefully and had realised that her best chance lay with Mma Ramotswe.

"I will do what you suggest, Mma Ramotswe. I will do that."

"Good," said Mma Ramotswe. "It is always better to settle things in that way. There is enough trouble in the world already, don't you think, Mma Sephotho?"

Mma Ramotswe waited for an answer, but none came.

"I said that there is enough trouble in the world already, Mma. Did you hear that?"

Violet now spoke. "I heard that, Mma."

"And you know what you must do if you wish to avoid further trouble? You know what you have to do?"

"I do," said Violet.

"Good," said Mma Ramotswe. "That is very good."

She turned to Mma Makutsi. "I think that we should go now, Mma. You have to be in the office and I have to be back at my place."

"You're not coming back to work, Mma?" asked Mma Makutsi.

"I am still on holiday," said Mma Ramotswe. "And I am now planning to go away to Mochudi. It is a good idea to spend your holiday away, if at all possible. It is not compulsory — I am not saying that — but it is definitely a good idea."

Mma Makutsi went off to the office while Mma Ramotswe returned to Zebra Drive. It was not yet half past nine, and yet she felt she had already crammed several days' work into a few hours. Once home, she prepared herself a cup of red bush tea and took it with her into the garden. The morning was a warm one, but the real heat of the day was yet to come and it was still possible to walk out in the sun without longing for shade.

She stopped to look up at the sky, remembering something her father had told her: "If you look at the sky, the things you need to think about will come into your mind." It was such a strange thing to say, and yet, on the odd occasion that she had done this, it had worked: she had thought about important things, and it had become clear to her what she had to do.

The sky was empty — a high, singing vault of blue that made her dizzy just to look at it. She closed her eyes, and then reopened them. If you looked up into that blue for long enough it seemed that the air was dancing, as air can do when it is heated and there are currents within it. She thought: *I have been unfair to Mma Makutsi. I have not*

trusted her to deal with things that she has
shown herself to be perfectly capable of han-
dling.

She looked down at the ground, at Botswana beneath her feet. The next time she
saw Mma Makutsi, she would repair the
situation. She would tell her how highly she
thought of her and say, too, that were it possible, she would promote her; but such
promotion was not possible, as she was now
a partner in the business. But then she
thought better of that; she would say nothing about promotion, because even if it were
not possible for Mma Makutsi to rise higher
in the agency, if she mentioned the idea
then Mma Makutsi would be sure to find
some way of achieving it. So she would
remain silent, for, after all, it is perfectly
possible to be both silent and grateful at
one and the same time.

CHAPTER FOURTEEN: HE WILL BE GIVEN A LOT OF LOVE

The night before she drove out to Mochudi, it rained. The storm hit shortly before midnight, announcing itself with a great explosion of thunder that cracked the sky, that shook the land. Mr. J.L.B. Matekoni slept through it all, but Mma Ramotswe awoke and lay in bed listening to that most blessed of sounds — rainwater drumming on the tin roof of a house. It was what the country desperately needed if the crops were to be saved and the cattle to flourish. It would heal the earth and soothe the minds of the people and the animals waiting for just this relief. It would lower the temperature and bring cool and green to a land that for months had been hot and brown. The blessing of rain was the one thing in Botswana that would unite those who might disagree about much else: *pula*, the word for rain in the Setswana language, also meant good fortune — *"Pula! Pula!*

Pula!" was the encouraging chant that children learned at school and carried in their hearts for the rest of their lives. "Pula! Pula! Pula!"

At first light she went out into her garden. The rain clouds had passed on, although there were still purple banks in the distance — the good fortune of somewhere to the west that would now be getting its share of the bounty. There had been a large downpour, and the ground was sated; here and there puddles had formed where the earth could cope with no more; here and there, rising from holes in the ground, came clouds of flying ants, wings aflutter, an irresistible target for the birds swooping in and out of the airborne feast.

She filled her lungs with the morning air, so clean now, so sharp and fresh, while at her feet the miracle of transformation was already occurring — tiny shoots of green, appearing between grains of sand, were making their presence known. Within hours there would be a green tinge to the brown; within days there would be fully formed blades of grass.

A few hours later she was on the way to Mochudi, following the road that she knew so well. Not far from the village, this road took her past a small burial ground, a short walk from the road, and she stopped and made her way to one of its corners. There she found the two graves that she had come to visit: the grave of her mother, lost to her when she was not much more than a babe in arms, and that of her father, the late Obed Ramotswe. She had erected a new stone to him a few years earlier, as the old one had been knocked over by a donkey and had split across the top. *Obed Ramotswe, A citizen of Botswana, A much-loved husband and father, now with the Lord Forever.* That was all it said, but it was enough. It might have said *Great Judge of Cattle;* it might have said *Miner;* it might have said *Witness to the Birth of a Country of which he was so Proud;* but it did not, for the words spoken by stone may be brief and to the point, and yet carry so much weight.

As was the custom, above the graves there was a small canopy, a tattered piece of canvas that she renewed every so often, stretched across a rectangle of metal bars that supported it. This provided shade for the sleepers below, and showed that they were still loved by those who kept their shelter there.

She touched this, then took a step back, wiped away her tears, and went back to the van. It became no easier as the years went by. People said that it would; people said that you forgot late people after a few years, that you forgot what they looked like and what they said; but they were wrong — she was sure of that. She had never known her mother, but every detail of her father was etched in her memory — the old hat he wore, the way he looked at her when he spoke, the things he told her about his life. She would never forget all that because it was now part of her, as familiar to her as the weather.

Continuing her journey, she arrived on the outskirts of the village and drove to the house of the cousin with whom she would spend the next few days. She always got a warm welcome there, as she and the cousin had grown up together and had many memories in common.

The cousin embraced her and then asked her what brought her to Mochudi.

"I am on holiday," said Mma Ramotswe. "I have been on a sort of holiday for a little while; now I am on a full-blown holiday."

"So you want to do nothing?" asked her cousin.

"I want to do nothing," confirmed Mma Ramotswe. "Nothing except talk to you and drink tea and help you with the children and maybe sweep the yard. And cook, of course. I will go and buy food at the store and I shall cook it for you. That is the sort of holiday I am on."

The cousin showed her pleasure at this response. "That sounds perfect to me. I was hoping that somebody would come along and say just what you've said."

"Then let's start my holiday with a cup of tea and a chat about what's been happening in Mochudi."

"A very good idea," said the cousin. "I have some very interesting stories to tell you. You remember that girl who was at school with us, whose father was a brother of the Chief? Do you remember her? Well, she found a husband at last. She has married a man who owns a delivery truck. They have two small children now, and those children have both got very large noses."

"Just like her," said Mma Ramotswe.

The cousin nodded. "I have always said that our faces tell everything that needs to be known about our history. I have always said that."

"I think I remember you saying it," said Mma Ramotswe.

"And then there is a new teacher. This one has got two diplomas, they say — one from the University of Botswana and one from the University of Cape Town. We have not had a teacher with two diplomas ever before."

"Then the children will end up knowing twice as much," said Mma Ramotswe.

The conversation continued in this vein while they drank tea. Then it was time for lunch, cooked by the cousin: rice, peas, and chicken, which is what the cousin always made for Mma Ramotswe, because they had eaten that dish on Sundays when they were children and it brought back memories.

"I am a bit tired," said Mma Ramotswe after she had done the washing-up.

"Then you must go and have a sleep," said the cousin. "In this hot weather a sleep in the afternoon is always a good idea."

She led Mma Ramotswe to her room, at the back of the house, where it was cooler and shadier, and where Mma Ramotswe sunk onto the bed and closed her eyes. It seemed to her that the unwinding that should have happened at the beginning of her holiday, but that for various reasons had not taken place, was now beginning. Her limbs felt heavy; her mind gloriously empty; her skin cool thanks to the breeze that blew in through the house, entering by the front door, moving through her room, and passing out of the back.

She dozed, entering into a world half of

dream, half of wakefulness. She thought of her garden at home, and saw the first green leaves; she thought of the children making their way to school; she thought of Mr. J.L.B. Matekoni cooking for them in her absence — he had assured her that he would cope perfectly well. She thought of rice, peas, and chicken, and of how much she loved that combination. And then she thought of Clovis Andersen's *The Principles of Private Detection;* she saw the book on her desk, and she thought of its author, far away in Muncie, Indiana, which he had told her had great cornfields about it, and she saw those too, the plants waving very gently in the wind. And then, quite unexpectedly, a phrase from the book came to her: *Don't believe everything anybody tells you,* he said. *There are people who will tell you lies because they take a secret pleasure in misleading you.*

She suddenly thought of a small boy called Samuel. She saw the woman who had been using him, and she heard her saying, *That woman is late.* She had said that; she had told her that Samuel's mother had died a year before, but she had not told him of this. And then she heard Mma Potokwane saying, *That boy is inconsolable.*

A shocking thought occurred. What if it were not true? What if that woman had not wanted her to find Samuel's mother for whatever reason — either because she feared retribution or because she did not want her claim on the boy to be challenged by a real parent?

The thought made her sit up. It was entirely possible. And now that poor little boy had been told that his mother was dead: yet nobody had checked up on that. She had simply accepted the facts as they were told to her, but Clovis Andersen would surely say that she should have verified them.

It was a very uncomfortable realisation, and it made an afternoon sleep out of the question. It meant, too, that she had to say to the cousin, "I know I'm on holiday, but something has cropped up and I need to go back to Gaborone."

The cousin was disappointed, but did not demur when she heard the nature of the emergency.

"You must go, Mma. There is no doubt about it — you must go."

She did not go back to the house on Zebra Drive, but made her way directly to the office. There was nobody in the garage, Mr. J.L.B. Matekoni having driven off in his tow-truck on an emergency call, and in the agency itself there were only Charlie and Mr. Polopetsi, seated at her desk and Mma Makutsi's respectively.

Charlie looked at her reproachfully. "Mma Makutsi said you were on a real holiday now, Mma," he said.

She reassured him that she had no objection to his using her desk while she was away. "Don't worry, Charlie," she said. "I have not come to check up on you. I have come because I need you and Mr. Polopetsi to help me do something."

"We're ready to help," said Mr. Polopetsi. "We'll do anything required, Mma."

She explained that what she had in mind would take several hours and that they might not be home until nine or ten at night. "We have to go to Lobatse," she said. "Once we are there we have some enquiries to make." And then, in order to sweeten the pill, she told Charlie that he could drive if he wished. This cheered him up, and after a few minutes of tidying up in the office they left in the tiny white van, with Charlie at the wheel, shooting out into the Tlokweng Road at what Mma Ramotswe considered an excessive speed. She did not criticise him, though, her mind being on what lay ahead at the other end of the hour-long drive to Lobatse.

"Tell me," she said to Mr. Polopetsi. "You worked down there, didn't you, Rra — when you were a government pharmacist? You know the bars in Lobatse, I take it?"

Mr. Polopetsi looked concerned. "Not really, Mma. I am not a big man for bars. I never really went to those places."

"But you know where they are?"

"Yes, I heard people talking. Some of the young men in the hospital would talk about them sometimes."

"And they mentioned the bad bars? Did they talk about the bars where bad women like to go?"

Charlie laughed. "You shouldn't be asking Mr. Polopetsi things like that, Mma! He is a very quiet man. He wouldn't know any bad women."

Mr. Polopetsi looked at him askance. "I am a man of the world, Charlie. You think that just because you're young and the girls all like you that people like me are no good."

Charlie apologised. "I was not saying that, Rra. It's just that if you want to know where the lions go to feed, you shouldn't ask a hedgehog."

Mma Ramotswe intervened. "I don't think any of this helps," she said. "Now, do you know the names of the bars where a certain sort of woman is most likely to be found?"

341

"There are two, I think," said Mr. Polopetsi. "I have been to neither, but I have heard that one of them, in particular, is full of bad women all the time and the other is less full of them, although they do go there too."

"What is the name of the one that is full of these ladies?" asked Mma Ramotswe.

"It's called the Good Times First Class Bar," said Mr. Polopetsi. "I can show you where it is — although, as I said, Mma, I have never been inside."

Charlie sniggered. "I hope not, Rra — otherwise I would have to tell your wife next time I saw her."

"Well," said Mma Ramotswe. "You are both going to be going there tonight. Anonymously, of course. Now, if you listen to me I shall tell you what I want you to do."

By the time they reached the Good Times First Class Bar in Lobatse it was already dark. It stood at the end of a street in the middle of the town, beside a large jacaranda tree. Behind this tree was a car park for the patrons, and this was almost full when they arrived, making it necessary for the white van to be parked very close to the entrance — not the most discreet of positions, and one that any arriving or departing guests of the bar would have to walk past. *If you need to be discreet, don't park in obvious places,* advised Clovis Andersen in *The Principles of Private Detection.* But there were times, such as this, when one had no alternative, thought Mma Ramotswe. Perhaps it was easier to be discreet in Muncie, Indiana.

Mma Ramotswe repeated their instructions before they got out of the car. "I shall stay here," she said. "I would look out of place in there. You two go in and buy a drink — here's the money." She handed them two hundred pula. "Find a lady who looks as if she wants to be bought a drink. Not a very young one — an experienced lady."

"They're all experienced in there, Mma," said Charlie, with a snigger.

"You know what I mean," said Mma Ramotswe. "Find a lady who looks as if she knows everybody. She'll look at home in the bar. She'll have been around. She'll know just about everybody in Lobatse — that sort of lady."

"I know what you mean," said Mr. Polopetsi. "Worldly wise."

"Exactly. Find that lady and then ask her if she knows anybody — any lady who goes to bars and likes men — who had a son called Samuel about nine or ten years ago. Understand?"

"A son called Samuel," said Charlie. "And if she does?"

"Then ask her how we can get in touch with that lady. Give her money for the information. Say, fifty or sixty pula." She nodded towards the bar. "All right, you should go in there now. It's beginning to look crowded."

"This is a very good way of earning your living," said Charlie. "Going to bars. Ordering drinks. Talking to ladies. This is much better than being a mechanic."

She looked at her watch. Half an hour had elapsed from when they had gone inside. From the bar there drifted music, a regular thumping sound, the sort that gave Mr. J.L.B. Matekoni a headache if he had to listen to it for more than a few minutes. It was too loud, but then music in bars was always too loud, particularly in bars like this, with their special clientele. She closed her eyes and tried to think of Mochudi. It would be quiet in the cousin's house now, and had she still been there they would have been talking about the old days while the cousin knitted. She was a famous knitter, and her bonnets for babies, made in the national colours of Botswana, were justly famous throughout Mochudi.

She was disturbed by a tapping on the windscreen. Opening her eyes, she saw Mr. Polopetsi standing outside the van, his face close to the glass. She lowered her window.

Mr. Polopetsi spoke with the breathlessness of the excited messenger. "She is inside," he said.

She caught a faint whiff of beer on his breath.

"You've found a lady who knows her?"

He shook his head vigorously. "No, Mma Ramotswe — we have found *her.* We have found the lady herself."

Mma Ramotswe felt a jolt of excitement. She had hoped that they might elicit some information that would give them something to go on; she had not imagined immediate success.

"Can you bring her out here?" she asked.

"I will go and ask Charlie. He is talking to her a lot. They are getting on very well."

"I can imagine that," muttered Mma Ramotswe. "Break up the party, Mr. Polopetsi, and bring her out here. Tell her that there is something to her advantage. Those ladies understand that sort of talk."

While he was inside, she composed herself. She wondered whether she should talk to the woman inside the van, but decided that it would be easier outside. And so she got out of the van and stood by the engine, waiting for them to arrive.

A man walked past. He glanced at her, took a further few steps, and then turned round and came back towards her.

"Hello, honey," he said. "You are a very nice fat lady. I like a soft mattress."

She drew in her breath. "Then go home and lie down on your bed," she said. "Go back to your wife. I know her, by the way."

The man gave a start, extreme alarm registering on his face. "You know my wife, Mma? You know her? I am just trying to be funny. That was a joke, you know."

"I am not laughing," said Mma Ramotswe. "Go back to your wife."

"Yes, yes," said the man. "That is where I am heading. I was not going into that bar, Mma. I can tell you that. These places are a shame on Botswana."

Mma Ramotswe said nothing more, and the man scuttled off. A few moments later, Mr. Polopetsi and Charlie appeared at the entrance to the bar, followed by a woman in a shiny red dress. They paused while Charlie pointed to the van and to Mma Ramotswe. Then they began to make their way towards her.

"So you are the lady who wants to speak to me," said the woman. "What is this about? I am very busy, Mma."

Mma Ramotswe signalled to Charlie and Mr. Polopetsi to go and stand under the jacaranda. "It will not take long, Mma," she said. "You had a son, I believe. You had a little boy called Samuel?"

The woman shrugged. "So what? He is being looked after up in Gaborone. There is a lady there who is very kind to him. She is a sort of auntie."

Mma Ramotswe nodded. "I have met that lady."

"So, Mma, why do you want to talk to me?"

"Do you not want to see your son, Mma?"

The woman looked down at the ground. "I haven't seen him for a long time, Mma. It would just make him upset. I cannot look after a child down here."

"You don't have to," said Mma Ramotswe. "He is now being looked after in a much better place."

"Then why bother me, Mma? I must go soon. I cannot stand here and talk about children."

Mma Ramotswe reached out to touch her on the forearm. The woman looked down at her hand, almost with disgust. "I can offer you some money, Mma. All you have to do to earn five hundred pula is to come up to

347

Gaborone tomorrow morning, just for an hour or so. You can be back down here in the early afternoon. You will say hello to your son and then you can come back. Nobody will make you do anything or pay anything. There are no conditions."

The woman stared at her. "And you will give me five hundred pula?"

"That's what I said, Mma."

The woman shrugged. "All right. If that's what you want."

It had been far easier than Mma Ramotswe could possibly have hoped. Now she signalled to Charlie and Mr. Polopetsi and told the woman they would meet her the following morning at nine, outside the bar. "And I'm sorry, Mma, but you did not give me your name."

"Stella," said the woman.

"That is a very nice name, Mma," said Mma Ramotswe.

Stella looked at her with some surprise. She hesitated, and then said, "Thank you, Mma. I am proud of my name." There was a further moment of hesitation, during which it seemed to Mma Ramotswe that Stella was searching for the words to say something that was not easy for her to say. Up to now she had been dismissive, even to the point of rudeness; now, after Mma

Ramotswe's compliment on her name, that had disappeared.

"I had to do it, Mma," she muttered. "Sometimes — often — my heart has said to me that I should see Samuel, but then I've thought: Do I want him to see what I've become? Do I want him to see that I am a woman who waits for men in bars? Do I want him to see me after some man has hit and hurt my eye? Is that what I want him to see?"

Mma Ramotswe did not reply immediately. Words that are full of hurt sometimes need to be left in the air where they have been spoken. But after a minute or so, she said, "I know, Mma, that in your heart you are a good mother. I can see that, Mma."

Mma Potokwane had been notified, and was ready for them when they arrived at the Orphan Farm the next day at eleven o'clock. The party consisted of Mma Ramotswe, Stella, and Mma Makutsi, who had been brought up to date early that morning and had expressed a desire to be present. Mma Potokwane welcomed them in her usual manner, leading them into the office, where a tray of tea had been set out, complete with slices of fruit cake.

Mma Ramotswe glanced at Stella. She

detected a certain nervousness and she sought to reassure her. "Mma Potokwane makes very good cake," she said. "Some say it is the best in all Botswana."

"I say that," said Mma Makutsi. "And so does Phuti Radiphuti."

Mma Potokwane shrugged off the compliment. "Oh, you are too kind," she said. "There are many ladies making excellent cake in Botswana. I am just one of them."

They sat down while Mma Potokwane poured the tea. "Now there is one thing I need to say," began the matron. "There is no pressure on any person to take their child away from this place. We understand that there are some people who cannot look after children. We do not sit here in judgement. We do not shake our finger at them. We say nothing about anything of that nature." She looked at Stella. "Do you understand that, Mma?"

Stella bit her lip and nodded.

"So this little boy will stay here," said Mma Potokwane. "That will be the best thing for him. He will get a good education. He will be given a lot of love. We will help him to grow up into a good citizen of Botswana."

Mma Ramotswe turned to Stella. "Do you understand all that, Mma? You must tell us that you understand."

Stella nodded again. "I understand," she muttered.

Mma Potokwane drained her teacup quickly. "We should not sit here too long," she said. "We should go outside in a moment."

They finished their tea without further conversation, leaving the cake untouched. Then, following Mma Potokwane, they went out of the office and began to make their way towards a small thatched summer house — a hut without walls that was used for meetings.

"Has he been told that she is not late?" whispered Mma Ramotswe to Mma Potokwane.

"Yes," said the matron. "He has been told. He is . . . well, you will see what he is like."

They approached the hut. There was a woman sitting inside — one of the housemothers — and she had her arm around a child. They were close now, and as they approached the housemother stood up and pointed. The boy who had been crouching on the floor got to his feet. He turned his head.

Suddenly he broke away from the housemother and dashed out into the open, running towards them. Stella stood stock-still.

She looked at Mma Ramotswe, uncertain what to do.

"This is your little boy," said Mma Ramotswe. "This is Samuel." And with that she pushed her forward, gently but firmly. She pushed her towards her son.

The boy stopped in front of his mother. He looked up at her. She opened her arms and bent down to embrace him, and they saw that she was crying, as he was too.

Mma Makutsi said something that Mma Ramotswe did not catch.

"What was that, Mma?" she whispered.

Mma Makutsi repeated herself: "I said I do not think we need to be here, Mma."

Mma Potokwane agreed. "I think we should go back to finish off the cake," she said.

afrika
afrika afrika
afrika afrika afrika
afrika afrika
afrika

ABOUT THE AUTHOR

Alexander McCall Smith is the author of the No. 1 Ladies' Detective Agency series, the Isabel Dalhousie series, the Portuguese Irregular Verbs series, and the 44 Scotland Street series. He is a professor emeritus of medical law at the University of Edinburgh in Scotland and has served with many national and international organizations concerned with bioethics. He was born in what is now known as Zimbabwe and was a law professor at the University of Botswana. He lives in Scotland.